THE BRIGHTER THE STARS

THE
BRIGHTER
THE
STARS

BRYAN PROSEK

CamCat
Books

CamCat Publishing, LLC
Brentwood, Tennessee 37027
camcatpublishing.com

Hardback ISBN 9780744301380
Paperback ISBN 9780744301236
Large-Print Paperback ISBN 9780744303667
eBook ISBN 9780744301243
Audio ISBN 9780744301878

Library of Congress Control Number: 2020937864

Cover design by Maryann Appel

5 3 1 2 4

To my mom, who is no longer with us,
but who was my biggest fan while writing this book

And to my dad, who watched all the late-night
action and science fiction movies with me when I was growing up,
inspiring me to write this book

FOREWORD

Earth Times Journal
Today's Date: July 8, 2200

This is Nigil Diggs reporting on the history of hilaetite (pronounced hill-a-e-tight) crystals, the adoption of intergalactic Treaty 5274, and the treaty's impact on the Planet Earth. As you may know, hilaetite crystals grow similar to living organisms, like a fungus, but they are not alive in any sense. They are classified as rock. No planet is able to reproduce them or grow them domestically, and once a crystal is picked, no new one ever grows in its place. Once removed from their host rock, they stop growing. For these reasons, fifteen years ago, in the year 2185, all known deposits of hilaetite crystals in the galaxy had been depleted.

But let's take a step backwards and give you a little history. By 2140, all diseases and cancers on Earth and throughout the galaxy had been wiped out through the discovery of hilaetite crystals. Hilaetite crystals were discovered in a small number of places throughout the galaxy and used in different forms for medicinal purposes.

These crystals were also very volatile and could cause massive explosions without being mixed with any other elements or compounds, thereby leaving behind no aftereffects, unlike the old nuclear weapons used on

Earth. So planetary governments began using them in their weapons systems. The possibilities were endless. The larger the hilaetite crystal, the more power it had. It was thought that weapons could be developed that could destroy entire planets given a large enough crystal.

PROLOGUE

Two men stood in the blinding snow and raging, bitter cold wind. They were dressed from head to toe in saber-toothed bear hide suits from the planet Andromeda—the best and most expensive cold-weather suits in the Milky Way galaxy. Only snow goggles protruded from slits in their head-pieces. Any exposed skin would be frozen solid in seconds.

From the cockpit of his spacecraft, Sloan watched the two men on the video screen. *Men will put themselves through anything if the price is right,* he thought. Sloan turned toward the pilot. "Will the scanners give me a video feed anywhere on the planet?"

"Anywhere that the chip goes," the pilot replied.

Sloan turned back to the screen and leaned his tall, solid frame back in his seat. The chip would go everywhere the two men went. He had inserted the audio-visual chip into the latch of the small case strapped over the shoulder of one of the men, Johnson.

Sloan leaned closer to the com. Johnson's shouts were barely audible over the howling wind.

"No wonder this planet is uninhabited," Johnson said. "They say this is the climate everywhere, year round! How far are we from the coordinates? I want to get this done and get out of here!"

Martino looked down at the transponder screen in his hand. "About half a click!" he shouted. "That way!" He motioned with his fur-clad arm.

Johnson continued to shout. "It better not be much farther! We won't last much longer out here!"

Sloan watched the men intently. If they didn't get moving, they would freeze to death before they accomplished his objective. What an inconvenience that would be; he would have to get new men and start all over. He watched the men struggle with each step, their heavy boots weighted down in the knee-deep snow. As far as Sloan could see on the video screen in any direction, the landscape was the same, hill after hill of nothing but snow, broken up occasionally by a few mountains, also mostly covered with snow. Ice mountains, as he had heard them referred to, made of ice and rock. That's what he was looking for.

The transponder beeped. Sloan watched as Martino scanned the landscape in front of him.

"I think that must be it!" Martino shouted, and he pointed to the faint outline of the mouth of a cave appearing through the snow.

It was a small opening in the side of one of the ice mountains. *Perfect*, Sloan thought. Its location relative to the wind was keeping it from filling up with snow, just as he had been informed. That was the only reason it was accessible.

He watched as the two men trudged the last few steps through the snow and into the cave. The opening was narrow. Once they were through it, the cave was probably ten feet tall at the highest spot, Sloan estimated. The walls looked like they were more ice than rock.

"Finally, we're getting somewhere," Sloan said, more to himself than to the pilot.

Once the men were inside the cave, the wind and blowing

snow subsided. Sloan could still hear the wind through the com, but he could hear the men more clearly now, speaking in normal tones. Martino pointed down the long, dark cave tunnel. The transponder was still pointing that way. The men reached into their packs and pulled out their light cylinders. Once activated, the greenish light extended about ten feet down the tunnel.

Johnson said, "I wonder why Sloan wouldn't tell us what we're after? Just, 'You'll know it when you see it.' What's that supposed to mean?"

"He's paying us ten quads each to figure it out," Martino replied. "And I have a pretty good idea."

Sloan grinned slightly, satisfied with himself. By agreeing to pay the two men a mere fraction of what he would make, he got them to risk their lives in one of the harshest climates in the galaxy, without telling them where they were going, what they were after, or what it was for. Who else could have done that but him?

Johnson turned toward Martino. "Do you think we can trust Sloan? He gave me the creeps, the way he stared at us when we met."

"At this point, we don't have much choice," replied Martino. "Besides, I brought along a little insurance." He pulled a small plasma gun from inside his coat.

One side of Sloan's mouth turned up in a cold grin. "Thanks for the warning," he whispered.

Johnson said, "I don't like this at all. Something doesn't feel right."

"Come on," Martino replied. "When you're sitting in the sun spending your quads, it'll feel right."

Sloan watched the men slowly press on. Their feet slipped constantly on the uneven floor, slamming into protrusions, and they struggled to keep their balance.

After making their way deep into the cave, the men came around a bend where the tunnel opened up into a larger cavern. They held up their lights. Sloan couldn't quite see the farthest side of the cavern, but he could tell that this was probably the end of the tunnel, or at least the end of the portion of the tunnel that was large enough to walk through.

Martino looked at the transponder. "This is it. Do you see anything?"

Johnson slowly moved his light cylinder from side to side. As he moved it to his right, something glared bright against the cave wall.

Sloan leaned closer to the screen. "Can we increase the brightness? I can barely make out anything down there."

The pilot shook his head. "I'm sorry, sir. That's the best I can do."

Sloan's heart began to speed up as the men drew closer to the brightly shining object. It was a large clear crystal, about twenty-four inches in circumference, growing out of a protruding rock about two feet off the ground. It was rounded but not smooth, with many flat edges. Sloan edged his face even closer to the screen. This was it. Finally, they'd found what he had come for. His latest plan was coming to fruition— a plan that would make him rich beyond imagination. But that was just the icing on the cake. Power was the real goal. In the end, he would control the two most formidable military powers in the galaxy. That would give him even more power than he now possessed, and he would use that power to control and manipulate anyone he wanted to, anywhere, beyond anything he had ever achieved. He nodded his head slightly and smiled.

Johnson spoke in an awed voice. "A hilaetite crystal. And it's huge."

Martino stared at it. "I had an idea we might be after a crystal, but I never thought it would be this big. This might be the biggest one ever found."

Johnson said, "Rumor has it that the Vernitions first uncovered some twelve- to fifteen-inch crystals way back when, but I never heard of anyone finding any even close to this size. Unbelievable! No wonder Sloan wouldn't tell us what we were after. I'd hate to think what would happen if the wrong people knew about this thing. This baby could be sold for medicinal processing for a fortune."

"And would be worth a hundred times more as a weapon," Martino added. "Can you imagine what type of weapon a crystal this size could power? No wonder Sloan's paying us each ten quads. That's chump change compared to what this thing's worth."

"But hilaetite crystals were mined out decades ago," Johnson said. "No one has found a single crystal for years. Earth, Craton, Vernius, and a half a dozen other planets have the technology to locate crystals ten times smaller than this and they haven't been able to locate any. How did Sloan find this one?"

"The less we know, the better," replied Martino.

"Do you suppose there's more in here?" Johnson asked. "These things usually grow in bunches, and Sloan only gave us the coordinates for this one. The rest could be ours."

"No," Martino replied. "It's not unheard of for a single one to grow, and if there were more, I'm sure Sloan would be having us snatch them up, too."

"What if we keep this one?" Johnson said. "We tell Sloan we couldn't find it. He'd never know."

Martino gave Johnson a hard stare. "Double-cross Sloan? I don't think so. You're the one that said he gave you the creeps. The man looked as fit as a Cratonite, and I'm sure he's packing the latest weaponry. If half the stories about him are true, I don't want to be the one who crosses him. Let's be happy with our ten quads."

"Good decision," Sloan whispered. He knew that his ability to manipulate came most often through fear. He liked how he could use his reputation to instill fear into those he needed to use, and when necessary, he didn't mind setting a new example.

Johnson set down the case. "Sloan said everything we need is in here."

Martino removed his mittens, flipped the latch, and slowly opened the case. It was empty, except for heavy padding on all sides and a small, separate compartment in the front. Martino reached into the front compartment and pulled out a thin, pencil-sized laser cutter. He examined it critically. "This looks like new technology since my last job, but I believe it will work just fine. You hold the crystal steady, and I'll cut it off. Whatever you do, don't drop it."

Johnson took off his mittens, blew into his cupped hands, and then placed both hands on the crystal. Martino twisted the end of the laser cutter, and a red beam shot out. He slowly worked the beam around the crystal in precise strokes. With every stroke, he cut deeper into the ice and rock.

Sloan watched intently, but his sources had been right—the man knew what he was doing. He could see the skill in Martino's workmanship.

If Martino so much as nicked the crystal, that would be the end of him, and if it was more than a nick, the end of the entire planet, with a crystal that size.

Sloan turned toward the pilot. "You better take us up another couple hundred feet."

"Are you sure you know what you're doing? Is this safe?" Johnson was asking. "I've heard plenty of stories of hilaetite crystal miners being blown sky-high. This thing's big enough to take out the entire planet. One wrong move and we're finished."

Martino didn't look up, but kept on working the laser. "Why do you think Sloan hired me for this job? I used to be a hilaetite crystal precision miner. When the machinery couldn't remove a crystal, they called people like me in to take care of it. Risky business, but it paid well."

"Not as well as this job's going to pay," replied Johnson. "If we live through it."

"Shut up and pay attention to the crystal," Martino said. "Why did Sloan hire you?"

Johnson replied, "Maybe he hired me to keep an eye on you."

Martino, finishing the final few cuts, did not respond. The crystal fell free into Johnson's hands. Sloan again leaned close to the screen as Johnson very slowly and gently placed the crystal in the case. It fit snugly in the padding. Martino closed the lid, which had the same padding on the underside, and latched the case. Sloan sat back in his seat, folded his arms and smiled.

Martino straightened up, picked up the transponder, and punched a few buttons. "That should reverse the coordinates and direct us back to the evacuation point. Sloan will be waiting for us."

"I hope," added Johnson.

Martino picked up the case. "With this baby on the line? He'll be there."

As the two men started walking toward the narrow tunnel that would lead them out of the cave, the picture on the screen began to vibrate. Sloan tried adjusting the screen, but then he saw the two men holding their lights up and slowly turning completely around, as if looking for the source of the vibration. It must have been something in the cave. Sloan could see nothing within the range of the light. After a few seconds, the picture vibrated a second time, and a few seconds later, a third time. With each vibration, he could see the floor and walls shake harder.

"Let's get out of here!" Martino said.

Both men bolted for the tunnel.

Just as they reached the opening, a huge hairy creature crashed through the back wall of the cavern. Among the flying ice and rock, Sloan could make out a rat-like head and a mouth full of teeth. It let out a hissing sound that caused the cavern to shake even more, bringing down more ice and rock.

With that, the men broke into a lumbering run. Sloan's eyes widened and he pulled back from the screen. His heart began to race, not out of fear for the men, but for fear of losing the crystal. He could hear a low growl mixed in with vibration after vibration, faster and faster. The beast was closing the gap. The picture on the screen shook. The vibrations gave way to thuds, as the weight of each step drew the beast closer and closer. Flying chunks of rock and ice filled the screen, with intermittent glimpses of the creature crashing through the sides of the tunnel.

"Faster! Faster, you fools!" Sloan shouted at the screen.

"Should I take us in closer to prepare for evacuation, sir?" the pilot asked.

"No, not yet." Sloan's eyes never left the screen. "It's still too risky. They're bouncing that case around like it's a rubber ball. At least Martino has the box and is in the lead. He just needs to outrun Johnson."

The picture on the screen began to steady. Sloan could see some daylight. They must be approaching the entrance, where the tunnel floor was smoother and wider. Sloan kept his eyes fixed on the screen. "Okay, move us down one hundred feet, but keep us a hundred yards or so from the cave. She could still blow. That distance should give us enough time."

Johnson's foot caught hard between two rocks, and he fell face first. Sloan grimaced. He could hear Johnson's ankle snap. Martino, who was starting to open up some distance between himself and Johnson, paused and looked back.

"Don't stop!" Sloan snapped, still looking at the screen. "This is your chance to get away while that thing has a meal."

Johnson lifted his hand toward Martino. "Help me," he pleaded.

The creature bore down on Johnson, and Sloan got a full view of it for the first time. It had a long tube-like body covered with coarse, dirty white hair. It ran on ten stubby legs, each ending with paws containing four or five very long and sharp claws. The creature's head looked like that of a giant rat, with a long snout. Large, crooked teeth protruded from its open mouth, dripping with saliva.

Martino pulled out his plasma gun, aimed it at the beast, and squeezed. Nothing happened. He looked at it, made an adjustment, aimed, and squeezed again. Still nothing.

Johnson shouted, "It's too cold for a plasma gun. Help me up! Quick!"

Johnson scarcely finished the sentence before the jaws of the beast clamped down on him. The scream that came from Johnson made the hair on the back of Sloan's neck stand up. He had heard a lot of dying screams, but this was one of the most hideous.

Martino turned and ran out of the cave. Sloan knew Martino had little time. At the pace the creature was devouring Johnson, it wouldn't take long for it to finish off its appetizer and go after the second course.

When Martino exited the cave, he had to slow to almost a walk. Sloan shook his head in disappointment, but he knew that was probably Martino's only option. The snow was still knee deep and blowing as fiercely as when the two men had entered the cave. Sloan watched intently. Martino made his way through the snow, glancing down at the transponder.

The creature was finished with Johnson and was now chasing Martino. With its short stubby legs, it was just as slow in the deep snow as Martino. *He might have a chance,* Sloan thought. *That thing isn't built for wandering outside.*

Sloan turned toward the pilot. "He's clear. Take us in for evacuation."

The pilot replied, "Yes sir, but the wind is too strong to land. We'll have to make it a hover-evac. Fifty feet's about as close as I can get."

"All right," Sloan said. "Make it so."

Sloan made his way rapidly down to the cargo bay, zipping up his heavy coat. He looked down at Martino through the open door and lowered the ladder. Everywhere he looked it was white. White snow on the ground, white snow on the mountains, white snow in the air. The ladder was swinging wildly in the wind. As it whipped by, Martino leaped up and grabbed it. He pulled himself up until his feet could rest on the lowest rung. He turned his head. The beast was no more than ten yards from him now, growling and occasionally letting out its hideous hiss.

Sloan watched Martino climb toward the open hatch, the wind still whipping the ladder. The beast raised the upper half of its body and lunged for the ladder. The spacecraft rose ten feet just in time, and the beast missed, its head crashing down into the snow. It let out a vicious hiss and stared up at Martino, mouth open. Never had Sloan seen teeth like that— large, jagged, almost stacked on top of one another.

The wind continued to blow and swirl. Sloan thought, *Hang on, Martino. Hang on. I've come so far. One slip and you'll be the next meal for that creature, if the crystal doesn't blow us all up.*

As Martino reached the top, Sloan bent down on one knee. He leaned over the open hatch, held out a gloved hand, and shouted, "Let me take the case?"

"Go ahead," Martino replied. Martino lowered his head and lifted one hand off the ladder to allow Sloan to remove the case from over his shoulder. Sloan watched as Martino reached for the handholds on the floor of the cargo bay. He grasped, but nothing was there.

Sloan stood up, staring at Martino and shaking his head. He had removed the handholds earlier.

Martino looked up at Sloan and his eyes widened. "Give me a hand."

Instead, Sloan turned and knelt by the case. He flipped open the latch and slowly and gently opened the lid, then reached in and touched the crystal. "Well done." He closed the lid and moved the case away from the open hatch.

"Now pull me up," Martino said, "and we can finish the transaction."

Sloan stood and walked over to the open hatch. Martino was still hanging onto the last rung of the ladder with one hand, his feet a few rungs down. His other hand reached up to Sloan.

Sloan bent one leg as if he was starting to kneel down to lift up Martino. Then, with a quick solid thrust, Sloan smashed his boot squarely into Martino's face. Martino's head snapped back, blood pouring from his nose. His free arm flailed and both feet slipped off the ladder. Sloan watched. He'd thought that one good kick would do it, but Martino was a little tougher than he had expected. Martino swung out over empty air, clinging to the ladder with one hand. Before he could swing himself back, Sloan stomped on the hand holding the ladder. Martino's finger bones crunched. Martino lost his grip. He snatched at the ladder one last time with his good hand, but all he caught was air. Sloan leaned out over the opening and watched Martino get smaller and smaller, falling through the white snow, falling toward the snow-covered ground, falling into the waiting jaws of the creature below.

Sloan flipped a switch on the side of the hatch. The ladder ascended up into the spacecraft, and the hatch door closed. Sloan then pressed the com button on the cargo bay wall. The spacecraft's pilot came on. "Yes, Mr. Sloan?"

Sloan replied, "Take us out of here."

"Where to, sir?" the pilot responded.

Sloan paused for a moment and then replied, "Earth."

The Planet Earth is no longer divided into countries, but rather into five geographic regions, called sectors. Scientific advances have enabled space travel to all parts of the Milky Way galaxy. Many of the stars in the galaxy were found to contain solar systems similar to the solar system of the Earth's own Sun, with inhabited planets. The inhabitants of some of those planets were hostile and had developed weapon systems far beyond those of Earth. As a result, the world leaders of Earth agreed to set aside all religious and political differences in order to protect their planet. By 2145, through the development of a new planetary defense system, Earth had avoided any takeover by other planets and developed a united society.

1

SURPRISE!

Fourteen-year-old Jake Saunders flattened himself against his bedroom wall, next to the auto-furnish console. He could hear Cal coming down the hall, slow and cautious. That was Cal, always the cautious one, the thinker, the planner. But this time, Jake had the plan. Not one of his spur-of-the-moment, just-wing-it decisions. Keep coming, Cal. Just a few more seconds . . . there. Cal was just outside the door. Jake made a small, deliberate noise to give away his position. As soon as he heard Cal move, Jake punched the "armchair" button on the console and dropped to the floor.

Cal swung into the room, his mock-plasma gun pointed in Jake's direction. The fake laser beam aimed straight ahead. It was powered by the latest in ion capacitor technology. "Surrender, Earthling, or face the wrath of Romalor. Your Earth Legion is no match for the Cratonites."

The armchair module slid out of its wall cavity and mushroomed to full size, right into Cal's line of fire. Jake rose to one knee and, using the armchair for cover, shot Cal with his sepder gun replica, powered by the same technology as Cal's plasma gun. Cal twisted at the last minute, and the fake plasma beam from the sepder clipped his shoulder instead of hitting his chest.

Cal glanced at his shoulder. His black game vest lit up yellow where the beam had hit. "It's not red," he said. "Just a minor flesh wound."

Jake flipped the lever on his mock sepder and the sword blade extended, just like a real sepder. Time for hand-to-hand combat. "Die, then, Romalor!" he shouted and dived over the chair. His foot caught on the arm, and he crashed into Cal, sending both of them to the floor. Each vest lite up red where the other's weapon had poked it.

"Ow!" Cal said. "You big lug. You trying to kill me for real?"

Jake's Aunt Jane called up the stairs, "Jacob Saunders, are you trying to knock the house down? Your uncle will be here any minute. Have you finished wrapping his birthday present?"

Jake forgot about his game with Cal immediately. He had been waiting forever to give Uncle Ben his present. Jake had lived with the Walkers in the Sector Four Legion headquarters, in the Owami Desert in former Nigeria, ever since his dad was killed in a quantum fighter explosion. His mom had died when he was born, so Uncle Ben and Aunt Jane were like parents to him. He called back, "I'm sorry. I was taking a break. I'll finish up and be right down."

Jake finished wrapping Uncle Ben's present and raced Cal down the steps. As they hit the landing at the bottom and saw the house full of guests, he grabbed Cal and came to a sudden halt. He hadn't realized how long he and Cal had been playing, but he could never resist the chance for a make-believe battle with his mock sepder. He searched the crowded room for Aunt Jane. There she was, over by the gift table. Jake made his way through the crowd to her.

"You look like you were in a war, Jake," Aunt Jane said, patting his hair down with her hand.

"I'm good," Jake said, pulling his head away from her reach. "Here's my present. I hope Uncle Ben likes it." He carefully placed the present on the table.

Aunt Jane squeezed his shoulder gently and smiled. "Like it? Your Uncle Ben's going to love it."

Someone shouted her name from the kitchen. She turned in that direction. "Be right there." She turned back toward Jake. "No more wars, at least not until after your uncle gets here." She smiled.

Jake scanned the room to see what was going on. The family robot was rolling through the room, carrying a platter of drinks. Turning neatly on its pivoted wheels, the robot made its way among the guests, stopping momentarily at each one to give him or her a chance to take a beverage. Jake noticed that his aunt had retracted all the furniture into the walls, so that the guests could mingle more easily. The television and video com screen on the far wall had been retracted as well. Darn. He had been hoping that he and Cal and could watch a show until Uncle Ben arrived.

"Jake, over here!" Cal yelled.

Jake turned quickly, bumping into someone's forearm, causing the person's drink to spill down the front of the person's shirt. "I'm sorry," Jake said.

He looked up, holding his breath, prepared to be scolded. Then he let out his breath and relaxed when he saw it was Bernard Danielson, Cal's father. Bernie was a Legion soldier just like Uncle Ben and Jake's dad, and Jake felt as comfortable around Cal's family as he did around his Uncle Ben and Aunt Jane.

Bernie shook his head with a rueful smile. "It'll wash off, champ. But you better work on those reflexes. A Legion soldier could have reacted quickly enough to miss the arm."

"I'll work on that," Jake said. He signaled the robot. "Spill protocol," he commanded as it reached them. The robot's sonic cleaning arm extended and removed the stain from

Bernie's shirt front, and then from the floor. Finished, it trundled off to deliver more drinks.

"Hey, your birthday isn't too far off, is it?" Bernie asked. "And it's a big one. Fifteen makes you old enough to get a driving permit."

Jake straightened up. "Yep. Cal and I want to take the driving test together since we'll be turning fifteen about the same time."

Bernie smiled. "I imagine that can be arranged."

Jake nodded respectfully. "Thanks."

"Jake, come here!" Cal shouted.

Jake made his way through the guests toward Cal. He could see Cal's sister standing next to him. Jake immediately slowed down, straightened his back, and smoothed down his hair.

Diane was so beautiful. She was tall, taller than he was. But that didn't matter. He was growing a lot anyway. Her cheekbones were set high, making her look like an old-time Indian princess. He liked her dark hair, so different from his blond hair and blue eyes. And there was something about those eyes, how they seemed to stare right inside him. They were mesmerizing.

Lots of young Legion cadets hung around Diane, but ever since Mrs. Danielson died three years ago, Diane was too busy taking care of Mr. Danielson and Cal to pay much attention to them.

That was good—Jake didn't want her to fall in love with one of them before he got old enough to ask her out. Sometimes, she'd talk to Jake when she wouldn't talk to them. That was the best—even better than practicing to join the Legion one day.

Jake looked at Diane, ignoring Cal. "Hi, Diane. Glad you could make it."

"Oh, I wouldn't miss your uncle's birthday for anything," Diane replied, smiling.

Cal gave Jake a playful shove. "Come on, let's go play some robo ball before your uncle gets here."

Jake loved robo ball. It was a mental challenge combined with athletic skills. One person programs the robotic ball to hide and the other person has to track and find it before time runs out. But nothing topped talking to Diane.

Conflicted, Jake looked at Cal. "I think . . . I just want to talk."

"Since when?" Cal asked. "When would you want to talk rather than play robo ball?" Cal broke into a large grin. "Since Diane got here. Right?" He poked Jake in the arm.

Jake tightened his lips. "Can't you see I'm talking to Diane?"

Diane broke in, "Okay, guys. I need to see your Aunt Jane anyway."

Jake frowned at Cal.

"Oh, come on, Jake," Cal said. "She's too old anyway. She's nineteen, you know. Let's go play Legion combat or something else on the computer. That's something I can beat you at. And we probably wouldn't be allowed to leave the house to play robo ball anyway."

Jake glanced back at Diane walking away. "Let's have another armed combat battle." Real combat was much more fun than computer simulations. And he won more often. "You can even be the Legion soldier this time, and use my sepder."

"Are you serious? You haven't let anyone touch that thing since you got it," Cal replied.

Cal's right, Jake thought. His uncle had given him the sepder replica for his thirteenth birthday, and it was his favorite possession. He was always proud that he could immediately recite to anyone the technical name for a sepder: "sonically emitted plasma direct-energy ray gun." It was both a gun and a sword.

Jake even knew the details of how real sepders were made and how they worked. As a gun, a real sepder was a direct-energy weapon that used sonic blasts to emit plasma streams in the form of short, repeated rays. As a sword, its blade was composed of a mixture of various elements found throughout the galaxy, including a small trace of processed hilaetite. As he liked to tell anybody that would listen, "Hilaetite gives a sepder unparalleled strength and durability, providing resistance to breakage as well as a blade that rarely needs sharpening." His plan, for as long as he could remember, was to be a Legion soldier just like his dad and Uncle Ben, and to wield a real sepder of his own. He couldn't wait to get his Uncle Ben's sepder. Because of the hilaetite used in them, he knew that new sepders were no longer made. They were passed down through the ranks.

Aunt Jane shouted from across the room, "Everyone, here he comes! Get ready."

Jake saw Aunt Jane peeking out the window by the door. She was pulling the metal window blind closed by hand, so Uncle Ben couldn't see in. The auto-window console must be jammed again. He was going to help Uncle Ben fix that when Uncle Ben had some time. He hoped that didn't cause Uncle Ben to notice her in the window and give away the surprise.

Jake could hear the door code being entered into the keypad outside, and the automatic door slid open. He liked the newer sliding doors better than swinging doors, which were still around in some older buildings.

Ben stepped inside. The whole room erupted with a shout of, "SURPRISE!"

Ben stopped and smiled. "Oh my, you guys got me good!"

Jake saw that everyone in the room bought it, except him. He knew that look on his uncle's face. Uncle Ben was faking it. But then nothing surprised his uncle much anymore. He had been through too much. But Jake thought Ben was doing a great job at acting, and he appreciated the effort. Aunt Jane had done a lot of work and spent a lot of time organizing the party and trying to keep it a secret from Uncle Ben.

Jane, with Jake by her side, walked over to Ben and gave him a quick kiss on the lips. "How was your day?" she asked.

Jake noticed that the party guests were immediately back to mingling and talking to each other. Ben replied, "Oh, the usual. Mostly the same old, same old. A couple of new developments, but they don't involve me much." He smiled at Jane, and then at Jake. He rubbed Jake's hair. "How's my little buddy?"

At fourteen, Jake didn't feel so little anymore, but he liked that his uncle still called him buddy. "Great," Jake replied. "I have to show you the new sepder move I used on Cal."

Ben chuckled. "Sure, buddy. After the party."

The evening progressed with talking, some music, games for the kids, cake, and ice cream. Jake knew or recognized all the guests, as they were all Uncle Ben's colleagues or friends of the Walkers, and all lived at Sector Four Legion headquarters. Jake was having a blast, as he always did when Cal was around. He didn't mind that he had no siblings or that the Walkers had no children of their own. Cal was just like a brother.

Finally, Jake turned to Jane and Ben. "Is it time to open presents?" He still liked the excitement of guessing what was in a gift-wrapped box, even if the present wasn't for him.

Aunt Jane smiled. "All right, everybody into the living room!" she called out.

Jake plopped down on the sleek sofa right beside Ben. Ben's presents were piled on the table in front of them. He looked around. Most of the guests were still sipping drinks or nibbling on a snack.

"Let's save mine until last," Jake said. He picked up the small neatly wrapped gift and placed it to the side.

"Okay, then," Ben said. "Why don't we start with this big one right here?"

Jake watched as Ben opened gifts, finally getting to the last gift before his. Some of the presents were boring, useful items, and others were some form of a joke, poking fun at Uncle Ben turning fifty. Jake reached over and picked up his gift. "Okay, Uncle Ben. It's time to open mine."

As Ben began to unwrap it, Jake could feel his heart beat faster and the excitement swell up inside him. He had worked so long and so hard making it, anticipating this moment, trying to imagine the look on his uncle's face when he opened the gift. Now, the moment was finally here. It seemed to be taking forever for Uncle Ben to get the wrapping paper off.

Finally, Ben slowly opened the small box and pulled out a gold-colored chain necklace with a flattened piece of shiny gold metal dangling from the chain. Jake noticed how bright the metal shone in contrast to his uncle's rough, callused hand. It was the hand of a Legion soldier that had seen plenty of action.

Ben turned the metal piece over and read the inscription out loud: "To Uncle Ben. The best dad ever. Love, your little buddy, Jake."

Ben reached over and hugged Jake. "Thank you. You're the best little buddy ever."

Jake, with a huge smile on his face, said, "I made it in shop at school. I've been working on it all year. Do you like it?"

Ben smiled. "Do I like it?" He slipped it over his head and let it drop around his neck. "I love it. I don't think I'll ever take it off."

The entire population of Earth is now under the command of one leader, the president of Earth United, who is the supreme commander of the military and head of state, both on the planet and intergalactically.

As for hilaetite crystals, given the far greater need for their medicinal use than in weapons, in the year 2180, all inhabited planets in the galaxy agreed to an intergalactic treaty known as Treaty 5274, which banned the use of hilaetite crystals for any use other than in medicine. Treaty 5274 required all remaining stores of hilaetite crystals and any new discoveries to be sent to the planet Pergan, a formerly uninhabited planet in the center of the galaxy. Two representatives of each planet in the galaxy were to make up the council, which was to oversee the medicinal processing of hilaetite crystals and the storage and distribution of the resulting refined powder.

2

TREATY 5274

For security purposes, the Presidential Sector had been established in the former Middle East. The location made it the easiest area of Earth to defend, from the Legion's standpoint. For additional protection, the Presidential Mansion was constructed in the northeast part of what was formerly the country of Saudi Arabia, in the city of Buraydah, which was close to the center point of the Presidential Sector. While Buraydah was the largest city in the sector, all cities in that sector were smaller than most cities in other sectors because the Legion limited the number of people that could live and work in the Presidential Sector. The president lived and worked out of the Presidential Mansion. New technology had enabled Legion contractors to discover and tap a previously inaccessible water supply deep beneath the surface of the region, creating a tropical oasis of sorts around the Presidential Mansion.

On this particular evening, the West Room of the Presidential Mansion was full. President Jack Buchanan was seated behind his desk. The others in attendance were still organizing their notes and getting situated, while Jack observed them carefully. This was easily the most important meeting in his young presidency.

Why did this have to happen so soon, he thought, *in just the fourth month of a ten-year term?* He'd barely had a chance to get his staff in place. At least he had a good staff—a very good staff. He looked to his left, where Armin Dietrich was seated. Armin was the perfect chief of staff, the perfect personal advisor. Sure, the position didn't come with any real decision-making authority, but Armin didn't need real authority. He had a knack for convincing people that he had it anyway. Armin had been at Jack's side since the early part of his political career, when he first ran for the Senate. Armin was an easy choice for him, but he knew the choice wasn't without controversy. Many people viewed Armin as somebody that had latched onto his coattail early and never let go—somebody who was using Jack to promote his own interests. Part of the problem, he felt, was merely Armin's appearance and mannerisms. People, in general, didn't like it that a short, pudgy man without any charisma had made it to where Armin had. Sure, Armin's nasal voice and arrogant attitude irritated even Jack sometimes, and he could be abrasive. But, no matter how Armin got to where he was or how annoying he could be, Jack knew nobody could dispute Armin's intellect or that he was a brilliant strategist. That showed during Jack's hard-fought campaign for the presidency. Those qualities, along with his obvious ambition to rise to power, made Armin an important strategic ally and a dangerous opponent.

Jack looked to his right. Seated there, reviewing her notes, was his chief civilian advisor, Clarisse Chirac. He and Clarisse had served together in the Senate for years. She wasn't afraid to take a hard line stance on difficult issues. If not for her efforts in pulling the sectors of Earth together, Earth might have never ratified Treaty 5274. That amazing political prowess had made her an easy choice for the role of his advisor on Earth's civil matters.

Marco Veneto, the chief Legion advisor, was still standing in front of his chair. Jack hadn't known Marco personally for very long, but Marco's staunch military background and unblemished Legion record made him the perfect choice for advisor on galactic matters. After all, who better to serve as the highest ranking Legion officer than a former Legion commander? In fact, he was the highest ranking law enforcement officer, period, since the Legion was Earth's sole law enforcement agency in addition to being its military. And Marco was self-made. He had worked his way up through the Legion ranks from private to guard to one of four superior guards in the sector to the commander of Sector Three, the highest rank in the sector.

Next to Marco, talking to him, stood Aretha Brown, the Senate leader. He admired Aretha almost as much as he did Clarisse. She was tough, yet fair. With two senators, including herself, from each main sector, she had the unenviable task of keeping seven of the most influential people on Earth in line. At the same time, as the only check on the power of the president, she had to keep the president in line. Jack believed that Aretha had been instrumental in broadening the Senate's oversight authority and expanding the well-defined list of matters that required Senate approval. Depending on the direction he would take in the current situation, he knew that his decision could end up needing Senate approval. In that event, he would need Aretha on his side.

Edgardo Ramirez, the only non-governmental person to be involved in the discussions, completed the circle. Edgardo was sitting down, talking into a personal silent audio com. Jack shook his head slightly. It still amazed him that the president and CEO of EarthNX Corporation, a private company, had become so politically powerful that he was sitting in a meeting with the highest level government officials on Earth. Jack glanced up at the two "business advisors" standing behind Edgardo—arms folded, eyes alert, faces stony. He knew they had been stripped of their weapons, but he still liked to glance occasionally at his own armed bodyguards standing by the door, for reassurance.

Jack quickly scrolled through a number of documents on the portable data pod on his desk until he found what he was looking for. Ready or not, he had better get things started. He needed to take control of the meeting immediately and remain in control. This was his meeting, his presidency at stake. "All right, we better get started. Thank you all for coming here on such short notice and at this hour of the night. I trust that you all have had a little time to familiarize yourselves with the report and why we're here? I'll skip the niceties and get right to the point." He turned to Edgardo. "So, Mr. Ramirez, just how did your company come into possession of the hilaetite crystal?"

Jack kept his gaze fixed on Edgardo. He wanted to make clear his disdain for EarthNX Corporation, and more so, its CEO. He felt guilty for not taking a position contrary to EarthNX during his campaign, knowing about all its questionable practices. But his advisors kept telling him that to do so would be political suicide. They told him, "Just look in the other direction like all the other successful candidates before you. EarthNX brings unparalleled strength to a candidacy when it's the candidate's ally, and the financial backing it'll bring you will assure your victory." How short-sighted he had been. Sure, EarthNX was the largest and most successful company in Earth's history. But even as a young senator, he'd had to laugh at its official, publicly stated purpose, which was "the development and advancement of technology and technological products for the betterment of mankind." What a falsity that was. Ninety percent of the technology and products that EarthNX developed were weapons. It was, by far, the Legion's leading contractor in the development and production of military weapons and other equipment. But he would sacrifice his morals no longer. He knew that Edgardo had the ability to take over and dominate a meeting. If that happened here, he would be finished. He had to stay in control. He smiled to himself. At least he'd already been elected, and one term was all a president got. He didn't have to worry about support for re-election. *Edgardo might be able to make things a little difficult,* he thought, *but he can't get me out of office.*

"Mr. President," Edgardo replied, "you know I can't reveal my sources. Nor can the government compel me to do so. The . . ." Edgardo paused thoughtfully, then grinned and continued, "let's call it, 'discovery,' of the crystal is a corporate trade secret, protected by Senate Bill 55."

Jack kept eye contact with Edgardo. Edgardo's arrogance never ceased to amaze him. But he did have to admit, for a man in his mid-sixties, Edgardo still possessed a stern, imposing look. He never saw Edgardo dressed in anything other than a three-piece suit that always looked freshly pressed, any time of the day or night.

"So, you're saying you bought the crystal from someone?" Jack replied.

Edgardo, sitting perfectly straight in his chair, ran a hand through his gray but still thick hair, perfectly combed. He answered, "I said nothing of the sort."

Jack leaned forward, his arms stretched out on his desk, hands folded. "I don't care if you found it, bought it, or stole it. Just possessing it alone is enough to be in violation of Treaty 5274."

Edgardo smirked. "Look, Jack—I mean, Mr. President. You wouldn't be sitting in that seat if it wasn't for me. I've been sitting in meetings like this and dealing with people like you since you were just a schoolboy. If that's a threat, I would advise against it." Edgardo relaxed his posture and adjusted his tie. "Besides, I no longer possess the crystal."

Jack could feel his chest tighten as Edgardo spoke. He clenched his hands together. He wanted to lash out with every documented and undocumented legal and ethical violation by

EarthNX that he could think of. No, no. This was a business meeting. They were here for a purpose, and it wasn't a fight with Edgardo. He would have to save that for another day. He took a deep breath. Relax, he told himself. "So where is the crystal now?"

Marco raised a hand slightly and caught Jack's attention. He spoke before Edgardo could answer. "Sir, it's at Sector Four Legion headquarters."

Jack looked at Marco. Marco was the one person in the room who looked threatening enough to stop Edgardo from speaking. Like all chief Legion advisors before him, Marco was officially a civilian, but Jack liked the fact that unlike all previous chief Legion advisors, Marco never dressed in civilian clothing. He always wore a Legion uniform. It gave Marco a presence that was very useful in situations like this.

"Commander O'Reilly is in charge there, isn't he?" Jack asked.

"Yes," replied Marco. "He has personally assured me that the crystal is under heavy guard and is still in the anti-detection box."

"The anti-detection box?" asked Jack.

"That's right, sir," said Marco. "EarthNX has developed an anti-particular coating that prohibits ninety-five percent of all hilaetite detection devices from sensing a crystal. And the five percent that can sense it, only pick up a faint signal, and only when the crystal is large enough."

The president turned toward Edgardo. "So this is how you managed to keep the crystal hidden from our detection system. And I suppose the only reason that it's at a Legion headquarters now is because Vernius was able to detect it. When you found out we were looking for it, you got worried. Am I right?"

Jack half expected Edgardo to come out of his chair at him. To the contrary, Edgardo sat up, straightened his suit, and replied softly, "Mr. President, you are correct. That's how we kept it hidden, but it's only in your military's possession now because of my goodwill."

Jack didn't buy the goodwill part for a minute. He'd read the briefing report. The detection hadn't come from Earth sensors. Vernius had detected the crystal. Since Vernius had no combat units, the Imperial Majesty of Vernius had notified the Legion, asking if they would investigate. The report indicated that the Imperial Majesty said that the signal was faint and originated from a region on the other side of the galaxy, where there hadn't been any reports of hilaetite crystals for decades.

"Are there any other crystals where this came from?" asked Jack.

Edgardo replied, "My sources tell me no. This is it."

Jack almost asked Edgardo about his sources, but then thought better of it. It would be a waste of everyone's time to go down that path again. Instead, he turned toward Armin. "Mr. Dietrich, does Vernius know that we have the crystal?"

"No, sir," Armin replied. "That's why we still have it in the anti-detection box. But that was against my advice. I wanted to inform the Imperial Majesty immediately. But the majority of the others now present thought that you might want to act differently. I informed them that you wouldn't."

Marco added, "And we have kept our patrols out, supposedly looking for it, so that Vernius wouldn't get suspicious."

"Four patrols, right?" asked the president.

"Yes," answered Marco. "One from each sector headquarters."

Jack sat back in his chair and rubbed his eyes. He was in a bind now. He could see where this was heading, right into Edgardo's hands. The last thing he wanted was to give Edgardo what Edgardo wanted. But that might be the best solution for the planet. It always seemed that Edgardo set things up perfectly so that what seemed best for the planet was also best for Edgardo. There had to be another way. But before he could figure that out, he would have to see the rest of Edgardo's cards.

Jack straightened himself up and looked at Edgardo. "Edgardo, Mr. Dietrich tells me that you, or your company, that is, want to sell the crystal to the Legion. Armin didn't give me a price, but I assume that it would be substantially more than the council pays. Is that correct?"

"Maybe," answered Edgardo. "But I want what's best for everyone on Earth. We can work out the financial terms later, once you give this your okay."

Clarisse Chirac slammed her hand on her leg. "I can't believe that we are even sitting here having this conversation. Treaty 5274 is very clear that every hilaetite crystal discovered must be immediately delivered to the council in exchange for the standard compensation. Period. If this crystal is as large as I've heard, it could save millions of lives. And Vernius is our closest ally. They stuck by our side throughout the galactic war and we couldn't ask for a better friend today. Are we going to deceive them? Mr. President, pardon me for being so blunt, but you know what kind of man Mr. Ramirez is. Why are you even discussing this with him? Earth has agreed to the terms of the treaty. That should be the end of the discussion."

Armin jumped in. "That was my position as well, sir."

Jack noticed the puzzled look Armin shot at Edgardo. Jack looked at Aretha Brown. "You've been quiet so far, Aretha. What's the Senate's position on this?"

"Well, Mr. President," Aretha paused for a moment, "I believe the Senate will follow your lead on this, since this is your first big decision. But be careful, sir. As you know, any action taken by you that contradicts an intergalactic treaty must be approved by the Senate. If you make a mistake, it'll be a big one, and you'll likely lose the Senate's support from here on. That'll make for a long nine-plus years."

That's what made Aretha so great at leading the Senate, Jack thought. What a perfect position. She was fair, by giving him a long rope. But she was also tough. He had the ability to cut the rope by making a mistake, and then he would be on his own.

Clarisse turned toward Aretha. "You can't be serious, Aretha. You mean that you would support breaking the treaty?"

"I didn't say that, Clarisse," Aretha replied. "What I am saying is that I believe the Senate will give the president the benefit of the doubt."

Armin pointed a finger toward Aretha. "You mean that *you* will give the president the benefit of the doubt. You're pushing the president unto dangerous political waters."

Edgardo held up his hand toward those arguing, palm down, and then spoke in a soft tone. "First, just hear me out. As you all know, two or more hilaetite crystals cannot be used together in a weapon. They are too volatile. Therefore, the only way to increase power is to find a larger crystal. There's no way to enhance or diminish a crystal's power. Except, of course, when it is ground to powder for medicine. That destroys its internal chemistry, making it useless in weapons. A crystal the size that we are talking about can power a weapon the likes of which has never been seen or thought of. That is, until now. EarthNX is in the initial design phase of a weapon that, if powered by a crystal of this magnitude, could destroy entire planets. Now, don't get me wrong, the weapon is still years from development, but we have never discovered a crystal of this size before, and probably won't ever again, if we even find any more crystals at all. So we should hang onto this one. Everyone in this room knows, as well as I do, that galactic peace isn't going to last forever, especially once the current stores of processed crystals are depleted. Planets will start warring again, in search of new ways to better their lives, as disease starts to spread once more. Even now, you can't possibly be so naive as to believe that other planets aren't hiding crystals for when that time comes. And I am sure they are working on weapons that will penetrate Earth's defense shield. I mean, look, I was able to hide the largest crystal that has ever been seen from every planet but one. You can't think that Romalor on Craton and a half a dozen other rulers like him aren't hiding crystals as we speak, can you? So why not do what they are doing? Ignore the treaty this once, buy the crystal, and let EarthNX develop the weapon."

Jack sat there, absorbing what he had just heard. He had no doubt that Edgardo was telling the truth about developing such a weapon. After all, the largest success of EarthNX was the development of the impulse shield technology and the production of Earth's defense shield. That discovery by Edgardo's father had made his father, and now Edgardo, one of the top five wealthiest people in the galaxy. He also had no doubt that Edgardo's sole motive here was to increase his wealth, not to protect Earth. After all, that's all Edgardo really cared about: money. Jack could not dispute the need for the defense shield, or the fact that without it, there likely would be no president of Earth United, or even an Earth United at all. But he disagreed greatly with the means by which EarthNX developed technologies and otherwise did business.

Clarisse turned toward Jack. "Jack, you can't possibly be buying this story. Think about what Earth stands for. The platform on which you campaigned. Turning the crystal over to the council is not only the right thing to do. For you personally, it's the smartest thing, politically, to do. You have to do it."

Armin looked at Jack. "Sir, I'm still not saying you should break the treaty, but Mr. Ramirez may have a point. I think maybe we should consider it."

Clarisse stood up and walked behind her chair. Her hands resting on the back of it, she leaned toward Armin. "Armin, that's just like you. As soon as you see something positive in it for you, you switch sides."

"Now, Clarisse," Armin said, tilting his head to one side, "I'm not switching sides. I'm always on the president's side. I just want what's best for him. This may be just the opportunity to put Earth in front of every planet in the galaxy. And that would be an excellent *political* move, in my opinion."

Clarisse sat back down, drew in a deep breath, and spoke slowly. "Armin, you couldn't care less about the president's political career. All you care about is how far you can ride that career with him. All this talk is nonsense."

Before Armin could respond, Jack stood up. "Okay, enough." He paused, then continued, "Marco, what do you think?"

"Well, sir," Marco said, "I think that both sides of the argument are well founded and have much merit. Being a military man, I myself prefer making our Legion the strongest fighting force in the galaxy. On the other hand, we do have the treaty to consider."

Clarisse spoke up again. "To consider? There is nothing to consider! Following the treaty is a requirement!"

Jack sat back down. "All right, I've heard enough. I know where each of you stands on this. I will consider everyone's points very carefully. We will meet back here in two days. I will inform you all of my decision then, and we can proceed accordingly from there. Thank you all for your time and input. And people, it goes without saying, not a word of these discussions leaves this room."

Armin stood up and walked to Marco. "Mr. Veneto."

Marco stood up to meet him. Jack noticed the height difference in the two men and the overall build of each man. One, a towering military figure; the other, well, someone the bullies would like to pick on.

Marco answered, "Yes?"

Armin said, "Please keep the patrols out pending the president's decision. We still don't want Vernius to grow suspicious and wonder why we stopped searching for a crystal."

Marco looked disgusted. Jack knew very well that of all the people who disliked Armin Dietrich, nobody had as much disdain for him as Marco Veneto. It was impossible not to notice how they competed for his approval. *Armin, why do you do that?* Jack thought. The chief of staff had no authority to give an order of his own, especially to the chief Legion advisor. But Armin liked to give orders that he knew Jack would agree with, or that Jack was about to give himself. Jack assumed Armin liked the feeling of power it gave him. But he didn't have time to referee a fight between two of his top advisors. He would let it play out. Hopefully, Marco would remain under control and not shoot Armin on the spot.

Marco replied, "Understood."

The meeting had gone just as Jack had thought it would. A divided room. No clear answer. No easy decision. He really didn't know what he would do. Clarisse was right. By law, they had to turn over the crystal to the council. And he hated to think of doing what Edgardo wanted. But was turning over the crystal to the council in the best interest of Earth? After all, he'd taken an oath of office to protect Earth and its citizens first and foremost.

As everyone was exiting the room, Jack caught up to Clarisse. "Sorry about Armin's comments and behavior. He means well. He's just looking out for me."

"You don't have to apologize to me," Clarisse replied. "I'm a big girl. I can take care of myself."

Jack smiled. "I'm sure you can. That's why I picked you for this job."

EDGARDO AND HIS TWO BODYGUARDS WERE THE LAST TO LEAVE the room. As they exited, Edgardo turned left down the hall. All of the others had turned right. Right led to the south entrance and the hover car parking lot.

One of the bodyguards spoke up. "Mr. Ramirez, the car is that way." He pointed toward the south entrance.

"We aren't going to the car," Edgardo replied. "I have to meet someone." He continued down the hall toward the north entrance with one bodyguard on each side of him.

One guard opened the door and Edgardo stepped out. The night air felt cool and refreshing. He loosened his collar slightly, then straightened his tie. He started down the short sidewalk leading to the visitors' aircraft landing pad, which was surrounded by trees. As he walked toward it, the landing pad lights blinded him, causing him to fix his gaze lower toward the ground. The pad was large enough to hold three or four aircraft, but tonight there was only one lone, small transport parked on the back edge of the pad near the trees. He could make out a pilot in the front and one passenger in the back. *That must be him*, Edgardo thought.

Edgardo said to his bodyguards, "You two wait here." He knew the reputation of the man he was about to see, and he wouldn't appreciate bodyguards hanging around. They wouldn't necessarily be a threat, given that reputation, but they would be considered a nuisance. In any event, he needn't fear for his personal safety with this man, at least not yet.

Edgardo approached the transport and the door opened. He stepped inside and sat down facing the passenger. "Edgardo," the man said. "How did it go?"

Edgardo shook his head and replied, "As you suspected, Mr. Sloan."

Edgardo knew his own power, politically with his connections, personally with his wealth, and militarily with his control over EarthNX's private security force, which he often thought resembled a Legion division more than a group of security officers and bodyguards. He was afraid of nobody, not even the president. But this man, Sloan—he was different. With all his connections, Edgardo still couldn't learn where Sloan came from, where he lived, or who he really was. He seemed to come and go as he pleased, with access even to the landing pad at the Presidential Mansion. Nobody contacted

Sloan. He contacted you. And as for Sloan's enemies, they just seemed to disappear. Edgardo always followed a policy that he worked with nobody that he couldn't control, with either money or fear. That is, he'd always followed that policy until now. But he couldn't resist. Sloan had proven to be a very valuable ally. They both had profited well from their relationship.

"So he isn't going to buy the crystal?" Sloan said. "Just as I thought."

"He said he would consider it," Edgardo replied, "and that he would let us know his decision in two days. But his answer will be no. Too much pressure from Chirac to do the 'right' thing. And you know Buchanan, he'll end up doing the 'right' thing."

"Well, it was worth a shot," Sloan said, "if only for what we learned about Buchanan. The alternative will be more complicated and risky, but we must hope the rewards will be satisfactory."

"You're not seriously still thinking about selling the crystal to Romalor?" Edgardo said. He wasn't sure why he'd asked that question. Of course Sloan was serious. He never joked. And now he'd showed Sloan some of his doubts, even though he didn't yet know Sloan's entire plan.

"Yes," answered Sloan.

"But how will you convince him to buy it without a weapon in which to use it?" Edgardo asked. "And assuming you do that, how will we ever deliver it to him? The Legion has the crystal now. It's under guard at Sector Four headquarters. I say we just take the standard fee from the council and be done with it. I didn't get to where I'm at by taking foolish risks."

Sloan leaned forward. The cold stare Edgardo saw in Sloan's eyes sent chills up his spine.

"Locating this crystal was the opportunity of a lifetime," Sloan said. "I don't intend to give it away. We're going to make a killing on this. Do you think I haven't thought this through? I had a backup plan before we turned over the crystal. As for your first question, Romalor will buy the crystal because *you* will also promise to design and build him a super weapon, powered by the crystal. And when the weapon is complete, *you* will sell that to him as well, at a premium, of course. In the meantime, we have nothing to fear. Craton is far from having the technology to develop a super weapon on its own. Their most advanced weapons are extras that *you* sold them. And might I remind you that those weapons sales violated at least six Senate and presidential bills, and those are just the bills that I can think of off the top of my head. So this isn't any road that EarthNX hasn't traveled down before."

"All right," said Edgardo, "but when Romalor is in possession of the super weapon, what's to keep him from using it to destroy Earth, or holding us hostage?"

Sloan sat back and smiled. To Edgardo, the smile seemed even colder than the stare.

"Edgardo, my friend," Sloan said, "here's the real beauty in all of this. At the same time EarthNX is developing the super weapon, it also will be developing a defense against the weapon. An upgrade to the current defense shield, or something brand new. I don't know what, but you'll come up with it. Then we leak the fact that Romalor is about to complete a super weapon. When the Legion hears of this, it comes to you know who to come up with a defense. And bingo, you sell the Legion the defense. You see, Edgardo, this crystal is the best investment ever. It just keeps paying one huge dividend after another."

Edgardo thought that maybe he should stop making inquiries, but he had one more burning question. He cleared his throat. "Mr. Sloan, may I ask what's in this for you, besides the money? It's my understanding that you never work for only monetary compensation. You always have an angle."

The silence was eerie. Sloan stared at Edgardo. Edgardo

thought he had pushed his luck and asked one question too many.

Sloan smiled again. "As I just explained, throughout all of this, both Craton and Earth will be in need of military intelligence from the other. I plan on providing that intelligence to each one, unbeknownst to the other. In exchange, I will demand a certain level of authority over their military." Sloan leaned forward and folded his hands. "And when I deliver in the manner that I plan on delivering, they will both grant me that demand." Sloan leaned back. The smile left his face, replaced by the cold stare again. "Now, Edgardo, are you with me or not?"

Edgardo wasn't sure if he really was on board, but he knew what Sloan's question really meant. He didn't have a choice. With everything that Sloan had just revealed to him, the question Sloan was really asking was whether he wanted to partner with Sloan to complete the plan or disappear like so many enemies before him.

"When you put it that way, Mr. Sloan," Edgardo said, "how can I refuse? But you still didn't answer one of my questions. How do you plan on getting the crystal out of Sector Four headquarters and into Romalor's hands?"

"We won't," answered Sloan with a grin. "Romalor will come and get it."

While all planets in the galaxy agreed to Treaty 5274, some were more reluctant to sign than others. However, no planet opposed the treaty as strongly as the planet Craton and its young ruler, Romalor Leximer. Long before its discovery by Earth and the signing of Treaty 5274, Craton had a proclivity for war. Romalor and his people saw the unlimited potential for the use of hilaetite crystals in weapons. If they could develop the super weapon before any other planet, they could rule the galaxy.

3

ROMALOR

J ake always enjoyed dinner at home, just him, Uncle Ben, and Aunt Jane. With Ben's position in the Legion, it seemed that they were always at someone's house or had guests over for dinner.

"Uncle Ben," Jake said, "can you tell us the story again of how you took out the Centans?"

Ben smiled. "The battle at Centaur is where I got this old war wound." He slapped his bad leg. "That was my last fight. You like that story?"

Jake sat up straight. "Yeah, I do. They got your leg with a plasma gun, but not before you destroyed four Centans with one swipe of your sepder!" Jake swung his fork over his plate, barely missing his glass of milk.

"Okay, I will, but not right now," Ben replied. "I need to get moving."

"Why?" Jake asked. "You have someplace to go tonight, don't you? I thought this was a little early to be eating dinner."

"Yes," replied Jane. "Your uncle has an important meeting he has to get to tonight."

Jake looked back at Ben and tilted his head. "What's it about? Will you be home in time for us to finish our Quantum

Light Fighter game on the computer? I love that game. It's so realistic!" The three-dimensional holographic images emitted from the computer were much clearer and more detailed than other computer games. Jake felt as if a miniature fighter was flying in his house.

"Not tonight, buddy. This will likely be a long one," Ben replied. He took a bite of his roll.

"Okay," Jake said, poking his fork in his roast beef. Roast beef was the one food he really didn't like. And with this news, he had even less of an appetite for it. "Then can Cal spend the night?"

Jane shook her head. "Sorry, Jake, but his father is still away on patrol. And you know he doesn't let Diane or Cal stay anywhere or have anyone over when he's gone. Diane doesn't need another boy to take care of, even though I'm sure Cal and you give her no trouble." She smiled and raised an eyebrow.

Jake lowered his chin and laid his fork down. "I know, I know." He knew Cal's dad's rule, but he had never really liked it. Cal's dad seemed to be gone more than he was home.

Jane looked at Ben and then at Jake. "But Cal can come over here until dark."

Jake smiled. A perfect evening for a game of robo ball.

Jane looked toward Ben. "Where is your meeting?"

"In the headquarters building," Ben replied. "The meeting was supposedly called by the president himself." Ben took another bite.

Jake's eyes widened. "Will the president be there? Will you get to meet him? What will he talk about?"

"No, no," Ben answered. "Nobody from the Presidential Sector is coming. The content and orders for the meeting were given to Commander O'Reilly. He'll run the meeting."

"Do you think they'll send you out on patrol like Cal's dad?" Jake asked. He picked up his fork and took a bite of roast beef. He chewed slowly and swallowed hard.

"No," Ben replied. "They don't send a cadet trainer out on patrol. My active days are over, buddy. And I'm not too disappointed. It's more time that I can spend with you and your aunt." Ben finished off his roll and meat and took a drink.

"But they value your uncle's opinion very much," Jane said, smiling at Ben. She looked at Jake. "That's why he goes to meetings like the one tonight."

"I don't know about valuing it," Ben said, "but they do ask for it, I guess. Maybe to make me feel good." He laughed. "Now, I have to run."

Ben wiped his mouth quickly with his napkin and got up, rubbing his leg. He gave Jane a kiss on the lips, then squeezed Jake's shoulder and limped to the door.

Jake laid down his fork again. "Aunt Jane, I think I'm full. I'm heading outside to find Cal. Do you need any help cleaning up?"

"No, I have it," Jane answered. "Go on."

———————

"YOU CAN HUNT FIRST," CAL SAID AS HE TWISTED THE SILVER metallic ball, separating it into two halves, exposing the small programmable computer screen.

Jake picked up the rectangular tracker. It fit nicely in the palm of his hand. He pressed the screen to activate it.

"Finished," Cal said. He twisted the two halves back together.

Jake pressed and held the sync button on the tracker until it blinked green, indicating that it was synced to the ball. A local GPS map popped onto the screen and the blinking dot marked the tracker's—and therefore Jake's—location. Jake loved the real-time images of the GPS. He could make out his house if he zoomed in close enough. The number 'twenty' appeared in the top right corner of the screen.

"Twenty minutes!" Jake shouted. "You only gave me twenty minutes?"

Cal grinned. "It's an easy route. I didn't program it to go through or around *too* many obstacles."

"Sure," Jake said. "I don't believe that for a second."

Cal released the ball into the air and it immediately shot off past Jake's house, out of sight.

Jake looked down at the tracker and then up in the direction that the ball flew. He then took off at a sprint, holding the tracker out in front of him.

Jake followed the path of the ball on the tracker's screen. Concentrating on the tracker, he ran straight out into the street. He heard a roar and looked up, ducking instinctively. A hover car swerved just in time to avoid flying directly over his head. Even at that distance, the air pressure from the bottom of the car felt like a giant weight dropped on his shoulders. His knees buckled and he landed in the street.

He pulled himself up into a sitting position and sat there for a moment, checking himself out. Everything seemed to work, and no pain. *Wow, that was close*, he thought. If Aunt Jane had seen him running into the street without looking, she'd skin him alive. Even little kids knew enough not to do that. What a dope! And he'd lost valuable time, too. The timer showed twelve minutes remaining.

He got up, looked at the tracker again, and then surveyed the other side of the street in the direction the tracker showed the ball had gone. He had to squint against the bright setting sun reflecting off the white domed houses. He shielded his eyes with his hand and looked closer. It looked like he'd have a pretty clear path. Maybe Cal wasn't making him navigate around too many obstacles. This would be a first.

He gave chase again, running out of the residential section and into the military section. As he passed each of the white domed buildings, he checked the tracker. It was still a straight shot. First was the mess hall, then the training facility, on to the barracks, past the spacecraft and weapon hangars, and finally to the Legion office buildings.

Jake stopped abruptly. The tracker took him right to the wall of one of the buildings. The tracker showed the ball going up, but not over the building. That was odd. Jake looked around. "You have to be kidding me," he said out loud as he eyed a drainage pipe running up the side of the building. Whether on purpose or by accident, Cal had programmed the ball to go into the drainage pipe. Jake glanced at the tracker again. Six minutes.

Jake looked around. He had been concentrating so hard on the tracker that he hadn't paid attention to where he was. But he recognized the large white domed building instantly. He was standing right beside the Legion headquarters building.

A SMALL SQUADRON OF TEN CRATON FIGHTERS DROPPED OUT of quantum drive as they approached Earth. They were positioned near the Sector Four defense station, but out of visual range. For the moment, they were out of the range of Earth's sensors, as well. The fighters were not small combat fighters, but larger transport fighters. They would be of little use in a dogfight against quantum light fighters, but they could do plenty of damage to ground troops, and each transport fighter could transport ten men besides the two pilots. Craton was located in a solar system near Earth's. Like Earth, Craton was currently one of the more formidable military planets in the galaxy. Unlike Earth, however, Craton had not become powerful through the use of its own resources or alliances with friendly planets. Craton took whatever it needed or wanted from other planets by force.

Romalor Leximer was in the lead spacecraft, in the captain's chair. His six-foot six-inch frame, which was large even for a Cratonite, filled the chair. He stood out from the others on the ship, in dark red and black, the colors always worn by the ruler of Craton. Like all Cratonites, men and women, he had a dark complexion and long dark hair. This made Cratonites attractive, even to other species. And he had a large muscular chest due to a third pectoral muscle that all Cratonite men possessed.

Romalor turned to his first officer, Raxmar, who stood at the control station. "Have you confirmed the intelligence that we received?"

"Yes, General," Raxmar replied. "There are four Earth defense stations orbiting just outside the atmosphere. One for each of their so-called sectors. Each defense station emits some sort of impulse shield, connecting it to each of the other defense stations, creating a shield around the planet, just as we were told. Any object that touches the impulse shield is probably disintegrated immediately. The only way to pass into and out of Earth's atmosphere is to go through one of the defense stations."

"Very well," Romalor said. "We will proceed as planned. Tell me when you receive the signal."

"Yes, General," Raxmar said.

An officer at the helm turned toward Romalor. "General, are you sure we are in the right position? Did you get the coordinates correct?"

Romalor lowered his hands to the arms of the chair and squeezed. He looked at Raxmar.

Raxmar quickly turned toward Romalor. "General, he's new. This is his first assignment."

Romalor stared at the officer. His mind raced: ignorance, insubordination, stupidity. Questioning Romalor. How did someone like that ever make it into the military, let alone become an officer? He wanted to lunge out of his seat and terminate the officer permanently. No. At least, not now. He needed every hand for the mission. He couldn't afford to lose a helmsman so early. He would have to deal with him later.

But he still needed to put the officer in his place, if for no other reason than to keep the rest of the crew confident that he was in control and, of course, to keep them intimidated. Since advancement in the Craton military often came by the elimination of a person's direct superior, it was important that he maintain a certain level of fear. He knew it generally took more than a few men to overthrow a general, but he wouldn't take any chances by showing signs of weakness. "Do you question me?" he thundered. "Have I not led Craton in more battles than you can count? Taking anything and everything we want! If you ever so much as look at me with a question on your mind, I will terminate you where you stand!" The officer shrank back in his seat, shaking.

"I'm getting a signal now, General," Raxmar said. "It's an all-clear for entry."

Romalor felt the tension leave him. He grinned. "Excellent." He slowly fingered the assortment of ropes, chains, and necklaces hanging down the front of his steel-coated black military vest. Some were plain, and others had medallions, symbols, wood carvings, or other trinkets hooked to them. He had a custom of taking something from everyone he killed— or at least, from everyone he killed that wasn't disintegrated— and making it into a necklace. He had hundreds of them. He wished he could wear all of them at once. He slowly ran his fingers over one particular necklace, the saber-toothed bear claws. He remembered vividly the victim from whom he took the necklace, and the look on the man's face as Romalor ended his life. "Soon I will add to my collection. Proceed at once."

CAPTAIN ABSOLAN WILLIAMS SAT ALONE IN HIS QUARTERS IN the Sector Four defense station, staring out his small window into the darkness of outer space. His first command. *But then again, let's not get too excited*, he thought. Commanding a defense station wasn't a glamour assignment. But there were only four stations, so he was one of only four captains chosen for such a command. Not bad.

His thoughts were brought back to his room by a voice coming over his com. "Sir, this is Hart. Something appears to be wrong with the defense shield."

Private Amy Hart was currently operating the main terminal in the central control room of the defense station. A good soldier, but green. He wasn't concerned. Young privates always had a tendency to overreact. He pressed the com. "What is it, Private?"

"Well, sir, the defense shield appears to be down between the Sector One defense station and us," Private Hart answered.

Absolan pressed a different com control. "Su, run a diagnostic on the system. I'm on my way." He had better go down there, if for no other reason than to instill some confidence in the privates.

"Already on it, sir," Private Cheng Su replied.

Absolan walked into the central control room with quick, long strides and immediately took his seat in the center of the room. "What do we have, Su?"

"Everything's coming up fine," Private Su replied. "There's nothing wrong with our system. The shield must really be down."

"Let's not jump to conclusions too quickly," Absolan responded. "It takes four different codes to access the defense shield system, and those codes are all held by four separate people. The president is the only person who possibly could obtain all four codes. But even then, there are numerous backup fail-safes." He could feel a few beads of perspiration forming on his forehead. Maybe this wasn't the slow, behind-the-scenes assignment he thought it was. But there had to be an explanation. There hadn't been a defense shield failure since EarthNX developed it. "Run a diagnostic on the diagnostic program."

"Already done, sir," Private Su said. "Everything is coming up clean."

Absolan wiped his forehead with his arm. "Okay, we know that any spacecraft attempting to enter or leave Earth's atmosphere anywhere other than through one of our defense stations will be disintegrated when it hits the impulse shield. If the shield is down, we're vulnerable. What or who could be causing the problem, or trying to make us believe there's a problem? Are there any foreign spacecraft currently being inspected or detained in the gatekeeper cell?"

Private Hart replied, "No, sir. And I just received a report of our external sensor readings. All indications are that the shield is definitely down between us and Sector One."

"All right," Absolan replied.

He had to remain calm and in charge. This situation was exactly what all of his years of training were for. He would continue to follow protocol. A solution would have to arise. He started running through the possible problems and the protocol for each in his mind.

Besides the central control room of the defense station, each defense station's computer system could be controlled from the defense station's Legion headquarters down on the planet, and from the combat room underneath the Presidential Mansion. The next protocol was to contact sector headquarters and then the Presidential Mansion. He turned to another Legion private at the communications station, Max Troutman. "Troutman, get me in touch with Sector Four headquarters."

"Sir," Private Troutman said, "communications are down."

Absolan pounded his fist on the arm of his chair. "Then get me the Presidential Mansion."

"Sir," Private Troutman replied, "I mean, all communications are down, not just communications to headquarters. We can't send or receive any communication signals. I've been trying to contact the Sector One defense station to see if they are getting the same readings we are. But I can't get a signal out."

"Captain," Private Hart interrupted before Absolan could reply, "I'm picking up a sensor signal. It's detecting ten spacecraft entering Earth's atmosphere. Coordinates zero-one-hundred-fifteen. That's about two miles from us. They appear to be headed for Sector Four headquarters."

Private Su jumped in. "I've checked every system on the station. Whatever's happening to us is being controlled from Sector Four headquarters or the Presidential Mansion. It's nobody here, sir."

"Scramble every quantum light fighter we have on the station," Absolan demanded. "Send them after those spacecraft. If the spacecraft don't respond and retreat, the order is shoot to destroy."

"Yes, sir," Private Su responded.

"Captain," Private Hart said, punching controls on her computer terminal, "the signal's getting stronger. The spacecraft clearly are headed to Sector Four headquarters."

Absolan noticed Private Su's eyes widen as he stared at the screen in front of him. "What is it, Su?"

"Captain," Private Su paused for a moment, "it appears the quantum light fighters' docking locks have malfunctioned."

"What!" Absolan jumped up, this time hitting both fists on the arms of his chair. *Is this some kind of a test?* he thought. Surely all of this couldn't go wrong for real. Maybe Legion headquarters was testing him. No, the Legion didn't operate like that. This was a real problem, and without communications, it was his problem.

"The fighters are locked down, permanently," responded Private Su. "The computerized locking mechanisms are being controlled by whoever is controlling the station. They won't release the fighters. They seem to know every single one of our protocols."

"Then have the pilots work the manual overrides at each dock and physically open the locks," commanded Absolan. This might be a new command, and his first command, but he wasn't going to give up. Wherever those spacecraft were from, he couldn't let them get through, not on his watch.

"They're already working on it, sir," replied Private Su. "But whoever is doing this has changed the manual override codes. All of them. It's going to take some time for us to crack the codes to be able to work the manual overrides. Headquarters' system has the ability to crack codes like this in minutes, but since we can't access headquarters . . ." He paused again. "Well, it'll take longer."

Absolan shook his head and turned away from the others, gritting his teeth. He took a deep breath, then turned back. "How long, Private?"

"Twenty minutes. Fifteen if we're lucky," Private Su answered slowly.

Absolan looked at Private Hart. "Hart, what's the ETA for those spacecraft to hit Sector Four headquarters?"

Private Hart turned to Absolan. He could see from the blank look on her face that he wasn't going to like what he heard. The answer came softly. "Five minutes, sir."

The room was eerily silent. Absolan had one last question, one last chance, but he knew what the answer would be. "The station's plasma guns, Private Su?"

Private Su shook his head slowly. "The spacecraft have never been in range, sir."

"They even had that calculated to perfection," Absolan

replied. He felt the weight of defeat pressing on him. Earth was being invaded on his watch, and there wasn't a thing he could do about it. "Who is doing this, and why?"

JAKE LOOKED AT THE PIPE. IT WAS JUST BIG ENOUGH FOR HIM to fit in on his hands and knees. He had just knelt down to crawl inside when he heard voices coming from the front of the building. He saw two Legion guards, heavily armed, checking very closely the credentials of everyone entering the building. He cocked his head in their direction, but it was no use. He could hear voices, but couldn't make out what they were saying. Should he crawl into the pipe or not? Any movement in that direction could give him away to the guards. Maybe he should play it safe and head home. No, he still had six minutes left. He wasn't going to give up and let Cal win so easily.

Once inside the pipe, there was enough light coming from the outside that he could see up ahead. He would just go as far as there was light, he told himself. He checked the tracker. Sure enough, the ball has to be in here. Three minutes left. The farther inside he got, the slower he crawled until he hit the end of the light. The pipe turned and headed straight upwards. He could see light at the top and it lit the sides of the pipe. There were ladder rungs on one side. It was made for climbing. He could feel his heart start to race and his hands getting damp with excitement and nervousness. He really shouldn't be in here. But he still had time to snatch victory. He started up.

As Jake slowly climbed the pipe, he started to hear faint voices from inside the building. As he reached the top where the light was entering, he discovered that the pipe was hooked to a large air duct. Jake checked the tracker. The ball had gone in the direction from which the voices were coming. One minute remaining. Jake crawled into the air duct toward the ball and the voices. He wondered what was going on inside.

Jake crawled slowly. He didn't want to make any noise. The slightest tap on the metal duct seemed to vibrate all along its surface. He proceeded in the direction of the voices and noticed where the light was coming into the air duct up ahead. As he reached the light source, he could see that it was a vent in the ceiling of one of the rooms. The tracker beeped as the timer hit zero, startling Jake. He bobbled the tracker and fumbled for the off switch.

He quickly found the switch, turned the tracker off, and froze, hoping whoever was in the room didn't hear anything. The volume and number of voices did not change. After a moment, Jake relaxed. They must not have heard him.

So much for winning the robo ball game. The right thing to do was get out of there. But Jake found his attention turning to what was going on in the room below. It was a weird place for activity this time of day, wasn't it? He carefully moved into position to see through the vent. He was forced to squint as he moved his head into the light. He blinked a few times until his eyes adjusted. He could make out the people in the room. They were Legion soldiers. And there was Uncle Ben. This must be his secret meeting!

Jake saw that his Uncle Ben was talking with the Sector Four commander, Ted O'Reilly. Mr. O'Reilly had been over for dinner plenty of times. They were close enough to the vent that when Jake focused on them, he could make out their conversation.

"So Ted, you don't know why this meeting was called?" Ben asked. "But the briefing notes sent to me from the Presidential Mansion said that you were in charge and that you had the agenda and orders. I spoke with a couple of other officers as well, and they said the same thing. I assume it's about the crystal, right?" Ben motioned toward a small case sitting inside a glass enclosure at the back of the room.

"Like I said," Ted responded, "my briefing notes came from the same place, but they said that one of the officers had been briefed and would provide me with the details. I've been trying to find out who that is."

"It's not me," replied Ben. "And besides, why was every officer and most of the guards at the headquarters ordered to attend? That breaches every protocol I know, as well as common sense. One division is still out on patrol, and another is on R and R. That leaves two here, and one of those is mostly made up of cadets. Who in their right mind would then put all of these officers and guards in one room?"

"Easy, Ben," Ted said. He put his arm on Ben's shoulder and grinned. "You would be right in wartime, but since we're at peace with every planet, those protocols are relaxed. I'm sure the Presidential Mansion knows what it's doing. Now, let's find out who knows something more about this meeting than we do. I'm the commander of this sector and I don't even know what's going on." Ted chuckled.

"And you're telling me to take it easy," Ben said with a slight smile.

———

THE CRATON SPACECRAFT APPROACHED SECTOR FOUR headquarters with Romalor's fighter still in the lead.

"They have finally detected us, General," Raxmar said, watching his monitor. "You were right. They're too late."

"Yes," Romalor said. He stood up. "The Legion has become complacent. They're so used to nothing coming close to any of their headquarters without first being notified by one of their defense stations. Their overconfidence has worked well for us."

"Shall I take us in, General?" Raxmar asked, looking up at Romalor.

Romalor clenched his fists. "Yes, we need to hit them

before they can sound an alarm. They're so arrogant, sitting underneath their precious defense shield. The guards are probably sleeping right now." Romalor pointed to the central command building on the viewing screen. "Are those the coordinates that we were given?"

"Yes, General," Raxmar replied.

"Then fire!" Romalor commanded.

Romalor watched as four blasts from the fighter's plasma guns obliterated the Sector Four central command building. "Excellent. That should stop any alarm from sounding or communications from going out." His fighter turned and he saw a number of Legion soldiers scrambling toward the closest quantum light fighters. "Take out those fighters before those soldiers get to them."

Raxmar fired the plasma guns. Romalor watched as the other fighters opened fire as well. The ground seemed to explode as all the quantum light fighters in sight went up in balls of flame, along with any Legion soldiers unfortunate enough to have made it to the fighters or who were too close.

"Where are the meeting coordinates?" demanded Romalor as he turned back toward Raxmar.

"Right there," Raxmar replied. He pointed toward the headquarters building.

"Land in the front," Romalor said. "And signal two more fighters to land with us. Leave the other seven in the air. Tell them to take out any Legion fighters trying to get off the ground. They can't let any get airborne." He knew that if they let any quantum light fighters get off the ground, his larger, less mobile transport fighters would be no match for them.

Thirty Craton troops exited three spacecraft ahead of Romalor. Raxmar was at his side. Immediately, the headquarters' guards and a number of other Legion soldiers scattered about opened fire with their sepders.

"Stay in formation," Romalor yelled. "Take them out, quickly." The longer it took him and his troops to get in and out, the more chance Legion troops would assemble and over-take them. The attack was perfectly timed and orchestrated, though, with two Legion divisions gone and most of the command trapped inside. Just as he had been told. He felt very confident in their chances of success. Everything was going as planned. His troops were well prepared, and the Legion soldiers were disorganized. He watched his men quickly dispatch the Legion soldiers.

JAKE COULD HEAR THE PLASMA GUNS AND SEPDER BLASTS. What was going on? He could feel the sweat beading up on his forehead. He had to run. He had to get out of there. But what if they were coming up the drainage pipe? No, surely not. He had to go. But he couldn't. He couldn't make himself move. What would happen to Uncle Ben? Would he fight the invaders? Jake watched as the Legion officers and guards inside the meeting room began to organize. A loud blast came from outside the room.

An officer shouted, "Whoever it is has just entered the building!"

Jake watched, his eyes frozen on the scene below him. Ted O'Reilly immediately took control of the meeting room. "Guards, give any extra weapons to any unarmed officer. Divide in half. You men, get to that side of the door." He motioned to his right. "You men," he signaled to the remainder, "take the other side."

Jake could see that there was only one way in or out of the room, and there were no windows. Jake knew from his many video games that this was a bad situation for the Legion. The room was designed to be a highly confidential meeting place, not to defend against an enemy attack. Jake also knew that the double doors at the front of the room opened automatically, but only by entering a code from one side or the other.

Ted continued to shout orders. "Each side, form two lines. Everyone in front, kneel. Everyone in back, fire over their heads. Angle toward the door so you don't hit each other. The rest of you get back here with me." Ted pointed to four guards and Ben, who weren't placed beside either door. They ran to the back of the room and crouched down in front of the hilaetite crystal.

Ted leaned over to Ben's ear and spoke softly. "If we're lucky, they will be afraid to shoot toward the crystal for fear of blowing themselves up along with us. That might buy us more time to take them out."

"Depending on how many there are," Ben added.

Jake heard a shout outside the door. "Clear!" Jake knew what that meant. He pressed the palms of his hands against his ears. The sound was deafening. The sight was worse. Half the guards positioned on each side of the door were blown up when the plasma bomb detonated. The door and three feet of the wall on either side of it took out a few more guards as they were hurled through the air. The remaining guards near the door had stumbled backwards. They pulled themselves up, shaking their heads. Jake thought, *Hurry up, shoot.* The invaders poured through the opening, firing. Jake recognized them as Cratonites from their large size and protruding chests. But Cratonites? Here?

A few of the guards got off a couple of shots from their sepders and smaller plasma guns, and a few Cratonites fell. But what were left of the guards by the door fell quickly.

Ted, Ben, and the four guards at the back of the room opened fire on the Cratonites. Jake watched in terror as the mass of Cratonites struggled to squeeze through the opening and over dead bodies. It didn't seem real. This couldn't be happening.

The delay from the crush in the doorway helped the six Legion soldiers to finally start knocking off the Cratonites. *Yes,* Jake thought. *Now the Legion will win. They have to win.*

But a few Cratonites started to fire at the six remaining Legion soldiers, hitting two of the guards before a very large Cratonite burst through the opening and shouted, "Don't shoot, you idiots! That's the crystal. You'll blow us all up."

Jake's eyes widened when he saw the large Cratonite. He recognized him from news photos and even computer games. Romalor Leximer, the Cratonite ruler. He had never seen anyone so big in person. But how could Romalor be attacking the Legion headquarters? How could he have gotten through Earth's defense shield?

The Cratonites immediately dropped their plasma guns, pulled out their goliaths, and charged. Ted, Ben, and the remaining two guards were able to take out a few more of the Cratonites before they were overtaken. Once the Cratonites were upon them, they stopped firing and turned their sepders to swords, engaging in hand-to-hand combat. Jake held his breath. The four remaining Legion soldiers were outnumbered almost six to one at this point. The two remaining guards who were out in front went down first, a goliath penetrating each of them, one in the chest and the other in the throat. Ted was fighting the one Jake had heard called Raxmar and two other Cratonites, and his Uncle Ben was engaged with Romalor.

"I have to help," Jake whispered to himself. "But how? I can't." He again tried to leave, to get help, but he still couldn't make his legs move. He just lay there, staring down into the carnage in the meeting room.

Jake's vision blurred, his eyes filling with tears. He angrily brushed them away. He would be brave, like Uncle Ben. Ted took a goliath stab to his left side, then another. His left arm went limp. Ted tried to defend himself with just his right arm, but Raxmar and the other two Cratonites were too strong. He took a stab to his right shoulder and his sepder dropped. He just stood there as Raxmar delivered the killing blow, driving his goliath deep into Ted's abdomen. Jake bit back a cry of horror. His uncle was fighting alone.

Uncle Ben was faring better, probably because he had more combat time and training, but there were still too many Cratonites, and Jake could tell that Uncle Ben's bad leg made it difficult for him to move. Come on, Uncle Ben. Come on!

Romalor delivered a stab into Ben's left bicep. His left arm hung limp. Ben raised his right arm and swung his sepder, but Romalor blocked it. With Ben's right arm in the air, blocked, there was nothing left with which to defend his body. Romalor brought his goliath around and struck Ben in the right shoulder. His right arm went limp and his sepder dropped. Ben stood there, helpless to defend himself, staring bravely into Romalor's eyes without so much as a flinch. Romalor drew his goliath back and then immediately surged it forward into Ben's chest. Jake didn't think. He shouted, "Noooo!"

His uncle crumpled to the ground. Jake lay in the duct, frozen, as Romalor slowly looked up and caught his gaze. Romalor smiled.

Raxmar reached up and yanked the ventilator grate out of the ceiling. Jake, stunned, fell at Romalor's feet. He couldn't move. "A child," Raxmar said contemptuously. "Do you want us to kill him, General?"

Romalor replied, "No, he won't give us any trouble. Besides, this will teach him a good lesson, not to mess with Craton. He can grow up with the fear of knowing what happens when you do. And he can teach all his little friends to fear us as well. I think his influence on the next generation will do us good."

Romalor walked over to Ben's body, lying on its back. He bent over and grasped the necklace that Jake had given Ben. With a quick jerk, Romalor snapped it off Ben's neck and tied it around his own. "This will do perfectly," Romalor said. Romalor looked at Raxmar. "Do you have the crystal secured?"

"Yes, General," Raxmar replied, pointing to a thickly padded pouch that he was holding.

"Then let's go," Romalor replied.

Jake's mind was blank. He couldn't think or do anything. He just lay there staring at his Uncle Ben's lifeless body.

As I end my news story, I leave you with one question to ponder. Has Treaty 5274 made the galaxy safer for Earth, or has it paved the way to the annihilation of our planet? This has been Nigil Diggs reporting for the Earth Times Journal.

4

OPPORTUNITY LOST

J ake quickly raised his sepder for a block. It was a weak blow, and he stopped it easily. The next swing would probably be low, and then one more high swing. His opponent was so predictable. Holding his sepder with only one hand, Jake dropped it low. Another block. Jake ducked, and as anticipated, his opponent's next swing went over his head. Jake lowered his sepder to his side. He wasn't a bit fatigued. He could do this all day. He needed a better challenge. Sure, his opponent was an officer with much more battle experience than him, but he could take the guy anytime he wanted. His opponent came up unexpectedly with a backhanded swing, and Jake instinctively jumped backwards. That was close. Time to go on the offensive. Jake countered with four swings: right, left, high, low, moving the officer backwards.

"Pretty good, Private," the officer said. "You know what you're doing. The commander warned me about getting into the ring with you. But now let's see what you really have."

The officer came at Jake with his sepder high, striking at Jake's head. *Clang, clang, clang, clang.* Jake blocked each blow but was driven backwards on his heels. The officer then did a complicated down-and-up move with his sepder. It was difficult to block, but Jake did so. He wasn't happy about it, though. He was completely on the defensive.

"That's what I thought," the officer said. "You can handle the standard stuff, but get a little tricky with you, and you're all mine."

Jake could feel his heart race faster. *I'm taking this guy out*, he thought. Jake faked a low swing, then turned a one-eighty to block the officer's counter. A tricky move, but the officer didn't counter as Jake anticipated. Instead, he kicked Jake in the chest. Jake didn't see it coming. The blow knocked him backwards into a roll. He'd been outmaneuvered.

Jake hopped up. "That's it!" He'd had enough of the officer's tricks and arrogance. He would show the guy what he could really do.

"What's the matter?" the officer said with a grin. "Can't handle an old man?"

Jake saw Romalor's grin on the officer. Eight years couldn't erase Romalor's face from his mind. He could feel the muscles in his face tighten instinctively as his eyes focused on the man's midsection. That was the kill zone. He really wanted to kill this guy. No, he couldn't kill him, but he also couldn't lose to him, not the way the guy was grinning and taunting him. He was going to finish this once and for all. Jake raised his sepder high, holding it in both hands, and began swinging as he moved forward into the officer. First to the left, then to the right. Swing left, swing right, faster, faster, swing harder, harder. The officer blocked each blow while continuing to back up, just as Jake planned. That was more like it. Jake quickly pulled his sepder above his head and put all his strength into a blow coming in high on his opponent. The officer blocked, but was knocked backwards by the force of the blow. With a roll-over move that Jake had never seen before, the officer came up under Jake and, with a backwards thrust of his sepder, knocked Jake's sepder out of his hands.

He stepped into Jake with his sepder pointed at Jake's chest. Jake stood frozen. He felt his chest heaving as he gasped for air. How did the officer do that move? How could I have lost to him? He's twice my age.

"Never come high and hard, Private," the officer said. "Anyone who knows what he's doing will turn it around on you." He lowered his sepder and held out his hand.

Jake shook it. "Thank you, sir."

"Nice fight, Private," said a deep voice from behind Jake. "Until the end."

Jake turned around. Captain Alfons Gorski approached them. He was a very large, heavy-set man in his mid-fifties. Jake had always thought that Gorski had clearly eaten his share of kielbasa and kishka, two of Gorski's favorite foods from his native region, formerly Poland.

"Sir." Jake saluted as Gorski approached them.

"I'm going to hit the showers," the officer said. Jake and Gorski stood alone at the side of the ring.

The familiar smell of sweat permeated the room. Jake liked it. He liked training. And with sepder training, physical fitness, and one-on-one, hand-to-hand and sepder fights in the ring, the training room was a sweaty place.

"Jake, I've been around this gym for longer than I care to remember," Gorski said. "And I've watched and trained more cadets, privates, and even officers than you can count. You're one of the best I've ever seen. That is, when you can control yourself. You would have won that fight if you hadn't let him get to you. You let the taunting get to you, and then you fight with anger, not with intelligence. At that point, you've already lost. Jake, in real battles, if you keep letting your enemies get to you, you're going to get yourself killed one day."

"Sir," Jake replied, "I just do what I need to do to win." He knew Gorski was probably right, but what else could he do? That's who he was. The anger gave him strength, and motivation. But for what? For Romalor. That's what.

"No, Jake," Gorski said. "You do what your opponents want you to do. They want you to get angry. They use that against you. Think about it."

Jake nodded, trying to look appreciative and respectful. Part of him knew that Gorski was right, but he wanted the anger. He needed the anger. "Thank you, sir."

JAKE SAT ALONE IN THE FRONT ROW OF THE LEGION headquarters meeting room. After a tough day, this was where he liked to go to think, and remember. The hole in the wall was repaired, new doors had been installed, and the other damage cleaned up. The room now looked exactly as it had from the air duct vent that night eight years ago. No memorial. Nothing. They even still used the room for an occasional meeting. Jake felt his pulse quicken and his fists clench. The government wanted to act like nothing had ever happened. They didn't want people to think about it. They didn't want people to remember. But he would remember. His Uncle Ben fighting to his last breath. All those Legion soldiers so outnumbered, taken by surprise, massacred. And Romalor's face as he killed Ben. Yes, he wanted to remember. He would always remember. Why else was he in the Legion? To protect the very government that covered up the events of that night? To protect the government that covered up his uncle's death? No, he was here to find the truth and make things right. He'd promised Aunt Jane. But did Aunt Jane really want that, or was it Jake who needed it? After all, Aunt Jane always said that all she wanted was to see him happy. He needed to visit Aunt Jane. She was all alone, living out in the country. He didn't make it out there nearly enough. But the country was a great place to grow up, after what he'd seen. That was Frank's idea. Frank had taken care of him and Aunt Jane ever since that awful night. His happiest times, after Uncle Ben died, had been the time he spent at Frank's house.

Cal's voice broke the silence. "I thought I would find you here. You know, you need to get out more. You spend too much time in this room."

"It's good to see you too, Cal," Jake said with a slight grin.

"Frank wants to see us in his office in fifteen minutes. Until then, I guess I'll take a load off my feet," Cal said as he plopped down in the chair beside Jake. "I'm serious. You eat, sleep, and live the Legion. You need to get out and have more fun. Why don't you go to dinner with me tonight? I was going to check out that new restaurant on the top floor of the Awori Tower in Lagos. Their motto is 'you can't dine higher anyplace on Earth.' You probably pay higher than anyplace on Earth too. But hey, I'm buying. What do you say?"

"I don't know, Cal," Jake replied. He leaned forward, putting his elbows on his knees, and clutched his head in his hands. "I just lost in the ring to an officer twice my age. What's my problem? I know I'm better than he is. Gorski says I have anger management issues."

"Well," Cal said, "it's nothing that a nice juicy steak in the sky can't fix." Cal grinned.

Jake knew that Cal was just trying to cheer him up. Cal was good at that. What would he do without Cal? He knew he wasn't an easy person to be friends with, but that didn't stop Cal. He was a real trooper. "Cal, it just doesn't make sense. That night. It doesn't make sense."

"Okay, buddy," Cal said with a sigh. "I see I'm not going to change your mind. You're in one of those remembering moods. Let's go through it again."

Jake leaned back. "How did Romalor penetrate our defense shield and attack a Legion headquarters? And the government inquiry, what about that? An attack on a Legion headquarters, and they investigate for only a week. Nothing was found and nobody was apprehended, and the investigation was signed and sealed by the chief Legion advisor, the president's chief of staff, and the president himself. For their eyes only. I was the only survivor that saw anything, but they didn't believe a word I said, or they said they didn't believe it. They said there was no evidence connecting Romalor or Craton to any of it and I was too young and too scared. That I probably just thought they were Cratonites from all the video games I played."

"I know, buddy," Cal said. He put his hand on Jake's shoulder. "You know that Frank, Diane, Dad, and I believe every word you said, but what can we do about it? We've been through this over and over."

Jake stood up and walked to the spot where his Uncle Ben had died. "The government was covering up its own blunders. They were in possession of a hilaetite crystal, and by all accounts, the largest one ever found, and they weren't supposed to be. If the government found out who stole the crystal, then they would have to explain to the council why they had the crystal in the first place. Why it wasn't immediately sent to Pergan. And putting the cover-up aside, where's the crystal now? Isn't anybody worried about that? And what about the Legion officers who were used as scapegoats? Captain Williams was dishonorably discharged from the Legion for his failure at the defense station. Where's he? I tried to find him once. He's off the grid. The government has him tucked away somewhere, if they haven't disposed of him. And Commander O'Reilly. The poor guy died trying to defend the headquarters and a crystal that shouldn't have been there. I saw him die. And it wasn't a pretty death. And the government runs his name through the mud. Putting the blame on him. What about his wife and kids?"

"Jake," Cal said, "you know I would do anything to help you, to help lift this burden from you, but we've been down every road, and each one leads to a dead end."

Jake turned toward Cal with a finger on his chin. "Maybe

we haven't gone high enough. I know Aretha Brown fought long and hard in the Senate to try to keep the investigation open. She believed there was more to it than a simple robbery. She pushed for an investigation, independent of the Legion."

Cal stood up. "Jake, she's the Senate leader and she still couldn't make that happen. What can we do?"

Jake shook his head slowly. "I don't know."

"Come on, we better get to Frank's office." Cal put his hand on Jake's back. "And did I mention that Diane will be at dinner tonight?"

Jake's head popped up and he turned to Cal quickly. "She will?" Everything seemed to change inside him when he thought about Diane. He couldn't let anyone know, though, especially her. His focus was on Romalor, his uncle's death, and those who had covered it up.

"I thought that would get your attention," Cal said with a smile. "I'll take that look as a yes, you'll be there. Eighteen hundred hours."

Jake half frowned, half grinned. "What look?"

JAKE AND CAL MADE THEIR WAY ACROSS AND DOWN THE STREET to the new Sector Four command center, construction on which had begun shortly after that night eight years ago. Jake looked down the street. It had changed so much in the past eight years. The buildings were still designed in the traditional style, white dome-shaped structures. However, there were so many new buildings, and the streets were bustling. People and hover cars were everywhere. Sector Four headquarters had truly become a city in and of itself. Jake instinctively ducked his head and winced from the roar as a spacecraft took off over their heads. He could tell a spacecraft from an aircraft just from the sound. He had learned that from his Uncle Ben. A spacecraft made more of a deep roar, as it was heavier and more powerful. The weight and power were needed to enter and leave the atmosphere of planets. Aircraft didn't need that ability just to travel around Earth.

They entered the building, went through the now standard security clearance checks, and made their way directly to Commander Frank Cantor's office. Cal knocked on the closed door.

"It's open," came a rough voice from inside.

Jake and Cal walked in. No surprise: Frank was seated behind his desk with an unlit cigar in his mouth, chewing on it as he always did. And the picture wouldn't be complete without Frank's trademark cowboy hat hanging on top of the coat rack in the corner.

How many of those hats did he have, and where did they all come from? Who still made such things? They looked like the military-style hats worn by the cavalry in the old United States western movies of the twentieth century that he and Frank used to watch all the time.

"You wanted to see us, Commander?" Jake asked.

"Yes, yes, have a seat," Frank said, gesturing toward the chairs without looking up from the work on his desk. "And close the door."

Jake glanced at the chairs, and was surprised to see Diane sitting there. "Diane, hi. I didn't know that you were going to be here." *Oh, that was real smooth*, he thought as he shut the door. Couldn't he come up with something a little nicer? But then, did it really matter? After all, they were there on business. But of course it mattered. It mattered to him. He had that warm, somewhat nervous feeling again, like he always did around Diane, like a silly schoolboy.

Jake and Cal sat on either side of Diane.

"Do you two know who the Imperial Majesty is?" Frank asked.

Cal replied, "Yes, that's the title that Vernius gave to its leader about eight years ago."

Jake jumped in. "They didn't think the title of Vernition Queen or King was politically correct anymore."

"Correct on both counts," Frank said. "And I suppose you know that they recently elected the new Imperial Majesty. She took office a couple of months ago."

"Yes, sir," Cal said. Jake and Cal both nodded.

Frank continued, "And when they elect a new Imperial Majesty, he or she picks a new ambassador from Earth, from our selected prospects."

"Yes, sir," Jake said, "but may I ask, what's all this have to do with us?"

"I have a new assignment for you two cowboys," Frank said. "You are to escort Earth's new ambassador to Vernius. What's more, you hit the trail at daybreak, so you'll need to pack up your saddlebags tonight. I don't have to tell you how important Earth's relationship with Vernius is. They're our closest ally. You'll take a small Legion transport. It'll have a couple of guns just in case, but it should be a smooth ride, seeing that everyone is at peace in that region. If I give you any more firepower, you could alarm the settlers in the area."

Jake didn't necessarily like the idea of going that far from Earth with nothing more than a transport, but he trusted Frank's judgment one hundred percent. After all, as commander, Frank was the number one ranking Legion soldier in Sector Four. Some people thought Frank inherited the position as one of the last officers standing after the attack, but Jake knew better. He hated it when he heard someone say that. Jake remembered Frank as a captain in Sector Four prior to the attack. He remembered how much Uncle Ben liked Frank and how hard Frank seemed to work. After the attack, with most of the Sector Four officers killed, Frank was promoted to the new Sector Four commander and given the unenviable task of trying to put Sector Four headquarters back together. He was the youngest Legion soldier ever to achieve the rank of commander. Jake laughed to himself. At almost fifty, Frank hadn't slowed down a bit and could probably whip just about any soldier in the sector in a fist fight. "Sounds good, Commander." Jake looked at Diane. "But why is Diane here?"

"You're looking at the new Vernition ambassador," Frank replied. "On her last visit, the Imperial Majesty interviewed everyone we put in front of her until she met Diane. She stopped right then. Diane was the one."

It took a minute for it to register with Jake. Then it hit him. Vernition ambassador. That's generally a long-term assignment. Very long term. He looked at Frank. "But is it safe, sir? Are you sure she should go?" As soon as the words left his mouth, he realized that wasn't a smart comment.

Diane looked at Jake with a raised eyebrow. "Really, Jake?"

"You're right," Jake replied. "That was out of line."

"Jake, this is what I've been working for," Diane said. "I want this. This is the opportunity of a lifetime."

Frank interjected before she could go on, "And I just said how important an ally Vernius is. If they want Diane and Diane wants to go, then we'll give them Diane."

Jake's day had just gone from bad to worse. He had to find some hope in this. He looked at Diane. "How long is the assignment?" He already knew the answer.

Diane started to answer, but Frank interrupted her. "Indefinitely. You know that the Vernition queen, I mean Imperial Majesty, is elected for life, unless she decides to retire. As long as she wants Diane and Diane wants to serve, then the position is Diane's."

Jake was speechless. He didn't know what to say. There would be little chance for him to see Diane. He would likely never have an assignment on Vernius. There was little need for Legion soldiers on such a peaceful planet. And an ambassador had little, if any, leeway or time to return home. Maybe Cal was right. He needed to have more fun. Cal used to always prod him to ask Diane out. Cal was always trying to set them up. Cal would say how he noticed how Jake looked and acted around Diane. Cal told him that Diane did the same thing around Jake. That they were a perfect match. But it always seemed that he, and probably Diane too, never had the time. Lately, Cal had pretty much given up trying, except for an occasional comment here and there. Jake stood up, extended his hand to Diane, and forced a smile. "Congratulations, Ambassador."

Diane rose, took his hand, and smiled back. "Thank you, Jake."

Jake stood there for a moment holding her hand. Her touch was soft, and her dark brown eyes still penetrated right through to his heart.

Cal hopped up, put an arm around each of them and smiled. "My big sister. An ambassador!"

"And," Frank said, also standing, "as an ambassador, she is officially part of the Legion. And ambassador outranks private. So you two better do what she says." He changed the subject. "Oh, yeah, Jake. Believe it or not, I found a John Wayne movie that we've never seen. *The Cowboys.* I never knew it existed. I've been saving it to watch with you. Want to come over and watch it when you guys get back?"

Jake knew how much Frank loved twentieth- and twenty-first-century western movies. Jake liked them too, but Frank actually walked the walk and talked the talk. Jake often thought back on how watching those movies for hours with Frank had helped him through his teenage years after the attack. Of course, most people didn't know who Clint Eastwood, John Wayne, or Clay Masterson were. Jake tried to crack a smile. "Sure, sir. Sounds good."

"Now I'm sure *The Cowboys* won't top his role of Marshall Rooster Cogburn, but we can give it a look-see," Frank said.

That was Jake's favorite of all the John Wayne movies, especially when Marshall Cogburn would call on the services of his sidekick canine, whom he appropriately called Dog.

"Yeah, sounds great." Jake knew it came out half-heartedly, but he really wasn't in the mood.

Jake noticed the puzzled look on Frank's face as Frank spoke. "All right, now you three mosey on out of here. I have work to do."

"The three of us are still on for tonight, right?" Cal said, looking at Jake and Diane.

Jake and Diane both nodded.

JAKE SIPPED HIS SODA. HE NEVER DRANK ALCOHOL. IT DULLED the senses. The senses needed for combat. He looked at his timepiece. Wow, he had gotten there fast. He would have to wait on Cal and Diane. The host had asked him if he wanted a table by the edge. He agreed, but after being seated, he wasn't so sure if it was a good idea. Sure, he had been in skyscrapers before, but he had never really just sat near an open edge and looked out. But he knew the technology was safe—and what amazing technology it was. An open-air design two hundred stories above the ground. Gravity beams to keep things—and people—in, and an invisible weather force field to keep inclement weather out. He was on the top floor of the largest building in the largest city in Sector Four, the capital. Jake stared out over the city. Wow, how Lagos had grown just since he was a kid. The lights from the smaller skyscrapers bounced off the white domed buildings nearer the ground, painting an eerie yet beautiful picture below. If it wasn't for the movement of the hover cars near the ground, he would have trouble judging just how high up he was. And what a magnificent view. The city lights stretched almost as far as he could see in every direction.

Jake fiddled with the candle in the center of the table. He liked how it flickered softly in the dim light of the restaurant. Diane would be there any minute. He turned slightly and glanced around the restaurant, looking for her. The way the large room was sectioned off made it feel comfortable and private. He liked that as well.

What was he going to say to Diane? Should he try to talk her out of leaving? No, she really wanted this. He couldn't put that kind of pressure on her. And besides, maybe she didn't feel the same way about him. Maybe he should just come right out and tell her how he felt about her. How he'd always felt about her. Cal used to tease him about having a crush on her when he was fourteen. And Cal was right. So what did he have to lose? She was leaving anyway. No, he couldn't just come out and dump all that on her the night before she was leaving. That wouldn't be fair to her. What should he say, then? Anything? If only Uncle Ben were around. He would know what to say. He always had. Jake had never known his mom and was too young to remember his dad, so Uncle Ben had meant the world to him. Sure, Aunt Jane was wonderful, and he wouldn't have made it this far without Frank, but nobody was like Uncle Ben.

"Hey there, want some company?" came a soft voice from behind him. Jake would recognize Diane's voice anywhere.

"Sure thing," Jake said, standing up and turning around. His eyes caught hers immediately. Her eyes were always the first thing he noticed. They drew him right in. He pulled out a chair for her. "Where's Cal?"

"He left me a message that he would be running a little late," Diane replied, sitting down.

As she brushed by him, he caught the familiar smell of her perfume. He loved how it lingered in the air just long enough for him to recognize it and know that Diane was there. He didn't know if it was the particular brand of perfume that he liked or if it was the fact that it came from her. But he loved the smell. "That's okay. We can wait, since he's buying," Jake said with a grin.

A waiter, dressed very neatly in a white suit, came to the table. "Are we still waiting for one more to join your party?"

"Yes," Jake said.

The waiter looked at Diane. "Madam, can I get you something to drink?"

"I'll have a frisco," Diane said.

Jake could have guessed that. Ever since she discovered that drink on Andromeda, she ordered it any chance she got.

"Yes, madam." The waiter said then left.

Jake looked across the table at Diane. The glow of the light on her face made her look even more beautiful, if that was possible.

Jake still could not muster up the nerve to say anything more than small talk. "How's your dad enjoying retirement?"

"Oh, you know how that goes," Diane replied. "You never really retire from the Legion, especially him. He's living in the country in Sector Four, but he's always doing some consulting gig or teaching or one thing or another at the headquarters, mostly with new cadets."

He decided to say something. He had to. He placed his hands on the table, then on his lap, then back on the table as he tried to think how to start. "Diane, you and I have known each other practically our whole lives. I mean, we grew up together."

"Yes, I know," Diane said. "I used to babysit you."

"Okay, you didn't need to remind me of that," Jake replied. "I'm trying to be serious and say something here."

"I'm sorry," Diane said with a grin. "Please continue." She rested her forearms against the table and leaned forward.

Jake adjusted his position in his chair, put both hands on the table, then started fiddling around with his fork, looking at Diane all the while. "Well, what I mean is that we know each other pretty well. Right?"

Diane nodded, and Jake continued, "There's been something I've been wanting to tell you."

"Here is your drink, madam," came the waiter's voice from behind Jake, interrupting him. "Would you two care to start looking at a menu?"

"Uh, uh, no, thanks," Jake answered. He wasn't the least bit interested in eating at the moment. He wanted to stay focused on what he was trying to say.

"Okay, Jake, you were saying?" Diane asked as the waiter left the table. Her gaze was intently fixed on him.

"Yes, where was I?" Jake put his fork aside and started messing with his spoon. "I was saying that there's something that I've been wanting to tell you for a long time, but I've never been able to get up the nerve. And well, today when Frank said that you are going to Vernius, well I felt, well, you know. I didn't want to see you go." He knew those weren't the right words. The right words were that his heart was crushed when he heard she was going. He leaned forward and continued, "Well, I just wanted to say that I . . ."

Before Jake could say another word, Cal's voice interrupted him from behind.

"Sorry I'm late. I hope you two haven't been too bored without me." Cal quickly pulled out a chair and sat down.

Jake and Diane were silent, staring at each other. Cal looked at Jake, then at Diane, then back at Jake. "Oh," Cal said. "You two were discussing something. I'm sorry. I think I need to use the restroom anyway."

"No," Jake said, slowly pulling his eyes from Diane and looking down at his spoon, now firmly gripped in his hand. "It's okay. Let's go ahead and order." What nerve he had gotten up was gone now. It was probably for the best anyway. He would have to chalk it up to another opportunity lost. Or a final opportunity wasted.

5

SPECIAL DELIVERY

J ack Buchanan sat behind his desk in his office in the Presidential Mansion. Armin Dietrich was seated on the couch. Nobody else was in the room. Things had been quiet, both on Earth and intergalactically. Too quiet. Things were going too well, Jack thought, too well for his presidency, now in its ninth year. He had just over a year to go. How would he be remembered? As the president that had a Legion headquarters successfully attacked during his first year, or as the president that served over eight, and hopefully ten, years of peace? He hoped for the latter.

"Mr. President," Armin said, "may I continue?"

"Yes, by all means," Jack replied. "You were saying?" Jack unbuttoned his collar, then stuck his forefinger between his neck and collar and tugged, first right, then left. He felt warm. The air in the room seemed stale. He wondered if the electro air system was working properly. Or maybe he was just tired of listening to Armin. The guy was great at what he did, and he had a gift for seeing two steps ahead of everyone else. That's one reason Jack had picked him for the job. But some-times Armin would look too long and hard in the wrong direction. It was those times that Jack dreaded hearing him out. This seemed like one of those times.

Armin continued, "As I was saying, I'm getting a little nervous that we've been at peace for so long."

Jack always felt odd holding one-on-one conferences in his office. Him seated behind his large desk, and the other person lost in the large half-moon couch facing him. He felt like he was supposed to be a king or something. Smaller, retractable furniture had never been installed in this room of the mansion. He guessed some former president liked the king feeling. "Nervous." Jack shook his head. "Why?" He really didn't want to ask that question, but he knew he had to.

Armin stood up. "Well, I fear that it's causing us to become complacent. I mean, our best inventions have come at the most critical times. When we were facing our darkest hours. When we *had* to design a solution. Look at the defense shield. EarthNX invented it at the height of the largest intergalactic war in history. Without it, Earth would have been eliminated. And since then—" He paused for a moment. "Well, EarthNX hasn't given the Legion anything new in the last eight years." Armin took off his suit jacket and laid it on a chair.

Jack leaned back in his chair, noticing the perspiration on Armin's white shirt. "What you mean to say is that EarthNX hasn't given the Legion anything new during my presidency."

"Well, yes sir," Armin replied. "Peace has caused even our greatest corporations and our greatest minds to become passive."

Now Jack saw where Armin was going with this. Maybe Armin wasn't as far off target as Jack had originally thought. This might end up being a very relevant discussion after all. He still felt hot, though. He made a mental note to have his assistant look into the solar panels. Electro air was a great invention for HVAC, despite the fact that it required all those white domed roofs, but it did occasionally malfunction. But you would think the Presidential Mansion would have top-of-the-line equipment.

Armin walked toward Jack's desk. "Jack, the next step is weakness."

Jack leaned forward, placing his elbows on his desk and folding his hands. "Armin, you can stop beating around the bush with me. You're not concerned about too much peace. You think that since I have openly disapproved of Edgardo's tactics, he is not supporting my presidency. He's not helping me out, so to speak. Am I right?"

Armin stepped back. "Well," Armin started to answer, then sat down. "Yes, sir. Never has EarthNX gone eight years without adding something new to the Legion's arsenal. I fear that Edgardo is holding back for the next president. And you'll go down in history as, well, just another president who got lucky during his term."

Jack knew Armin was correct to a certain extent, and he was pretty sure Armin's motives were pure, but there was no way that he was going to give accolades to or support a man of Edgardo Ramirez's character. Jack spoke softly. "Armin, I respect your opinion and advice, and I appreciate it, as always, but there is no such thing as luck. But even if you want to call it luck, I'll gladly go down in history as the 'lucky president,' if it means that we are at peace. If nobody is senselessly being killed."

"But Jack," Armin said, cupping his hands together and leaning forward, "there have to be new weapons or upgrades to existing ones. Offensive weapons, or defensive, like upgrades to our defense shield. We need to continue to secure peace, at least for Earth. It's been so long. Other planets have surely moved past us by now. I'm sure that someone has developed superior weapons." Armin leaned back, placing his hands on his lap. "I'm just saying, if a new defense upgrade, or any upgrade for that matter, is presented by EarthNX or by whomever, won't you consider it?"

Now he wasn't sure where Armin was going. Sure, he would consider anything new for the betterment of Earth. "Armin, I would be glad to consider upgrades to anything, even the potatoes served to our soldiers, but I will not publicly, privately, or in any other manner, condone the actions of EarthNX to get them."

There was a knock at the door, and Jack paused.

"Yes, come in," Jack said.

Marco Veneto entered and walked quickly to Jack's desk. Jack noticed how Marco intentionally ignored Armin, not even acknowledging him.

"Mr. President," Marco said, "we need to talk. Some new information just came to us from Vernius." Marco handed Jack a data pod.

Before the president could answer, Armin, still sitting on the couch behind Marco, spoke up. "Mr. Veneto, the president and I will gladly speak with you about this, just as soon as he and I are finished."

Jack could see the grimace on Marco's face as Armin spoke. He knew that the grimace wasn't so much from the interruption, as it was from the high-pitched tone in Armin's nasally voice. He also knew that Armin used that tone to add emphasis to what he was really saying: "I am the president's chief of staff and, well, you aren't." Or to drive the knife deeper into his colleague's back. Jack generally liked to just let it go and monitor how things progressed. He liked the differing opinions of his staff. They helped him make the best decisions based on all the facts. But Jack did wish that his chief of staff and his chief Legion advisor got along a little better. He thought that eight years of serving as two of his highest-ranking advisors would have softened their relationship. However, if anything, the two had grown to despise each other even more. He could tell that Marco loathed the fact that Armin was in a position to give Marco an order on behalf of the president. What made matters worse was the fact that their dislike for each other was no secret to others on his staff. The best he could do without terminating one of them was to try to keep the peace between the two of them.

"No," Jack said, reading the first page on the data pod, "we were finished, Armin. What is it, Marco?"

Marco, with his back still to Armin, grinned ever so slightly. "The Legion has received a report from Vernius. The Vernitions have apparently detected a hilaetite crystal. They sent us the coordinates and have asked us to investigate."

Armin spoke up while Jack was reading the information on the data pod. "Again. Why are they the only planet that seems to detect crystals? And maybe we should tell them to investigate it themselves. After all, they still don't believe that we found nothing in our investigation of the attack on Sector Four headquarters eight years ago."

Marco, still facing Jack, replied, "Mr. Dietrich, Vernius is our greatest ally. The Imperial Majesty has stated publicly that she unequivocally supports Earth and the Legion."

Armin stood up and walked to the side of Jack's desk. "That's because she's new and it's the politically correct thing to say. And besides, of course she's going to say that she supports us. Earth's Legion is the only thing standing between them and half the planets in the galaxy that would like to have a piece of Vernius. A planet without a military. What kind of operation is that anyway?"

Jack held up a hand. "Okay, that's enough. Let's stay focused on the issue at hand. Eight years ago was a unique situation. This time we don't have a crystal hidden at a Legion headquarters." He looked straight at Marco and then at Armin. "Do we?"

Marco cleared his throat. "Of course not, sir."

Armin folded his arms and leaned slightly against the desk. "How can we be so sure that the Legion hasn't done something to cause this? I think we should keep away from any investigation."

Marco looked at Armin and leaned on the desk with both fists. "Why are you so worried about an investigation? The Legion is clean. And you know the Vernitions haven't the ability to conduct such an inquiry off the surface of their planet, nor the resources to do anything about it if they did find something. They may be the most technologically advanced planet in the galaxy, but they haven't the transportation or weapons to move that technology anywhere."

Jack was becoming frustrated with their bickering. They weren't laying out options or discussing different sides of the issue. They were just arguing to try to one-up each other. And the warmth of the room was adding to his frustration. He could feel his armpits getting damp and a bead of sweat slowly rolling down the middle of his back. "Enough, I said! We will investigate if the matter warrants an investigation. It's part of our alliance with Vernius. But you know that already, Marco. Why are you bringing this to me?"

The room was silent. Jack stared at Marco's blank face, trying to read him. The news must not be good. Marco was hesitating too long.

Marco stood up straight. Jack watched him as his gaze went first to Armin and then to Jack. "Sir, the detection coordinates show the crystal somewhere on the planet Craton. And because of what happened eight years ago when Vernius detected a crystal," he paused for a moment, then continued, "the attack on Sector Four, our failed attempt to find a crystal, or, as far as Vernius knows, our failed attempt to even determine why we were attacked, Vernius doesn't fully trust us to conduct a thorough investigation."

Jack looked up at Marco. "But you just said that the Imperial Majesty supports us and asked us to investigate."

"She supports us," Marco replied, "but she doesn't always trust us."

"Well, I can't really blame her," Jack said. "Neither of you, nor the Legion, gave me much to work with. I wasn't too happy with the investigation into the attack myself."

Armin shot Marco a cold glance. Jack read that as Armin blaming Marco for the poor investigation.

"So, what does the Imperial Majesty want?" Jack asked.

"Sir," Marco replied, "she wants the new Vernition ambassador to investigate."

Armin winced and stepped back from the desk. "Diane Danielson? No, we can't send a civilian on such a mission, especially to Craton."

Marco kept his gaze directed at Jack. "Sir, our ambassadors are not civilians. They are Legion soldiers, and Legion trained."

"Not combat trained," Armin replied.

"No," Marco said, looking at Armin, "but they know the risks when they sign up for the job. I recommend that we send her. She's on her way to Vernius right now with two Legion soldiers as escorts. They'll give her the protection she needs. I think we should divert them to Craton, have them go to the coordinates, and take pictures and sensor scans only. If they come back negative, then we will have satisfied the Imperial Majesty's request. If they come back with evidence of a crystal, then we can discuss how to handle it."

Jack looked at Armin, knowing that he would have a counterposition. He wanted to hear both of them out before making a decision.

"I don't like the idea of investigating at all," Armin said, "let alone sending an ambassador with just two soldiers to Craton to do so. You know where I stand, Mr. President."

Jack thought for a moment. He didn't like the idea of sending an ambassador either. So many things could go wrong. And they needed to be completely open and honest with Vernius if something did go wrong. No, he didn't like it, but it was his best option. He wanted to honor the Imperial Majesty's wishes. He knew she had reason to not trust the

Legion, and he needed to earn her confidence in the Legion and in Earth United. He stood up, stretching his legs. He could feel his shirt stick to his back. He turned his back to Marco and Armin and walked to the one-way window behind his desk, looking out. "We need to comply with the Imperial Majesty's wishes. I don't like the idea of sending an ambassador to do this any more than you do, Armin." He turned and looked at Armin. "But I like Marco's plan. Only three people, under cover, with orders not to engage. That's about as safe as we can make it. Whose command are the soldiers under?" He turned toward Marco.

"Frank Cantor's, sir," Marco replied. "The commander of Sector Four."

"Yes." Jack nodded. He knew of Frank and remembered meeting him on one or two occasions. He was a good man. "Marco, notify Commander Cantor. Make this happen."

CAL WAS IN THE PILOT'S SEAT OF THE LEGION TRANSPORT. JAKE was to his right, sitting in what was normally the copilot's seat. But for now, Jake was using it as an easy chair. The copilot's seat to Cal's left was empty. A transport could be handled by a single pilot. However, the controls, including the weapons system and communications, could be turned over to one or two copilots in times of trouble or in an emergency. Although, most Legion transports, including this one, had minimal weapon capabilities. Diane was the only other person on board and was seated just behind Cal and Jake.

Diane peeked over Cal's shoulder. "What are you doing? You're not playing a game, are you?"

Jake, sitting with his head laid back and his hands folded on his lap, opened one eye and turned his head toward Cal. Cal was focused intently on the small portable transponder in his hands, with his thumbs moving frantically from button to button.

No problem, he thought. Playing video games anytime he could find a minute was normal for Cal. And he assumed the spacecraft was on autopilot. Jake turned his head back and closed his eye again.

Cal stared at his transponder. "Yes, it's a brand new game, *Intergalactic Combat*. It's the most realistic battle game yet. It uses real planets in the galaxy. Supposedly, the person who developed it had connections inside the military at various planets like Centaur and Craton, who gave him access to all the military technology and codes. He used them to make the game. I don't know who the guy was or even if he's still alive for doing it, but word is, he got rich off of black market sales."

Diane sighed. "Black market, probably illegal on every planet, and my brother, a Legion soldier, is playing it."

The game made an explosive sound. "Aaah, bad move," Cal said.

Jake opened one eye again and spoke with his head still laid back. "Could you keep it down a bit? Some of us are trying to sleep."

"All right. I'm dead anyway." Cal turned toward the space-craft's viewing screen and took the spacecraft off autopilot.

"That's better," Jake said, closing his eye. He started to think again, about Diane, about what lay ahead for him, and for her, on different planets. He didn't want to think about it. He changed his thoughts, as he always did when his mind wandered where he didn't want it to go. That's when he would think about his uncle's death, Romalor, the government cover-up. What he wanted to do if he ever met Romalor, or if he ever found out who was behind the cover-up. It could go all the way to the top. Even to the president himself. But what could he possibly do if that were the case? Jake Saunders against the most powerful man on the planet. The spacecraft jolted and then started to vibrate slightly. He opened his eyes. "Why are we dropping out of quantum drive?"

"Our sensors are picking up an odd distortion. Some sort of nebula, I'm guessing," Cal replied.

"There's never been a nebula reported in this region of the galaxy," Jake said. He sat up. "It's always been a straight, clear shot from Earth to Vernius."

Just as Jake looked out the viewing screen, he saw a bright flash and felt a plasma burst pound their spacecraft. All three of them bounced and shook in their seats. Jake grabbed the control panel to steady himself. The lights went off for a moment, then on, and then blinked off and on once more.

"What was that?" Diane asked. She pulled herself back into her seat, and then got up and plopped into the empty co-pilot's seat.

"I don't know," Cal replied, "but it took out our weapons, our quantum drive, and our long-range communications. It knew exactly where to hit us."

Diane looked toward Cal and Jake with a raised eyebrow. "We're being hailed."

Cal slowly turned their transport. Another spacecraft came into view. It had been behind them. Jake enlarged the viewing screen. The spacecraft was three times the size of their transport. It was rough looking, without much form or contours. Sort of like a long cylinder with a roughed-up surface that had been smashed a little on each end.

"That doesn't belong to any planet I know of," Cal said.

"Pirates," Jake said.

"They're hailing us again," Diane said. She turned on the video com.

Jake looked at the screen. It was apparently the space-craft's captain, seated in a chair, with what looked like two guards or officers, one standing on either side of him. Jake looked closely at their appearance, trying to determine where they were from. All three had dark green, scaly skin, with flat faces and no nose, only two nose holes. They had no hair, but rather, small spikes, covered with their scaly skin, sticking up on their heads where hair would be. They didn't have on uniforms. Each was dressed in similar brown clothes. And each of them had a multitude of different types of weapons hanging from their shirts and pants, from knives and sabers to clubs to various types of plasma guns.

The captain spoke in a rough, hoarse tone. "I am Captain Lionslarth. You are now under the control of the pirate space-craft *Labyrinth.* You foolish Earth creatures. You fall for the simplest tricks. Now your foolishness will cost you. What cargo are you transporting?"

It was obvious that the captain had done his homework. He knew that the spacecraft was from Earth and was a trans-port. He also knew where to strike a transport to disable all major functions in one blast. He would not have tried the same maneuver against a quantum light fighter, as they were specifically designed with multiple weapons functions.

Jake could feel his temper start to flare up. He was going to tell *Captain* Lionslarth a thing or two. But Cal held out his hand, down low out of sight of the video com, his palm toward Jake. Jake caught the signal. Cal didn't want him to say anything.

Cal whispered, "I have an idea."

"I'm waiting. What is your cargo?" Lionslarth grumbled.

Cal replied, "We are transporting Queen Diane back to her homeland. Our cargo hold is full of her diamonds, jewels, and precious gems."

What was Cal doing? The cargo hold was empty. The sole purpose of their trip was to deliver Diane and her few belong-ings to Vernius. Jake whispered, "Queen?"

Diane shot Cal a glare. Jake knew that look. She was telling Cal that he better know what he was doing or else. He had no idea what the "or else" could be in this predicament, but he was sure Cal got the message.

Cal spoke again. "Diane, won't you get a few samples and show them to the captain?"

Jake wondered what Diane was going to do now. She was playing along; she seemed to know what Cal was thinking. She went to her suitcases, out of the view of the video com, and pulled out what little jewelry she owned: a couple of pearl necklaces, a few rings with diamonds, jasper, and amethyst stones, and a number of bracelets with various mixtures of turquoise, rubies, emeralds, and jasper. She mixed them up in the palms of her hands and returned to the video com. *Very good, well done,* he thought. He would never have thought of that. But now what?

Cal turned toward the video com. "Captain, these are just a sample of what's in our cargo hold." He stretched out Diane's arms, pulling her hands closer to the viewing screen. "If we give them to you, will you please let us live? Please."

Pitiful, Jake thought. Cal's plan better be good. If he was going to die here and now, he didn't want to do it pleading for his life.

He wanted to go down fighting.

"Veerrrry niiiice," Lionslarth commented. "They will fetch a nice price on the black market. As for your lives, give me the jewels, then I will decide whether you live or die. Now open your cargo door. We will send a tractor beam into the hold to secure the cargo."

"Okay, Captain, but I need a little time to secure the jewels in their crates," Cal said.

"You have ten minutes," Lionslarth replied. He turned off his video com. Diane did the same.

"Okay, what's your plan?" Jake asked. "It better be good, or Frog Man over there is going to kill us," Jake paused for a moment, "in just about ten minutes."

"I don't have time to explain," Cal said. He quickly climbed down into the cargo hold. "When I tell you, move the quantum drive control to one quarter pulse."

"I thought you said the quantum drive is disabled?" Jake replied.

"It is," said Cal, "for going to quantum speed, but its power pulse within the spacecraft is still working. Just move it when I tell you!"

"Okay, okay." Jake could tell Cal was getting agitated at his questions. He did ask a lot of questions. But it was one thing to follow Cal's plans in a game or training exercise, and quite another when their lives—and Diane's—were at stake. He hoped his friend knew what he was doing.

After a few minutes, Cal yelled up from the hold, "Okay, move it now, to one quarter pulse, and no more."

Jake slowly moved the lever. He could hear the quantum drive power up. With his eyebrows raised, he looked at Diane. "I still don't know what he's doing."

"Me neither," Diane replied. "But you better just do what he says. You know Cal."

The hailing signal sounded.

Diane got up and stuck her head in the cargo hold opening. "It's Lionslarth."

Cal climbed out of the hold. "Okay, ready, put him on."

Diane sat back down and turned on the video com. Lionslarth spoke. "Your ten minutes are up. Now open the cargo hold."

Cal punched a couple of buttons. "There, done."

Lionslarth turned to one of his guards who had moved over to a control bank. "Engage tractor beam. Target their hold."

Jake watched on the video com. The pirate guard turned to Lionslarth. "Sir, we're not locking on to anything moveable. Their hold appears to be empty. No, wait, there, I've got something slightly moveable, but I'm not sure what it is, sir. It's not a crate or container."

Lionslarth turned to face his video com and yelled, "Where are the jewels? Your time is up. The game is over and you lose." He turned back to his guard. "Destroy them!"

Cal punched the quantum drive lever to full throttle.

A low rumbling noise filled the ship, growing louder and louder. The transport started to vibrate. Jake grabbed the back of his chair. Cal and Diane grabbed hold of each other. On the viewing screen, he could see the pirate ship start to vibrate.

The pirate guard turned to Lionslarth. "Sir, something's wrong."

The pirate ship's vibrations grew worse, then it started to shake violently. The pirates were hanging on to whatever they could to stand up, and those who couldn't find anything fell down.

Lionslarth turned to the guard, then looked at the control bank, and then turned back to his video com with his eyes wide. He shouted, "What have you done?"

Cal smiled into their video com. "Oh, I don't know. We're just foolish Earth creatures."

That was the last thing Lionslarth heard before the *Labyrinth* imploded in one massive explosion. As the fire cleared, Jake could see nothing but space in front of them, marred only by a few floating fragments of what was once the *Labyrinth*.

Jake and Cal high-fived each other. Diane looked at them and just shook her head. "Boys."

Jake plopped down in his chair. "What in the world did you do? That was awesome!"

"Just a little Cal ingenuity. Pretty brilliant, wasn't it? I just used our quantum drive, or what was left of it, against them."

"I still don't get it," Jake said.

"All right," Cal said, "let me spell it out for you slowly. Maybe you'll learn something. I rerouted the quantum drive system into a small control bank in the cargo hold and left the pulse signal in the bank open. With the quantum drive at one quarter pulse, it sent out enough power to create a signal, but not enough power to do anything. With nothing moveable in the hold for their tractor beam to latch onto, it latched onto the quantum drive pulse signal. Then when I moved the quantum drive lever to full throttle, every last pulse of the spacecraft's quantum drive power was sent to the cargo hold control bank and into the tractor beam. Are you still with me, or am I going too fast for you?"

Jake shook his head. "I have it. Keep going."

Cal continued, "The tractor beam then pulled all that power back to the pirate spacecraft. At the other end of the tractor beam, there was no place for the quantum drive power to go. It kept building up and building up until ka-boom! And without any shield to soften the impact of the blast, well, you saw the result."

"Not bad. Not too bad at all," Jake said. "When did you come up with that?"

Cal smiled. "Oh, about ten minutes ago."

Diane waved her hand between them. "Okay, if you two are finished with your ego trip, can we work on getting us going again? Queen Diane might not have enough jewels to save us the next time."

Cal patted Diane on the back. "Oh, yeah, you were key in this too. Good job."

Diane grinned and shook her head.

Cal got up and started back down into the cargo hold. "Okay, don't worry. I think I can get us going. But it'll take me an hour or two to reroute the quantum drive and fix the damage the pirates caused. Come on. You guys can help."

After about two hours of work, Cal sighed with satisfaction. "There, that should do it."

As they climbed out of the cargo hold, the hailing signal went off. Diane looked at the controls. "It's Frank." Diane flipped on the video com.

"What have you cowpokes been up to?" Frank said. "I've been trying to reach you for an hour."

Jake smiled. "Our stagecoach ran into some bandits, sheriff. But don't fear, they got no loot." He loved to talk "western" with Frank. He felt badly about his less than excited reaction to watching the new movie. Hopefully, he hadn't hurt Frank's feelings. He would make it up when they got back.

"Are you guys all right?" Frank asked. "Do we need to send out a posse or are the bandits long gone?"

Jake grinned a little. "I guess you could say that they've been eliminated, sir. We're set to continue now."

"Okay, you guys can give me a full report when you get back," Frank said. "Right now, I have a change in plans for you. This is coming directly from the Presidential Mansion."

"We're listening," Jake replied. That sure got his attention. The Presidential Mansion.

Frank continued, "It seems that Vernius has detected a hilaetite crystal and given us the coordinates. The president wants you three to go check it out. Only check it out. That means, go to the coordinates, and take a sensor scan and video com picture of it from long-range. Nothing more. Under no circumstances are you to engage."

"Engage what?" Cal asked. "And why us three? What's the secrecy?"

Frank paused for a long moment, then answered, "The coordinates are on Craton."

Jake's grin disappeared immediately. He looked at Cal, his eyes narrowed. Cal was staring right back at him. Jake could feel his heart start to race. Could this be his chance?

"No. No way, sir," Cal said. "We can't take that risk with Diane with us. Why would the president send us?"

Frank replied, "As I understand it, the Imperial Majesty no longer trusts Earth United or the Legion to investigate a detection alone. She wants her new ambassador to witness what is or isn't there, herself. And there's no time for you to return and then for the Legion to send another spacecraft there with Diane."

"But we only have a transport, sir," Cal responded. "What if we're attacked?"

Jake just sat there. Thoughts of his Uncle Ben, Romalor, the attack eight years ago, all raced through his mind. Then his mind jumped to Diane. Would she be safe going to Craton? After all, it wasn't a very hospitable planet—not the terrain, the weather, or the people. But they wouldn't be landing. And besides, Diane could take care of herself. He noticed the change in the tone of Frank's voice and the less than happy look on Frank's face.

"Look," Frank said, "I don't like this any more than you do, but it's an order directly from the president. I understand all too well the circumstances. That's why you are to get in and get out. No touching down. Pictures and scans only. Got it?"

"Yes, sir," Cal replied.

"Jake," Frank said, "you got it?"

Jake didn't answer for a moment. He knew the orders, but he didn't like them. He wanted to go, to have a chance to face Romalor. He wanted to land. He wanted the opportunity he had thought about for so long. But again, there was Diane to think about. He just wasn't sure.

Frank spoke again. "Jake, you got it?"

He hesitated a moment longer, then said, "Yes, sir, I have it."

"Good," Frank said. "After you get the pictures and scans, send them to me, then get back on your way to Vernius. I'll take it from there."

6

CRATON

"I hope Craton hasn't added any defense shields that we don't know about," Cal said in a half-joking, half-serious tone as their transport entered Craton's atmosphere.

"The coordinates Frank sent us show the detection somewhere in this vicinity," Diane said. She made a circle with her finger over the impulse detection grid on the spacecraft's control panel.

"Okay," Cal replied. "Let's get the long-range scanner online. The scanner will pinpoint the exact location and give us some readings. The video com will tie into the scanner signal and be able to bounce back a picture to us."

Jake moved the lever to power up the long-range scanner. Nothing happened. He flipped the backup switch. "The scanner's not coming online."

"Did you reconfigure the grid?" Cal asked.

"That's what I'm doing now." Jake typed in the reconfiguration commands, then moved the power lever again. "Nothing. It's not working."

"Let me see," Cal said. He leaned over to where Jake was working. "You're right."

Cal jumped up and quickly went down into the cargo

hold. A few moments later, he came back up. "All right. This mission is over. Call Frank."

"Why? What is it?" Jake asked. The mission couldn't be over. This was his chance. They had to do something. Maybe this was an opportunity. A reason to land.

"I missed it the first time," Cal said. "The pirate spacecraft also took out our long-range scanner. And without the scanner to link to, the video com does us no good."

"Can't you fix it?" Jake half wanted the answer to be no, not so they could leave, but so they could land and physically check out the coordinates.

"No," Cal said. "When I rerouted everything to get things back online, I left out the scanners. And before you ask, no, I can't reroute things again. If I do, there's a ninety percent chance that I weaken the circuits and cause a hyper-flux. In other words, a complete burnout."

"And that means what?" Diane asked.

"That means we have no quantum drive, no weapons, no long-range communications, still no scanner, and it could even take out life support," Cal replied. "So no, it can't be fixed. Not out here, anyway."

This was his chance, Jake thought. He just needed to convince one of them not to contact Frank—and to land. "We need to land, and go to the coordinates with the portable scanner and video com. If we don't, we'll be letting down the Imperial Majesty, again. That will really weaken our already fragile alliance with Vernius."

"No way!" Cal said. "That's way too dangerous and goes directly against Frank's orders. Besides, without the long-range scanners, we can't find the exact location of the coordinates, so we could be looking for days. The portable scanner will only get us to the general vicinity. That's no better than what we already have from the coordinates in the impulse detection grid."

"How general is general vicinity?" Diane asked.

Cal turned toward Diane. "About two square miles. And from the detection grid, those two square miles include Craton's military headquarters. So we might as well forget it. A search there would be impossible. Besides, Jake doesn't care about the Imperial Majesty or Earth's alliance with Vernius. He wants an opportunity to confront Romalor." Cal turned back to Jake. "Isn't that right?"

Jake thought. *Yes, that's right.* But he couldn't admit it. That would be the end of it. He had to convince Cal, or Diane, another way. "Wait a minute. Frank's first order was to get a scan and picture at the site of the coordinates. Frank's second order was not to land. When he gave the orders, we didn't know our long-range scanner would be out. It isn't disobeying an order if we have to work around the second order to achieve the first. And yes, it's dangerous, but that's what we signed up for. We're all members of the Legion. This is our duty. If this is the giant crystal that I saw Romalor take eight years ago, he could very well have some sort of weapon of mass destruction now ready to use it in. It makes sense. That's probably why Vernius just now detected it. If he has such a weapon, you can bet that it'll be pointed at Earth for its first test. This may be our best chance to find the weapon before it's operational, so that the Legion can figure out how to defend against it and stop him."

"This may be our only chance," Diane added.

Cal turned to Diane. "Diane, no."

"I'm sorry, Cal," Diane said, "but I'm with Jake on this one. I do care about the Imperial Majesty and about Earth. I am the ambassador between these two planets. This is my job. We have to find out what's going on down there. There's too much at stake to turn back. Earth is counting on us, and Vernius is counting on me."

Jake felt a relief come over him. He had done it. They would be going down. But then he thought about Diane. He'd just helped talk her into a mission that could very well kill all three of them.

"But what about locating it?" Cal said.

That was Cal's last chance to dissuade Diane, Jake thought. Should he side with Cal and get out of there? No, he wanted to go down to the surface more than anything. "That's easy, Cal. No matter the planet, politics are all the same, and the locals know more about what's going on than the government. We'll just ask around."

"Cal," Diane said, "whatever the reasons, Jake and I want to go down there. I am the ranking soldier here, but I won't order you to go with us. You can drop us off and then pull the spacecraft back up."

Cal shook his head. "Not on your life. If you two stubborn fools are going down there, then somebody with half a brain has to go to take care of you. But promise me that you two will do everything possible to obey Frank's third order, and not engage. That means no fights. This is still a reconnaissance mission. This is not the time for revenge, okay?"

Jake was silent.

"Jake, *agreed?*" Cal repeated slowly.

Jake replied, "Agreed." Part of him wanted the mission to be clean, with no road blocks. That would ensure the safety of Cal and Diane. But the bigger part of him saw this as the opportunity to finally face Romalor. He had no idea how he alone could end up facing Romalor one on one, though, when it would be the three of them against the entire Craton military if they were discovered. Despite that, somehow, some way, part of him hoped they would be discovered.

JAKE HAD NEVER BEEN TO CRATON BEFORE. HE HAD ONLY SEEN pictures and read about it. As the planet's surface came into sight on the viewing screen, he realized that it looked even worse than the pictures and descriptions. What he had already known was that it was a desert planet, with a few oases here and there. Its landscape was dry and desolate, made up of sand, dirt, rocks, canyons, and mountains. The mountain ranges in sight were small, but he had read that Craton had mountain ranges that would surpass the heights of the greatest peaks in the Himalaya range on Earth. What he noticed immediately, though, was that the mountains on Craton were not snow-capped like the mountains on Earth. "How does anything live on this planet?"

"Good question," Cal answered. "From what I understand, this is what it looks like everywhere. The air is constantly hot and thick, from the desert floor to the summit of the highest mountains. That's why there's no snow on those mountains over there." Cal pointed toward the mountain range on the viewing screen. "It's too hot, even at that altitude. And that climate makes most of the planet unlivable and it produces few natural resources."

"That's why it's such a military powerhouse," Diane said. "It has to rely on its military strength for survival."

"Most of the people live in Craton City, right?" Jake asked.

"Yeah," Cal replied, "because seventy percent of the water on or in the planet is located underneath Craton City. That's why it's the largest city." Cal flipped the viewing screen to long-range and pointed to a long, narrow mountain range just coming into view. "We want to stay clear of that range. Craton's military headquarters is located on it. We need to go in fast and low and away from those mountains so we aren't detected. We'll put down somewhere on the east side, outside Craton City."

"Why not the west side, and avoid Craton City altogether?" Jake asked.

Diane answered, "That mountain range cuts this part of the planet in half. Basically, the 'haves' live on the east side and the 'have nots' on the west. There's nothing on the west side but barren rock and sand deserts, inhabited by nomads, rebels, and bandits. It's too dangerous, and we'll never get the information we need to pinpoint the location."

Jake continued to watch the viewing screen while Cal landed the transport in a remote region of the planet just outside of Craton City. As they passed the outskirts of the city, Jake could see what a horrible-looking city it was, especially for the capital of one of the strongest planets in the galaxy. There was no green space, just concrete and steel stretching for miles.

Cal opened the transport's door. "I saw some houses over there." He pointed.

After climbing a couple of low rock hills, they came upon a small village with houses made out of rock and clay. *Wow, what a tough life,* Jake thought. "You call these houses, Cal?"

"This is where the Cratonites live who are too poor to live within the city," Diane answered. "But they're lucky, by Craton standards. They're fortunate enough not to have to live on the west side of the mountain."

Cal looked at Jake and Diane, scanning them from head to toe.

"We're going to have to fit in better," Cal said.

Jake pointed behind Cal. "Over there." There was a small house standing alone, with a rock fence around it. On the side of the house was a clothesline, full of ragged clothes, mostly brown and tan in color.

"Perfect," Cal said. "Let's see if we can borrow some clothes."

They bent low and crept to the stone fence. Jake peeked over the top. He didn't see anybody. "I'll go first."

Jake jumped up on top of the fence, then down to the other side. When he hit the ground, he landed on something that shot out from under his feet. The thing let out a loud honk, and his heart felt like it skipped a beat. He stumbled but kept his footing. He glanced at the house. Good, nobody had heard, or at least they didn't seem to care—there was nobody in sight. He was sweating, from the heat as well as his startled nerves. The thing he'd landed on looked like a gray chicken. It had a body and feet like one, and it flapped its wings, but it had fur instead of feathers and a long, tube-like bill instead of a pointed beak.

Cal and Diane jumped down beside him.

"Way to be nice and quiet," Cal whispered.

"What was that thing?" Jake whispered back.

"A peeky," Diane said. "The poorer people raise them for food and for their fur."

Jake noticed a number of them huddled in the far corner of the fence.

"Come on," Cal said. "Let's get some clothes and get out of here."

They each snatched some local clothes from the line and hung a couple of Diane's gem-studded bracelets on the empty clothesline hooks.

Jake felt fairly inconspicuous as they made their way into town wearing the native clothing. He couldn't help but wonder how some of the Cratonites could even survive in such desolate living conditions. Did Romalor take that much for himself that he couldn't provide anything better for his people? He had to wonder whether Romalor even provided these people with translator chips. Sure, by treaty, every baby born on every planet in the galaxy immediately was supposed to have a translator chip implanted into his or her ear to translate any language into his or her learned language, paid for by the government of the planet. But Romalor probably felt more in control if his people couldn't communicate with the outside universe. It would be a problem if they couldn't communicate with anyone, though.

Cal turned to Jake. "Where do you think is the best place to get information in a place like this?"

Jake looked around. They were still on the outskirts of Craton City, in the "slum" area. The buildings were run-down concrete and wood structures, standing side by side. They looked ancient, but probably weren't in much better shape when they were new. "The same place you get information in any city. The local pub. But how do we find it without asking directions and standing out like a sore thumb?" He looked around some more. The signs on the buildings, or what was left of them, were all in Craton.

"Right there." Diane pointed to a building down the street on their left.

Jake looked at her. "How do you know?"

"Craton is one of the ten languages I had to learn to read and write for my ambassadorship." She poked Jake in the shoulder and smiled. "It's amazing what you can learn if you're not swinging a sepder all day." She turned to Cal, lowered her chin, and raised an eyebrow. "Or playing computer games." She stepped out in front of them toward the pub.

Jake chuckled to himself and looked at Cal. Both of them shook their heads.

When they neared the pub, Jake found a large rock with some dried brush around it. "Here, let's leave the bag here. I assume we'll look pretty out of place in there carrying a portable scanner and video com."

The bright sunlight immediately vanished when they stepped into the pub. It took Jake's eyes a moment to adjust to the dark interior. He surveyed the room. There were no windows, only the opening behind them where a door had once hung. A few dim, flickering lights hung from the ceiling. The room smelled stale and thick with smoke and alcohol. It was mostly full of Cratonites, dressed even more poorly than they were. There also were a few characters from other planets seated here and there, who were probably living in a Craton village either by necessity or by force.

The bar was on the back wall. All the seats there were full. Wood tables were scattered throughout the room. Jake pointed to an empty table along the side and shouted to be heard over the noise. "Over there." Most of the Cratonites were drunk, half yelling, half laughing at each other. This was one time he wished he didn't have a translator chip. He would rather not have been able to understand some of the colorful language being thrown around. But this was the perfect place to find out what they needed to. These people were probably mostly from outlying villages. Unlike the wealthier inner city people, these people probably wouldn't be afraid to talk.

A Cratonite waitress approached their table. "What can I get you strangers to drink? You new around here?"

Jake looked up at the waitress and smiled. At one time, she was probably pretty attractive, but time and rough living conditions had clearly taken their toll on her. She seemed jolly and happy enough, though. "Just passing through. From the next village over." He nodded toward the south. "Give us your special. Whatever you recommend." Jake hoped that she bought it.

"Okay, that's easy," the waitress said with a smile. "Three purple drools coming up." She turned and gave Jake another smile as she walked away.

Yes, that meant she bought it. Great. Now to find someone to target. Someone who looked like he or she might have the information they were looking for, and who might be willing to share it—for a price of course. Jake noticed a very old man sitting alone in the far corner opposite them. By his clothes and appearance, he looked to be Cratonite, but he was so dirty, unkempt, and unshaven that it was hard to say. He was dark-skinned, or at least that was the best Jake could determine through the dirt and beard. Although, the man could have been from Earth for all Jake could tell. Jake leaned his head in toward the center of the table. "Over there." Jake nodded toward the man. "I'm going to try him. You two wait here for a minute."

Cal and Diane nodded.

Jake got up and walked slowly toward the man, careful not to draw attention to himself. He pulled up a chair and sat down. Up close, the man looked even worse. He had long, shaggy, gray hair, and a beard to match. His clothes were worn and torn. Not that anyone in the pub had nice clothes, but his were noticeably worse.

The man cupped his glass on the table with both hands and stared at it, not looking at Jake. "What can I do for you, young man? You aren't from around here, are you?"

Jake paused for a moment. The man had caught him off guard with his accurate comments. "No," Jake said. "No, I'm not from this village."

The man, still not looking up from his glass, added, "No, I mean you aren't from Craton, are you? You haven't been here long. A day at most. Am I right?"

That made Jake a little nervous. He didn't know whether to cut his losses and retreat, or to press on. If he pressed on, and the man was loyal to Romalor, the man could call him out in a moment, and there would likely be enough supporters to drag the three of them away to Romalor. For a moment, Jake pondered that idea. Maybe that wouldn't be so bad. He could finally meet Romalor face to face. But no, it would be too dangerous for Cal and Diane. He had to keep the safety of Cal, and especially Diane, foremost in his mind. He had to stay focused on the task at hand. Well, if the man wanted to call them out, he would have done so already. Jake decided to press on. "How did you know?"

"I know a lot," the man replied. "Isn't that why you have come over to me?"

It was becoming unreal. The man was either playing the greatest trick ever on him and he was doomed, or this was the best break they could ask for. A gift. Either way, he might as well go for it. "Yes, I guess it is. I'm looking for a weapon. A very powerful weapon, powered by a very large hilaetite crystal. The crystal has been detected on the planet and I have reason to believe that Romalor has developed a weapon in which to use it. It's in the vicinity of his military complex. Do you have any idea where it could be?"

"Hilaetite crystals are forbidden to be used in weapons," the old man said.

"I know," Jake replied, "but I believe Romalor has one anyway."

"Only a fool would walk into Romalor's military complex with only two other people, and try to find such a weapon, if one in fact exists," the man said, still cupping his glass and staring at it.

"Well, call me a fool," Jake said. Maybe it was neither a trick nor a gift. Maybe just a disappointment. "Look, I see you don't know or don't want to say where it is. I'm sorry to have bothered you." Jake began to get up. The man didn't look up from his glass, but grabbed Jake's forearm with one hand. He had a strong grip for someone who looked so old and frail.

The man let go. "I didn't say that I didn't know where it was and I didn't say that I didn't want to help, did I?"

Jake slowly sat back down. The man reached inside his ragged vest and pulled out a yellowish sheet of parchment paper, folded up. Still staring at his glass, he stuck the paper in Jake's pocket. "This will lead you to where you want to go. But son, before you decide to continue on your journey, think about one thing."

Jake hesitated, then asked, "What's that?"

The man, still staring at his glass, replied, "Be careful seeking what you think you desire. For it is the heart that is much wiser than the mind."

Jake didn't think long about what the man had said. Just an old man babbling. He stood up. "So you won't turn us in?"

"No," the man said.

"And what if Romalor finds out you helped strangers seeking his weapon?" Jake said. "Will you be okay? I'm sure they'll do whatever it takes to make you tell them what we look like."

"How can I tell them?" the man said, still staring at his glass and grinning. "I'm blind."

Once again, Jake had no explanation. How did the man know so much about him and the crystal and the weapon? How did he, Cal, and Diane end up in this very pub with the man? Jake had no idea. It was a gift, he guessed. He touched the man on the shoulder. "Thank you."

Jake started back toward his table. He saw four Cratonite men, all wearing the same weathered clothing that everyone else had on. They were surrounding Cal and Diane's table. They were rugged looking, but they looked more fit and less drunk than the others in the room. Everyone else appeared to be in the pub to kill time or to kill some sorrow or pain. These four looked like they were in the pub looking for trouble.

Diane and Cal were still seated. One of the men touched Diane's hair. "Hi there, pretty lady. What's someone like you doing in a place like this? There are some bad people in here. Why don't you come with me? I'll protect you."

Jake walked up to the table behind one of the men and looked across at the man who spoke to Diane. "I wouldn't do that if I were you."

The man looked at his buddies and laughed. "Why? Is the pretty blond boy going to do something about it?"

Jake shook his head. "No, I'm not."

"That's what I thought," the man said as he grabbed Diane's arm. "Now come on along with me."

Diane grabbed the man's forearm and twisted her other hand up and around the man's wrist. She yanked his wrist sideways and twisted both of her hands in opposite directions. The man's wrist snapped. He screamed and bent forward. Diane jumped out of her chair, bringing her knee up in a quick thrust that caught the man square in his nose. He screamed again and fell backward, grasping his crooked, bleeding nose.

Jake smiled. "But she is."

The other three men immediately pulled homemade swords from under their vests. Cal jumped up, and he and Jake pulled out their sepders. Cal blocked the sword of one of the men coming at him. Another swung at Jake. He blocked it. The third attacked Cal from behind, but Jake swung and cut him along the arm. That accomplished what Jake wanted. He came after Jake as well. Jake knew that he could handle two opponents much better than Cal. Jake could tell quickly from their fighting technique that the men were not military trained. They were simply backyard brawlers. He could probably handle two or even three of these guys at half speed.

Everyone else in the pub had cleared to the side. Jake didn't want to kill the guys or injure them too badly, as they likely didn't intend any real harm. They were just looking for a little trouble. And they certainly found that. Probably more than they were looking for, Jake thought. That made it a little more difficult to fight them, trying to put them out without doing any serious damage.

The two men kept working Jake backward until he was backed up against the bar. It was time to fight back a little harder. He ducked one swing and punched the man in the face, knocking him backward. Jake kicked the next man in the stomach. The first man came back with his sword raised. Jake kicked him in the stomach as well, then gave him another punch in the face. The man went down and this time he didn't get up. Jake saw a sword coming at the side of his head. He instinctively ducked and came up with a left hook that caught the man square in the jaw, sending him to the ground.

The man with the broken nose got up with his sword and took a step toward Jake. Jake heard him and turned just in time to see Diane break a bottle over his head from behind. The man's eyes rolled back and he hit the floor.

Jake turned toward Cal. Cal had backed his opponent into the corner and was punching him. The man slowly slipped to the floor.

The three of them looked at each other. "Let's get out of here," Jake said.

As they darted for the door, the waitress came from the kitchen carrying a tray of drinks. She observed the mess and the four men out cold on the floor. "I take it you won't be drinking these?" she shouted.

Cal grabbed their bag from behind the rock as they exited the pub. The three of them ran down the street and into an alley. Jake peeked back around the corner. "We're clear. Nobody's coming."

"Did you get anything out of the old man?" Cal asked.

"Here." Jake handed Cal the map. He decided not to tell Cal and Diane all the man knew about them, about what they had come for—about everything, it seemed. Since he couldn't even understand it himself, how could he explain it to them?

"Wow, jackpot!" Cal said. "If this is accurate, he has pinpointed the exact location of the weapon, and therefore, the crystal. It's in one of the military buildings on this side of the mountain, not too high up. How did he get this?"

Jake didn't know the answer, and didn't want to speculate. He didn't even want to address the question, and thankfully, he didn't have to.

Diane spoke before Jake could say anything. "That doesn't matter now. We need to move. It won't take long before word of us being here reaches Romalor. I'm sure these people don't see trained fighters wielding sepders every day. It won't take long for them to put two and two together. I'm sure Romalor gives some kind of reward for news like that."

"You're right," Cal replied. "I think I know how to get us to the weapon. Come on."

THE THREE OF THEM MADE THEIR WAY THROUGH CRATON CITY toward the military headquarters. Between the concrete buildings and metal skyscrapers, Jake saw glimpses of the mountain range to the west of the city, on which the headquarters was located. As they approached the mountains, in the western outskirts of the city, the buildings were much smaller. That enabled him to more clearly make out the complex of variously shaped buildings making up the headquarters on the side and top of the mountain. Some buildings were square, some domed, and some pointed, but all were built into the side of the mountain, except for one large, oval-shaped building that sat on the highest peak of the mountain range.

Cal pointed to a smaller round building about halfway up the mountain in the middle of the complex. "According to the map, it's in that building."

"That's not too bad a climb," Jake said. "That's quite a maze of buildings up there, though."

"That's not the half of it," Diane said. "There are just as many buildings on the other side of the mountain, and Legion sources say that for every building you can see on the mountain, there's a chamber at least as large built inside the mountain. Not to mention the tunnel system connecting everything."

"Yep," Cal said, "and that oval building on top is the central command center of the entire headquarters. Romalor's hangout. They say the entire dome of the building can be retracted to expose a glass roof underneath. Just so Romalor can watch over the city on this side, and whatever goes on over on the west side."

Jake stopped and stared up at the oval building. Romalor. He was so close to him now. He knew where he was. He could just forget about the mission and head straight for that building. It was what he'd been wanting since he was fourteen. It was what he'd spent the last eight years of his life training for. No, he still had Cal and Diane to think about. And besides, how could he ever get Romalor one on one inside his own military complex?

"Jake," Diane said. "Are you okay? We need to keep going."

Jake didn't say anything. He lowered his head and started walking again.

The mountain had a gradual incline up to about the halfway point, making their climb to the target building relatively easy. There were also enough brush and large rocks up to that point to keep from being detected. As they neared the building, Jake noticed that the roof was flat and appeared to be retractable. The design looked like it was made to allow weapons to fire through the open roof. Jake swallowed hard. The reality of the situation had just hit him. Until now, a weapon designed to utilize the hilaetite crystal he'd seen eight years ago was only a thought, a maybe. But if that same crystal was what Vernius had detected inside this building with its retractable roof, well, he didn't want to think about the consequences to Earth.

They reached the base of the target building. No guards were in sight.

"I don't like this," Cal said.

"Yeah," answered Jake. "Me either. It's too easy."

They found a side door. Cal took a small decoder from the bag, latched it onto the door keypad, and pressed the activation control. The lock popped. Jake opened the door and stepped inside. He looked around. The building appeared to be one large round room, with a flat ceiling at least fifty feet high. It was difficult to make out much in the darkness, but the room appeared to be empty except for a very large object in the center. What little light there was came from the object, which gave off a purplish glow. Jake moved toward it, motioning for Cal and Diane to follow. The purple glow increased as he grew nearer to the object. It appeared to be a combination of interconnected wires and tubes set up on a large circular platform, ringed by a flat, level console a few inches lower than the edge of the platform. He touched the console and it illuminated, giving Jake plenty of light to finally see what was before him. The entire platform was one massive weapon.

The bottom of the platform was about chest high. Jake estimated that fifty people, standing shoulder to shoulder, could fit around the circumference. The weapon components covered the entire platform and extended ten or fifteen feet above the platform. In the center of those components, at the highest point, was the massive hilaetite crystal. Even in the dim lighting, it was unmistakably the hilaetite crystal he had seen in the Sector Four headquarters building eight years ago. It was enclosed securely in a clear, transparent housing, attached to the component parts with a multitude of wires, like tentacles.

"That's it," Jake said. "That's the crystal." This vindicated him. Everything he knew to be true now really was true. Everything he had told the Legion, the investigators, anybody that would listen. The largest hilaetite crystal anyone had ever seen had been stolen by Romalor from the Sector Four headquarters. This proved it. And everyone behind it all—the attack, the massacre, the cover-up—would now have to be exposed. The Legion would have to come after Romalor, and Jake would make sure he was at the front of the attack. Now he had what he wanted, or at least it was within his reach.

"Let me get the scanner going," Cal said. He pulled out the portable scanner and video com. "Then we need to climb up there and get some close-ups with the video com."

"I don't think so," came a deep voice from behind them. The lights came on.

Jake instinctively pulled out his sepder and started to turn, ready to fire.

"I wouldn't do that if I were you," came the voice again.

Jake stopped partway into his turn, but kept his sepder in firing position. He was face to face with at least twenty Cratonite guards. He recognized the one giving the commands. Raxmar. He started to burn inside. He could take out Raxmar, and probably two or three more before they could return fire. Cal might be able to get a couple too. But what then? All three of them would be dead. Yes, all three, even Diane. This wasn't the time. He would have to wait.

Jake lowered his sepder to his side and let it drop to the floor. Cal followed.

"And the bag," Raxmar said.

Cal let it drop as well.

Jake thought for a moment. How could Romalor have known they were here? There hadn't been enough time for word of them to reach Romalor from the village. And these guards had been there waiting for them. Romalor had to have known they were coming before they ever landed on the planet. Their transport would have detected any sensors scanning them, so Romalor hadn't picked them up as they approached the planet. Was it the old man? Did he bait them into Romalor's trap? No, Jake didn't believe that. He had seen it in the man's face as they spoke. The man was honest. More honest than anybody he had ever met. Then who was it? How did Romalor know?

Cal whispered to Jake, "Somebody set us up."

"I know," Jake whispered back. "But who?"

FOUR CRATON GUARDS ESCORTED JAKE, CAL, AND DIANE, ONE leading the way and one walking behind each of them with plasma guns stuck in the smalls of their backs. They wound through the maze of tunnels. Jake could tell that they were going deep into the mountain and climbing upwards. He had no doubt as to where they were heading. To the central command center. To Romalor. But this wasn't how he wanted to face Romalor, unarmed, four guards with guns, and Cal and Diane right beside him in harm's way. Had he put them in this position? After all, he wanted to face Romalor. No, each step of the way after they landed on Craton, he'd always chosen the path to avoid Romalor. He'd consciously done so to protect Cal and Diane. But he had just answered his own question. Yes, he had put them in this position. Each step of the way *after* they landed. It was his fault that they had landed in the first place. Had he not wanted to, Diane would never have pushed for it. Now they all three practically had one foot in the grave—himself, his best friend, and, well, Diane. He couldn't even think about it. He had to get them out of this. He had to find a way, wait for an opening. He glanced over at Cal and Diane. Their eyes were fixed straight ahead. They didn't seem scared. And neither was he. Of course not. They were all Legion trained. Joining the Legion meant you knew that this moment could come at any time.

The guard punched a code into the keypad and the door slid open. The guards pushed them through the door by jabbing the plasma guns further into their backs. As they entered, the guards holstered their guns and drew their goliaths. Jake scanned the room. There he was, Romalor, seated at his desk, his back to them. Jake noticed that the desk had a computer and control panel built in. It looked as though Romalor could command any area on the planet from that seat, and probably spacecraft anywhere in space. Behind the desk, built into the wall, was a large video screen for conducting video calls. The screen took up the entire wall, almost fifteen yards high and twenty yards wide. That would put Romalor up close and personal with whomever he was speaking to. Jake glanced up at the roof. It wasn't retracted.

Romalor turned around in his chair, and his eyes immediately met Jake's. Jake suddenly felt cold. He saw Romalor's goliath piercing Uncle Ben. He saw Ben's lifeless body lying there. Jake's back straightened, his fists clenched. For eight years, all he had wanted was to face Romalor and kill him. Now he was standing right in front of Romalor. He wanted to make a move for the guard's gun. No, it was still too risky for Cal and Diane. And why had they holstered their guns anyway? For fear of hitting Romalor? No, probably not. But it didn't matter. He had to keep cool, if not for his sake, for the sake of Cal and Diane. He had to wait.

Jake looked at Diane. His face must have shown the regret he felt for getting them into this predicament. She looked at him, gave him a little smile, and shook her head slightly. He knew she was telling him it wasn't his fault. In a situation like this, how could she be so brave, so forgiving? What a fool he had been. Spending the last eight years of his life chasing Romalor. He should have been chasing Diane. And there was a good chance he wouldn't have tomorrow to make it up.

"So, are you enjoying your little visit to our planet?" Romalor asked. "I understand you were viewing our latest in weapons technology. Now what did you hope to accomplish? To stop me from using it? Or to stop me from using it against Earth?"

Nobody answered. Jake looked back at Romalor and grew cold again. He straightened his back.

Romalor looked into Jake's eyes. "I know what you're thinking. You shouldn't be thinking that, son. Somebody could get hurt." Romalor got up, pulled out his own plasma gun, and walked over to Diane. He put the gun to Diane's head.

Jake took a step towards Romalor and started to reach for the gun. Two guards grabbed his arms and yanked him back. Another grabbed Cal as he made a move for Romalor as well. Jake pulled and jerked. He had to get free. Romalor was insane. He was going to kill her right there on the spot. Of course, he really needed only one of them to question. "What are you doing?" Jake shouted. "Take me, not her. Shoot me, you coward."

Diane didn't flinch, didn't step back, nothing. She just stood there, staring straight ahead. A trained soldier.

Romalor looked at Jake, smiled, and pulled the trigger.

Jake shouted, "NO!"

Nothing happened. There was no blast. Nothing. Jake just stared. He couldn't believe it. First relief flooded him, then he felt joy. But only for a second. What a cruel joke. He could see his uncle's dying face. More clearly now than ever. Jake's hands started to shake. His eyes narrowed. He lunged again for Romalor, but the guards held him firm. He just wanted to strangle Romalor. He was so close to him now. . . No, now still wasn't the time. This wasn't how he was trained in the Legion. He knew better than to react emotionally in a situation like this. He had to be clear-headed. He needed to think. He slowly relaxed. He felt the guards' grip loosen.

Romalor smiled again. "How heroic of you, son. But you see, that was just a demonstration to get rid of any thoughts you might have of getting a gun and starting to blast away. It also shows you the advanced technology that you're up against. You see, this room constantly emits a reverse energy pulse, disabling any energy weapon while in the room. I designed it myself. It gives me—let's say peace of mind, should one of my enemies, or friends for that matter, desire to take over my position in a cowardly sort of manner." Romalor started to pace back and forth in front of Jake, Cal, and Diane while still looking at them. "Okay, now where were we? Why did you come?"

Still, nobody spoke. Cal and Diane were looking straight ahead. Jake stared at Romalor's face.

"I see we're not talking," Romalor continued. "I realize we aren't treating you like proper guests, but if you just answer a few questions, then we can make you more comfortable. How did you locate the crystal? Who detected it?"

There still was nothing but silence. Jake heard the questions, but he really wasn't listening. He had no intention of answering any questions anyway. He glanced back at the guards again. He had to find a way out. But their goliaths were too close.

Romalor broke the silence again. "Very well, then. I believe I already know the answer anyway. You see, I have sources in what you Earth people would call very high places. I was just giving you a chance to be friends. But I see it's useless. Why do you protect Earth anyway? Why do you risk your life for your government? Your own people don't even care. They would rather me kill you than let you return to Earth."

Jake knew the government was behind the cover-up eight years ago. Maybe Romalor knew something they didn't. Maybe he could keep Romalor going and find out more information. Who was involved, how many, how high up did it go? Maybe he could get Romalor to name some names, or at least provide some clues. Of course, it wouldn't matter if they couldn't find a way to escape. But he had to try. "That's a lie. Do you think we believe that you're working with our government?"

Cal looked at Jake, then shouted, "Be quiet! Don't say anything."

Jake knew that Cal knew what he was up to and would help. By arguing with Jake, Cal was trying to get Romalor on Jake's side. *Nice move, Cal,* Jake thought to himself. Jake looked at Cal and spoke. "No, I don't believe him for a second." Then Jake turned to Romalor. "If what you say is true, prove it, then maybe we'll talk."

"I need to prove nothing to you," Romalor replied, "but just so you know what your people think of you, I will do so. Then you can die knowing how worthless your efforts were. You will die knowing everything that you have done in your life was for nothing."

Romalor walked back to his desk and pressed a few controls. The video screen lit up. He pressed a few more buttons. "There, that should be it."

Romalor turned to face the screen and spoke again. "This was recorded just about an hour ago. Notice the time and date. I put the writing in Earth mode so that you could read it."

The video and audio began to play. It was a recorded video call of Romalor talking with a man seated behind a very large and, Jake could tell, expensive desk. There was part of a symbol or logo on the wall behind the desk. Although the man was seated, Jake could tell he was tall, with a dark complexion. He was about forty years old and wore a black suit and tie with a white shirt. Again, expensive-looking. He didn't recognize the man.

The man spoke first. "Romalor, why are you contacting me again?"

"It's General Leximer to you, Mr. Sloan," Romalor replied.

Jake turned toward Cal and Diane and caught their attention. They shook their heads. They didn't recognize him either.

"All right, what is it? I haven't much time," Sloan replied.

Wow. Whoever he was, he was either pretty stupid or pretty powerful to talk to Romalor like that. By the sound of the conversation, it was probably the latter.

Romalor could be heard on the recorded video. "Mr. Sloan, I have captured your planet's little band of spies. What would you like me to do with them?"

"You captured them?" Sloan shook his head. "When I told you they were coming, I said they were only there to take pictures, and all you needed to do was hide the crystal. They would find nothing and leave. If you hadn't had the crystal out in the first place, Vernius wouldn't have detected it, and we wouldn't even have this problem."

Romalor's voice remained calm. "Mr. Sloan, I take orders from nobody. We handle intruders our own way on Craton. Now, do you have any plans for them, or shall I dispose of them in the Craton fashion?"

Sloan paused and rubbed his forehead. "Let me think for a minute." After another pause, he spoke again. "Okay, here's what we'll do. I will fix the records of the two Legion soldiers here on Earth so it looks like they have been dealing in black market crystals. I'll make it look like they were trying to sell one to you, the deal went bad, there was a fight, and you killed them. The girl got caught in the middle and was just another casualty. I'll fix it so that the two soldiers are wanted here on Earth and are dangerous. Legion orders will be shoot to kill if they return. But they better not return. You dispose of them, all three of them. I've gone to a lot of trouble the past eight years to keep all of this quiet. Don't blow it now, Romalor. Oh, and one more thing. To help the cause, find their spacecraft and send it and one of your small hilaetite crystals back to Earth as a good faith gesture. You will be returning the Legion spacecraft and the black market crystal."

"What small crystal?" Romalor asked.

"Romalor," Sloan replied, "I know you better than that. Do you think for one minute that I believe that you have turned over every Craton hilaetite crystal to the council? I know you have some stashed away. Use one."

Romalor grinned. "I trust the value will be deducted from the weapon purchase price."

Sloan reached up and turned off his video. The screen went blank.

Romalor turned off the video and turned toward Jake, Cal, and Diane. "Now do you believe me? Now do you see what your very own Earth thinks of you? Sloan is just one of your people working with me. I could name more, but that would be useless, since you're about to die."

Cal spoke. "So when you learned from this man Sloan that

we were coming, you set us up with the old man in the pub?"

Romalor looked puzzled. "What old man, in what pub? I didn't have to set you up with anyone. I knew you would get here. I expected to have to intercept you in your spacecraft. I figured you would scan things from there. But when I heard your spacecraft had landed, well, let's just say I knew right then you would be foolish enough to find your way to the weapon and walk right up to me, all on your own. I needed no help from an old man or anyone else."

Jake knew Romalor was telling the truth on this point, by his reaction. The old man, whoever he was, was trying to help them or, more likely, warn them.

Who else? Who were the other names that Romalor had? He figured it wasn't the entire government, and maybe not even more than one or two people. But whoever it was, and whoever Sloan was, had no small part in killing his uncle, and now wanted the three of them dead. How could he keep Romalor going so he could learn more? More importantly, how could he keep Romalor going until he could find an opening to escape?

Then Jake noticed it. Hanging among the other victory tokens around Romalor's neck was the necklace he had given Uncle Ben on his fiftieth birthday. The one Romalor had taken from Ben. Jake forgot about the conspiracy. He forgot about Sloan. He forgot about escaping. He went back to that evening eight years ago.

He could hear the sounds of dying soldiers. He could smell the mixture of plasma blasts, blood, and death. He could see his uncle hugging him one minute and lying in a pool of blood the next. He stared at the necklace, growing cold once again. But this time he didn't want to let it go. He wanted it to consume him. He wanted Romalor now more than ever.

"What is it?" Cal whispered.

Jake didn't move, just stared at the necklace.

Romalor took a few steps toward them and spoke. "So, you see. Even your own government wants you dead."

Nobody spoke. Jake continued to stare, his eyes squinted.

Cal and Diane both looked at Jake. "Jake," Diane whispered.

Then Romalor caught Jake's stare and walked to within a few feet of him. Jake watched as Romalor followed Jake's eyes from Jake to his own chest. "Ahh, which one is it? This?" Romalor held out his favorite necklace made of saber-toothed bear claws . "No," Romalor said. He let it fall back against his chest. He followed Jake's eyes once more. "Yes, this is it." He picked up Ben's necklace and Jake's head lifted. Romalor turned it over and read, "To Uncle Ben. The best dad ever. Love, your little buddy, Jake."

Jake felt like Romalor had just reached in and smashed his heart. He felt short of breath, almost dizzy.

Romalor paused and smiled. "Yes, now I see. It was you in the ceiling. My, what a grudge you hold. Look at you. You're ready to explode. This wasn't just about the crystal. You wanted to come here. You wanted to kill me. Well, Jake, I'm sorry to disappoint you. I haven't time to drive a goliath through you myself. Although I can't imagine it would take long. You probably fight no better than your Uncle Ben, as you call him. He was an easy kill. He did seem to have a bad leg if I recall, but he still deserved to die like the Legion pig that he was."

Jake lunged at Romalor. This time, the guards couldn't stop him. He saw Romalor's throat and grabbed for it with both hands. Just before he closed his hands, he felt a solid blow to the side of his head. The pain was instant and severe. He went down holding his head. His ears rang. His vision blurred. He looked up and saw Cal. He realized that Cal had bumped the guard just enough to throw off his swing, causing him to hit Jake with the blunt side of his goliath rather than the cutting side. Then he saw Diane. She was struggling to get to him, but a guard was holding her back. It was all he could do to pull himself up to his knees. He could see the blood dripping from the side of his head to the floor, but he couldn't feel the pain any longer. The whole side of his face was numb. He tried to talk but words wouldn't come. Yet all he wanted was to fight Romalor, then and there. Finally, spitting a mixture of saliva and blood, he was able to talk. "Why don't you fight me, you coward!"

"Because I'm going to give you a chance to live," Romalor replied. "You see, here on Craton, we like to give our prisoners a chance. A chance in the Pit."

Diane looked at Romalor. "What's that?"

"Oh, you'll see," Romalor replied. "You will all see."

Romalor turned to the guards and pointed to Jake and then to Cal. "Get him up and get these two ready for the Pit."

"What about the girl, General?" one guard asked.

"Put her in the holding block, then bring her to me when they are ready for the Pit. I want her to watch. We'll keep her alive. She'll be very helpful in dealing with Vernius in the future. I understand that she's the new ambassador from Earth. Once Earth is destroyed, I will turn my attention to Vernius. It's a more valuable planet to me. I want to keep it intact. She will be useful in helping me do that. Vernius will be my first addition to the new Craton galactic empire."

The guard spoke again. "But, sir, Sloan said to dispose of all three of them."

Romalor walked up to the guard and spoke slowly and softly. "I don't care what Sloan said. I don't take orders from him and I don't take orders from my subordinates." Romalor drew his goliath quickly and stuck it in the guard's stomach. The guard grasped the handle. He fell to the floor, his eyes wide open.

Romalor looked at the other guards. "Any of you want to question my orders?" He looked each guard in the eyes. None of them made a sound. "Then get out of here!"

7

THE PIT

Frank was seated behind his desk, working on his computer. He heard a knock at his door. "Come in." He looked up and saw a young private, seeming a bit nervous, standing in the doorway holding a portable data pod. "What is it, Private?"

The private stepped toward Frank and held out the data pod. "A new report, sir. It just came from the Presidential Mansion."

"Well, what is it, Private? Go ahead and read it," Frank said. He had enough work to get done as it was. The private could at least read the report. That was standard procedure. Especially for unannounced reports, which were almost always routine.

The private pulled the data pod back, paused, then held it out again, then pulled it back. "Uh, well, are you sure, sir? It's not good news."

"Yes, yes. Now get on with it. I have a million things to get done," Frank said. "I assume you've read it already?"

"Yes, sir," the private replied.

"Then summarize it for me," Frank said. "I'll read the full report later."

The private laid the data pod on the edge of Frank's desk slowly and carefully. "Sir, it's a report on Jake Saunders and Cal Danielson. It says they were involved in a hilaetite smuggling operation. That they're now wanted by the Legion for treason for breaking Treaty 5274, and described as armed and dangerous criminals. They're also charged with kidnapping Ambassador Danielson and for stealing Legion equipment. The order in the report gives any Legion soldier authority to shoot to kill."

Frank sat back in his chair and stared at the private. He couldn't believe what he was hearing. He had just spoken with them early that morning. He hadn't heard a word about any of this. Of course he hadn't. None of it was true. But who had issued such a report? What had Cal, Jake, and Diane found on Craton, or what had they done? Why hadn't they reported to him? He should never have sent them there. He knew it was a bad idea from the start. Jake was too close to everything. Now, clearly, someone in the Presidential Mansion wanted them out of the picture. Okay, he had to think. He had to do something. "Thank you, Private. That'll be all."

"But there's more sir," the private said softly. "It gets worse."

Worse? How much worse can it get? Frank thought. "Well, don't just stand there. Out with it. What else does it say?"

"Sir," the private continued, "both Jake Saunders and Cal Danielson, along with Ambassador Diane Danielson, were killed on the planet Craton while Private Saunders and Private Danielson were trying to arrange a hilaetite sale with Craton General Romalor Leximer."

"What?" Frank blurted out, not thinking, just reacting. "Impossible. Let me see that." He leaned forward, picked up the data pod and read. He couldn't believe it. He didn't want to believe it. But it was true. It was all right there in the report, under the president's seal. He leaned back again, dropping the data pod on his desk. He put his face in his hands. His head ached. What was going on? They couldn't be dead. But they were. He didn't know what to think. He didn't know what to do.

The private broke the long silence. "Sir, the report says that General Leximer is cooperating fully with the Legion's investigation, that he has returned the Legion's transport ship stolen by Private Saunders and Private Danielson, and he has returned the hilaetite crystal that they were trying to sell him."

Frank picked up the data pod again, squeezing it tightly in his fist. "I'll bet he's cooperating. Right." Frank looked down at the report. He read, "General Leximer has shown an excellent display of good faith, which confirms what a very strong ally of Earth and the Legion General Leximer has become." Frank flung the data pod against the wall, shattering it into pieces. The private flinched and stepped back. Frank slammed his fist on the desk. The private moved backwards again. Frank closed his eyes. He had caused this. This was his fault. He had ordered them to go to Craton. Yes, but it was also the government's fault, even the Legion's fault. What had happened on Craton? Somebody other than Romalor didn't want the three of them to return to Earth. What did they learn? He would find out if it was the last thing he ever did. For what purpose, he didn't know. It wouldn't bring them back. But he had to clear their names. Somebody had to pay. He owed them that much. But who could he talk to? Who could he trust? He had to calm down and think. He would have to work from the bottom up. He would call in some favors. Call on people he had helped get into lower level Legion and corporate positions. These people he could trust. He could trust that they had nothing to do with this whole conspiracy or cover-up or whatever it was. And, more importantly, he could trust that they would keep his investigation quiet.

DIANE STOOD UNWILLINGLY BESIDE ROMALOR, LOOKING WEST out from the retracted roof of the central command center. There was nothing but desert and rock as far as her eyes could see, except for what Romalor referred to as the Pit. She could see most of it very clearly. It was a giant rectangular hole in the ground, about one hundred yards long and thirty yards wide and approximately ninety feet deep. The sides were solid rock, rising at ninety-degree angles from the bottom. Circling the Pit were crude bleachers made of wood and rock, as well as other makeshift seats. A rock tunnel stretched from the base of the mountain range directly below them out to the edge of the Pit, which was a distance of about thirty yards.

"I see you're taking it all in, Ambassador," Romalor said with a grin. "Isn't it exciting? Let me tell you how it works." Romalor pointed to the tunnel. "That tunnel down there connects to the mountain range and our military headquarters so that our guards can safely escort the contestants to the Pit. See that opening in the bleachers at the farthest end of the Pit?" He looked at Diane and pointed farther out. "That's where the spectators enter. And that wooden booth, manned by a Craton military officer." His gaze moved back out toward the Pit and he pointed to a small shack just big enough to fit one person. "That's used for placing bets."

Diane didn't speak. She didn't even look at Romalor. She just stared out through the glass. She noticed that beyond the entrance opening, there was a large flat area with parked hover cars, aircraft, and spacecraft, probably used by the Cratonites and visitors fortunate enough to own some type of transportation.

Romalor continued, "The only way in and out of the Pit is by a rope ladder, which the guards will lower down. And all that debris you see covering the bottom of the Pit, well, let's just say that the Pit also serves as our junkyard. But the parts make very nice weapons." He looked at Diane and grinned. "Very deadly."

Diane moved her gaze to the bottom of the Pit. She could see the farthest two-thirds of the bottom, but the high, steep sides impeded her view of the portion closest to her. The bottom of the Pit was full of rocks and rubbish, mostly scrap metal items, from discarded goliath swords and other weapons to poles, rods, and other metallic "junk," broken hover cars, and dismantled aircraft and spacecraft.

"You see," Romalor said, "the Pit serves for both punishment of prisoners and criminals, and entertainment for the spectators. What an invention. This is why we have little, if any, crime. All crimes are punishable by the Pit. Ingenious, right?"

Diane finally looked at Romalor. "Ingenious? Invention? This is barbaric. This is nothing but a Roman coliseum. We had them centuries ago on Earth. But then we grew up!"

Romalor smiled and then turned and walked toward his desk. "Come now. After all, your friends were spying, trying to steal military secrets. That's a crime punishable by death, by the standards of any planet, including Earth. But unlike Earth, we give such criminals a fighting chance." He turned back toward Diane. "Let me finish explaining how it works. It's quite simple. The prisoners enter the Pit with the champion Craton warrior and it's a fight to the death. Our current champion is a not-so-friendly chap named Hargar. If your friends kill Hargar, they may leave the Pit, free, and you can all go home. But of course, if they lose, well, then I guess you're stuck with me." Romalor smiled. "We have been administering this system for hundreds of years. It's simple and it's fair."

"Fair?" Diane said, gripping the handrail in front of her tightly. "What's fair about it? No chance for a prisoner to explain himself! No trial!" She shouted louder with each word. "No jury! You're insane!"

"Now now, you do get angry," Romalor said. "I like that. And I know what you're thinking, and you're right. It's pretty much impossible for a prisoner to win. But, it has been done. Prisoners have won." His smile disappeared. "However, unfortunately for your friends, Hargar has over one hundred kills to his credit, and, I'm sorry to say, no losses."

If the Pit was where Jake and Cal were going, she knew they didn't have much of a chance. Her heart ached for them, for both of them. Her little brother that she'd practically raised. How could his life end so quickly, so brutally? And Jake. Oh, Jake. The little boy who used to play at her house. Who used to act grown up just to impress her. Who grew up into a handsome young man. A young man she had fallen in love with. And she never told him. She never once told him how she felt about him. If only he knew. If only she could turn back the clock. If only. She would not let her feelings show to Romalor. She would not weep. She would not give him the satisfaction.

Diane looked down again, and there she saw Jake and Cal stumbling out of the tunnel, their hands and feet tied crudely with rope, prodded by two Craton guards carrying goliaths and plasma guns. Her heart ached even more. She wanted to cry out to them. She wanted to run down and hug them. She wanted to fight with them and, if necessary, die with them. But she knew she couldn't. So she would not make a sound. Nothing to give Romalor any pleasure. She just stared toward the Pit. She wanted to walk away and not watch. But that too would be what Romalor wanted. So she watched. The bleachers were full of rough, ragged-looking Cratonites. Most were dirty, wearing old leather and animal fur clothes and unshaven, with long, matted hair. Those who couldn't get seats were standing along the edge of the Pit. She could tell that this was probably their only entertainment.

"Oh, and I almost left out another important part of this sport," Romalor said. "This gives the poor Cratonites living in the west a chance to get wealthy. If they bet enough on an underdog and win, they just might be able to move to Craton City on the other side of the mountain. Your friends are scrawny. They are extreme underdogs and will make for a big payoff if they win. There will be fools who will bet on them, hoping for that payoff. There always are. But they'll lose."

The crowd erupted in an enormous boo when Jake and Cal exited the tunnel.

"See," Romalor said, "almost all of them have bet on Hargar, so they're booing your friends. That won't help your friends' confidence any." He smiled.

Then, as if the booing wasn't loud enough, the crowd erupted even louder with cheers. At the other end of the Pit, through the entrance opening in the bleachers, appeared an extraordinarily large Cratonite. In Diane's estimation, he stood a little over seven feet tall and had to weigh over three hundred pounds, mostly all muscle. Like most of the people in the crowd, he was unkempt, with long, tangled hair and a rough, unshaven face. He also appeared to be missing several teeth, and those he had were yellow. He had a caveman sort of appearance, wearing only an animal fur around his waist that hung to just above his knees. It was held up by one leather shoulder strap that ran diagonally across his chest. He stood for a moment, then raised his huge wooden club in the air. He shook the club as the crowd shouted, "HARGAR, HARGAR," over and over.

"That would be Hargar," Romalor said, again with a smile. "They love him. He's won them a lot of money, even though the odds are stacked in his favor. But a little winning is better than none, or better than losing."

JAKE AND CAL EXITED THE DARK TUNNEL. JAKE SQUINTED AND held his hand over his eyes. The bright light of Craton's sun, glaring off the sand and rock, blinded him. And the heat was intense. He had felt temperatures over one hundred before, but this felt even hotter. His eyes started to adjust to the light. He could feel the dried blood on the side of his face. The numbness was gone, replaced by a throbbing pain. He wished the numbness would return. He could hear the crowd chanting. He turned to Cal. "What are they saying?"

"I believe it's 'Hargar,'" Cal replied. "That must be our opponent."

Jake looked to the rim of the Pit on the far side. He could see Hargar shaking his club in the air.

The crowd continued to chant, "HARGAR, HARGAR." Jake could make it out now.

"How about you take this one, and I'll get the next one," Cal said with a slight smile.

Cal always was good at trying to calm people's nerves in times of crisis. But this was more than a crisis. This situation was next to hopeless. Jake knew they had little chance of getting out of this one alive. He surveyed the surroundings. The bleachers were packed with yelling, sweaty, unruly Cratonites. There were just as many people standing on the ground between the front row of the bleachers and the edge of the Pit, as were in the bleachers. Those standing were shoving and yelling at each other, probably trying to get a view down into the Pit. People in the front few rows of the bleachers were shouting at the people standing: "Get out of the way," and "Sit down, I can't see," and "Move or I'll come down there and toss *you* into the Pit."

The guards pushed Cal and Jake forward. The first guard spoke. "Come on. Get moving. Just think, all these people here, just to see you guys. Aren't you flattered?"

Cal and Jake shuffled their feet, which were still tied in ropes, until they reached the edge of the Pit. With plasma guns still aimed at their backs, one guard cut their hands and feet free. Another guard lowered two ropes into the Pit, secured to metal stakes in the rock-hard ground at the edge.

"The rules are simple," the second guard said. "Hargar's ladder will remain hanging in the Pit. If you try to climb the ladder before Hargar is killed, you'll be pushed over the edge back into the Pit, if not by guards, then by the people who have bet on Hargar. But Craton gives its prisoners a chance. All you have to do is kill Hargar. Then you leave by his ladder and are free." The guard cracked a sadistic smile.

The first guard spoke. "Now climb down or be pushed down. Either way, you're going to the bottom."

Logic dictated that they climb down, given that those were the only two options at the moment. So they each climbed down a rope. No sooner had their feet hit the bottom than the guards yanked up the ropes. Jake turned around. At the other end of the Pit, they could see Hargar make his way to the edge. He had a rope and wood ladder hanging down into the Pit, secured at the top in the same manner as Jake's and Cal's ropes.

"I guess that's our way out of here," Jake said, pointing to the ladder.

"Yeah, all we have to do is get through *him*." Cal nodded toward Hargar.

Hargar tossed his club into the Pit and slowly descended the ladder. Jake thought for a moment. They could just avoid Hargar altogether. They were likely faster than him. While there was too much debris to really run, he figured they could outmaneuver him and avoid any contact. He looked up. The sun was directly overhead, and it was hotter down in the bottom than up on top. No breeze at all. It was hot beyond belief. They wouldn't last long without water and he was sure water would be lowered to Hargar, but not to them. So they better fight. That would be their best chance. Fight him while they were still fresh, or in Jake's case, as fresh as one could be after being bludgeoned with a goliath. They would be able to run only so long before they dehydrated or were unable to move. Jake looked at Cal. "Let's split up and try to flank him."

"You know," Cal said, "even if we do kill him, they'll never let us go. You heard that Sloan guy, and you know Romalor."

"I know," Jake replied, "but first things first. We're going to have to get through Hargar before we have any chance of escaping."

Hargar slowly came toward them, holding his club in one hand and balancing himself with the other as he climbed over the debris. Cal slowly moved away from Jake to circle back behind Hargar. Hargar continued toward Jake. Jake searched around for a weapon. He tried to break a piece of metal free, but it wouldn't give. He pulled on another piece of metal. Too flimsy. Hargar was getting close. He had to settle for a long thick board. Jake tried to get to higher ground but kept slipping into the debris. He noticed that Hargar was a lot more agile for his size than Jake had anticipated. Plus he probably had practice down here. Just as Jake pulled himself up from a slip, Hargar reached him. Hargar grunted, brought his club back over his head, and swung. Jake held up the board with both hands. Jake's hands shook and stung from the force of Hargar's swing, which split the board in half and sent Jake tumbling backward. He heard the crowd roar. Most of them must have bet on Hargar. Jake scrambled up and started moving backwards, all the time watching Hargar and reaching behind him for anything to block the next blow. He had to find something. Anything. His hand grasped a metal rod. He quickly moved it in front of his face just as the next swing came. Hargar growled as he swung. Again, the force of the blow broke the rod and sent Jake tumbling back into a pile of twisted metal. The crowd roared again. Before Jake could pull himself up, Hargar was standing over him. Jake saw the club high over Hargar's head. The crowd shouted, "Kill him!" The club seemed to move slowly as it started to drop, straight toward his face.

The club froze in mid-air. A large board had smacked the back of Hargar's head and split in two. It was Cal. Hargar barely flinched. Thank you, Cal, Jake thought. But this is going to be impossible. Hargar turned toward Cal. Cal stumbled backward, off balance. Hargar swung his club around quickly. Cal started to duck, but the edge of the club caught the side of his forehead, sending him backward. The back of his head struck the rock wall of the Pit, and he went limp. Cal slid down slowly, blood trickling from his forehead, the back of his head leaving a bloody streak on the rock. The crowd roared. Jake could hear Hargar mumble, "One gone, one to go."

DIANE LOOKED STRAIGHT AHEAD AT THE PIT, NOT SHOWING A bit of emotion. She could see Romalor out of the corner of her eye, looking at her. Probably looking for a tear, sadness, something showing weakness. She wouldn't let that happen. She had just watched her brother be brutally murdered. She would grieve later.

"You act like you don't even care," Romalor said. "I thought they were your friends. I know how you Earthlings sympathize with each other. I know you care. You people always care. That's your weakness. That's what's going to destroy your planet."

Diane looked at Romalor. She intentionally kept her face expressionless, cold. "That's where you're wrong, Romalor. That's our strength. You're right, we care, but we're also willing to lay down our lives for our planet. For the freedom and values that we believe in. Jake and Cal are willing and I am willing. You can try all you want to make us believe that our whole government is against us, but we know differently.

There's only a few. And the actions of a few wicked will never defeat the power of the many righteous. Romalor, in the end, you will lose."

Romalor smiled. "My my, such strong words coming from someone whose very life is in my hands."

Diane turned back toward the glass. She felt almost numb. She couldn't stand being in the same room as Romalor. She couldn't stand watching Jake and Cal suffering, dying. But she forced herself to stay cold. She forced herself to remain emotionless. For the moment, she forced herself to not care.

JAKE SCRAMBLED UP AGAIN WHEN HARGAR TURNED BACK toward him. Reaching behind him and feeling around, he kept his eyes on Hargar. Not Cal! He should have been quicker. He should have had Hargar down before Cal had to do anything. But how could he? He had never fought anyone or anything like him. And this heat. He was quickly losing what energy he had left. His throat was dry and ached for water. His mind started to race. He was losing focus. Not out of anger, out of fear. Cal was gone, Diane was in Romalor's hands, his own planet had disowned him, and he had a behemoth of a Cratonite bearing down on him to kill him. He could find nothing to grasp hold of that would break free. Hargar swung. Jake ducked. Hargar swung again and Jake ducked again, this time down and under, coming up behind Hargar and punching him in the lower back. The force of the punch jammed Jake's wrist. He felt a sharp pain shoot up his arm. Hargar turned, smiled, and grabbed Jake by the throat with one hand and picked him up. He couldn't breathe. Pain shot up both sides of his neck. His lungs burned. His bruised head throbbed. He kicked his feet toward Hargar, but caught nothing but air. He grabbed Hargar's arm with both hands and tried to pry his throat free. No use. Too strong. His vision started to blur. Everything started to go dark. Then he felt himself flying backwards through the air. He landed hard on his back against a pile of debris. He rubbed his throat, coughing, gagging, and spitting. He could taste his own blood coming up from his throat. He tried to pull himself up, but his vision was still blurred. His head spun. He saw something coming at him, but it was fuzzy. He tried to react but couldn't. He felt a sharp intense pain in his face and everything went black.

DIANE WATCHED AS HARGAR'S CLUB CAUGHT JAKE SQUARE IN the face. Jake was flung backwards into a pile of scrap metal and wooden boards. As he hit the bottom of the pile, it toppled over on him. There was no movement. All she could see of Jake was one arm, limp and lifeless, and a small trickle of blood coming out from underneath the pile of rubble that buried him. The crowd roared louder than ever. She screamed, "NO!" She instantly caught herself, but the reality of the situation was pressing down on her. First Cal, and now Jake. Dead. She wanted to reach for Romalor's goliath and cut his throat. She didn't care if he ended her life. In fact, she wished he would. Then this nightmare would be over. She backed away from the window and looked Romalor in the face. She felt like she would explode. She looked at his goliath, then back at his face. No, it wasn't worth it. She turned and walked straight for the door. A guard grabbed her arm. She jerked herself free, shoving the guard backwards. The guard quickly drew his goliath.

"No," Romalor said. "Let her go. But see that she gets back to her room."

Romalor walked over to his desk and sat down in his chair. "Now that was entertainment." He pressed two controls on his desk and raised the retractable roof. "Now we have to get our ambassador prepared to help us with Vernius."

<hr />

THE MAJORITY OF THE CROWD WAS STILL CHEERING AS HARGAR made his way toward his ladder. Hargar shook his club in the air. That made the crowd roar even louder. "HARGAR, HARGAR." Hargar was soaking it all in. The Cratonites that had bet on Cal and Jake were angry. They started to push and shove those cheering for Hargar. Small skirmishes broke out here and there.

Hargar kept waving his club and turning his head from side to side all the way to the ladder. He stepped up on the ladder, but as he placed his second foot on the bottom rung, he heard a voice behind him. "You forgot to count to ten."

Hargar turned his head. There was Jake, holding a rusty goliath, his clothes torn and stained with dirt, sweat, and blood. His face was covered with a mixture of dirt and blood. But even with all of that, Hargar could tell there was something different about his opponent now. It was his eyes. They were no longer full of fear and despair. Now they were full of anger and revenge.

<hr />

JAKE FELT HIS ANGER BURN. IT WAS THE SAME ANGER THAT HAD driven him every day of his life since Uncle Ben's death. The same anger that his training officers continued to tell him he needed to control, to focus. And now he added more anger and vengeance for the death of Cal and the loss of Diane. He didn't want to control it. He just wanted to unleash it all on Hargar.

Jake gripped the goliath that he'd found on the bottom of the pile of rubble. It was old, but still sharp enough and solid, and it fit his hand nicely. Hargar growled and jumped off the ladder. Hargar picked up his club and headed for Jake. Jake didn't back up. Not this time. Hargar raised his club and swung. Jake ducked, then immediately leaped into the air, his feet toward Hargar. With a quick, swift kick, his right foot landed squarely in the middle of Hargar's face. Jake landed on his side. Hargar went tumbling over backward. The part of the crowd that had bet on Cal and Jake let out a roar. Not as loud as the roars from the others, but loud nonetheless. Jake felt his head throb for a moment. He ached all over and he would give anything just for a sip of water. But he was more angry than hurt. He climbed to his feet. Hargar got up and put his hand to his face, then looked at the blood on his hand. *He's probably never bled before,* Jake thought. *If he bleeds, he can be killed.*

Hargar snarled and growled even louder and came at Jake again. Jake jumped up on a pile of debris. As Hargar swung, Jake jumped up to a higher part of the pile. Hargar's blow struck the debris, sending metal and wood splinters flying. As Hargar drew back to swing again, Jake leaped forward at Hargar's head, again striking Hargar in the face with his boot. Hargar fell over again. Jake landed on both feet and immediately jumped backward up onto a rock. Jake winced. His head throbbed. A mixture of sweat and blood oozed down his face, turning the dust and dirt into a muddy paste. The crowd roared even louder. Jake looked up. Now the Cratonites that had bet on Hargar started to skirmish among themselves, and the earlier skirmishes were becoming fights.

Jake wouldn't let go of the anger. He didn't need to control it. He would let it work for him. It helped block out the physical pain and thoughts of Cal and Diane. He thought of nothing but killing the beast that was in front of him. Hargar got up, looking dazed, and headed at Jake yet again. Jake mustered up all the strength he had left. He leaped off the rock toward Hargar, his right knee and foot cocked, ready to kick. Hargar did exactly what Jake had hoped. Probably expecting another kick to the face, Hargar lowered and ducked his head to his left. But this time Jake didn't kick. Jake held his goliath in his right hand, the point aimed toward Hargar. As Hargar ducked to the left, he moved his head right into the path of Jake's goliath, which was exactly what Jake had hoped for. As Jake sailed past Hargar, he brought his right arm through, sending his goliath deep into Hargar's neck. Jake let go and landed on both feet. Hargar immediately dropped his club and grabbed the handle of the goliath with both of his hands, pulling on it to dislodge it. It was no use— the sword was run too deep, and Hargar already had lost strength. The part of the crowd that had bet on Jake and Cal roared yet again. Hargar stood motionless for a moment, his eyes looking hazy. His hands dropped to his sides and he fell over backward. Hargar breathed his last.

Jake turned and saw Cal trying to get up. But he was stumbling. "Cal!" Jake hurried to him, grabbed one arm, and pulled it around his neck. He put his other arm around Cal's back and helped him up.

"What happened?" asked Cal groggily.

"Not now," replied Jake. "We have to get out of here. Come on. We have to get to the ladder."

Jake continued to support Cal as they made their way to the ladder. The crowd above was in a frenzy. There was fighting everywhere. The Hargar supporters were angry. If they always bet on Hargar, they had never lost before. The Jake and Cal supporters had newfound wealth. They were pushing and shoving to make their way to the betting booth, probably in fear that there wouldn't be enough to pay all their winnings or that the Hargar supporters would simply steal their money back and run. The guards that had brought Jake and Cal out of the tunnel were still on the tunnel side of the Pit. Jake looked back and saw them pushing their way through the mob toward the ladder. He and Cal had been right. Romalor would never let them leave alive. Jake helped Cal onto the ladder first and supported him from beneath. They both started to climb. Jake looked back toward the guards. They were trying to aim their plasma guns at him and Cal, but too many people were in their way. Jake was sure that the guards weren't worried about shooting a few Cratonites too, but the shots wouldn't have a chance of getting through the crowd and hitting him and Cal. The guards kept pushing through the crowd, stopping every now and then, taking aim, but still no clear shot. The crowd was now in such a frenzy that people were being pushed over the edge, into the Pit. Jake saw the two guards motioning to the guards at the betting booth, near where Jake and Cal would be coming out of the Pit. Jake wasn't worried. Those guards could barely keep themselves alive amid the angry crowd, let alone make it to the Pit and apprehend them.

Jake shoved Cal up onto the rim of the Pit, then climbed out himself. He saw the guards from the tunnel still pushing toward them. "We have to make it to the parking lot before the guards get to us," Jake said. "Come on. This way." Jake put Cal's arm around his neck again and helped him.

"I'm okay now," Cal said and slipped his arm off of Jake.

The two of them pushed their way through the crowd toward the parking lot. The guards were talking into their coms, probably trying to alert the central command center. But it was too late. Jake saw some of the Cratonites, probably those that had bet on Cal and him, unable to reach the betting booth to collect their winnings, now mobbing the two guards. They took the guards' guns, communication belts, and anything else of value. Jake figured the people probably felt that if they couldn't collect their winnings in currency, they would collect it in goods from the guards. *Thank you,* Jake thought.

Jake and Cal made it clear of the crowd and into the

parking area. "We need to find some transportation that looks like it can handle space travel," Cal said.

Jake looked around. Nothing there looked like it could.

"This one," Cal said.

Jake went to Cal. It was a transport that sort of looked like a spacecraft, but also looked like it could simply fall apart at any minute. "Will this make it out of here?" Jake asked.

"I don't know, but it looks like it has the best shot of any of these," Cal said. "Come on. Get in."

"I'll drive," Jake said. "You start it and navigate."

Cal studied the instrument panels and computer system for a moment. "We're in luck. Looks like it has quantum drive," Cal said.

"Good pick," Jake replied. "Now let's go get Diane."

Cal stopped working the controls. "Hold on just a minute. We can't get Diane. Not yet. Not in this spacecraft. We need to go back to Earth and get help."

"Back to Earth!" Jake shouted. "We can't leave her here with Romalor. And how will we get help on Earth? You saw the video. By now, we're wanted on Earth as much as we are here."

"Jake," Cal said calmly, "look, she's my sister. I want to go get her as much as you do. But we have to be sensible about it. Any minute now, every guard at Romalor's disposal will be looking for us. We have no weapons. This spacecraft has no guns. It would be suicide. We can't help Diane that way. We go back to Earth and find Frank. He'll be able to get us some Legion support. And if this cover-up is bigger than Frank, he'll at least be able to get us the equipment to give us a fighting chance to get back here ourselves. And in the meantime, Romalor isn't going to do anything to Diane. She's too valuable to him right now. You heard him. He wants her to use against Vernius. And if we do get out of here alive, he'll want her for leverage to get us back or to use against Earth. We have time to regroup."

Jake sighed. He knew Cal was right. But it still hurt thinking that they were flying away, leaving Diane. And for all he knew, she assumed they were dead and would never be back. "Okay, you're right. Let's get out of here."

Cal quickly punched in coordinates on the computerized instrument panel. They were off, through Craton's atmosphere, and into space, undetected, within minutes.

8

ROOSTER COGBURN AND DOG

J ake could tell that the spacecraft he and Cal were in was a small transport spacecraft, pieced together from parts of various other spacecraft. To make matters worse, the other spacecraft from which it was made looked like they were manufactured on several different planets. That gave it an odd look and feel, giving Jake a very disconcerting feeling while piloting it. On a positive note, Jake thought, at least it resembled no known planet's spacecraft. In addition, he and Cal still wore the ragged Craton villager clothes, now even more torn and dirty and bloodied after the battle in the Pit. With the looks of their spacecraft and clothes, along with their battered, dirty, and blood-dried faces, nobody would recognize them as Legion soldiers, let alone Jake Saunders and Cal Danielson. The only problem they would face in trying to pass through an Earth defense station would be their names and identification. How could they get in touch with Frank without using their names?

"How are we going to get through?" Cal said as they approached the Sector Four defense station. "We can't use our real names or Legion IDs. We probably can't even say we're from Earth. Based on Romalor's video com, we don't know who we can trust."

"Yeah," Jake replied. "Somebody high up is at the bottom of all this. Whoever it is has some sort of control over the Legion, or at least parts of it. I'm sure the Legion is on the lookout for us. I wouldn't be surprised if their orders are to shoot to kill. We have to get through to Frank somehow, though. He's the only person we can trust right now."

"Agreed," replied Cal. "But this spacecraft has no long-range communications. And I've been monitoring all airwave frequencies. As I assumed, the Legion is monitoring them as well. If we get close enough to contact Frank, then as soon as we speak, the Legion will be all over us. So using the radio or video com to reach Frank is out of the question."

"I have an idea," said Jake as their spacecraft pulled into the defense station. "Just follow my lead."

Jake slowly maneuvered the spacecraft into the siding dock and opened the hatch. Jake and Cal remained seated as a Legion soldier walked up to the spacecraft. He was holding a portable data pod in one hand and a stylus in the other. He was punching various buttons and numbers on the data pod. Jake knew that it was standard procedure to log all spacecraft entering and leaving Earth. The soldier looked dubiously at the spacecraft, from one end to the other. Jake knew the spacecraft was clearly in a state of disarray. *Here we go with the questions,* Jake thought.

"This thing actually flies?" the soldier asked in a sarcastic tone. "Where are you headed?" The soldier turned his attention back to his data pod.

Jake wanted to come across stern and confident. A man on a mission. "To see Commander Frank Cantor."

"Is he expecting you?" the soldier replied without looking up. He continued to record information.

"Well . . ." Jake hesitated. "Sort of." That wasn't a smart answer. Not very confident sounding. What if his plan didn't work? Could they retreat? He looked behind him. A line of spacecraft had formed. And the docking bay doors were closed. Escape would be difficult.

The soldier paused and looked up from the pad toward Jake and Cal, who were still seated in the spacecraft. "Can I see some ID?"

Jake hesitated for a moment, and then responded, "Well, we kind of lost our IDs." This was getting worse. He looked at the soldier's belt. He could probably get the soldier's plasma gun if he could draw him close enough. He could then force him to order the docking bay doors be opened using the com. He really wouldn't shoot a Legion soldier. But could he convince the soldier that he would shoot? No, if the soldier was trained properly, which he probably was since he was in Frank's sector, then he would die before opening the doors. That would be the protocol. So the plan had to work. Retreat wasn't an option, and going forward meant getting blasted to smithereens with the defense station's plasma guns.

Cal leaned over and whispered, "I thought you had a plan."

Jake whispered back, "I do. I do."

The soldier looked at both of them with one eyebrow raised. "Okay then," he said slowly, "where are you from?"

"We aren't real sure," Jake said. He grimaced, waiting for the soldier to lose his temper. But the soldier didn't.

"Okay," the soldier said even more slowly, "what are your names, or do you not know that either?"

Jake paused, and then straightened up. He felt more confident. Now he could kick in his plan. "I'm Rooster Cogburn, and this guy here," he pointed to Cal, "he's Dog."

Cal lowered his chin to his chest, rolled his eyes, and whispered, "This is your plan?" He shook his head.

Now the soldier looked irritated. "Mr. Cog-burn," the soldier said slowly, "what kind of names are those? I don't believe they fit any planet in the galaxy. Look, I don't know who you are or why you're here, but Commander Cantor is a very busy man. He has no time for irritants like yourselves. I have a line of spacecraft waiting to get through the station. Would you kindly turn your spacecraft, or whatever this is, around and go back to where it is you came from?"

Now, step two of the plan. Time to plead and beg. "Sir, please," Jake said. "Just call Commander Cantor and tell him we are here. It'll only take a second. What do you have to lose? Besides, if he finds out you turned us away, and he really wanted to see us, don't you think he'll be quite upset?"

The soldier stared at Jake. It seemed like forever. Jake stared back. Not an "I'm going to take you out" stare, but a "please do me this one favor" stare.

The soldier finally replied, "Okay, if it'll get you out of here quicker." He reached down and pressed the com button on his belt. "Joey, get me Commander Cantor on the com."

There was a pause, and then a reply over the soldier's com. "Got him on com one."

The soldier pressed another com button on his belt and spoke. "Commander Cantor. This is Private Alexander at the Sector Four defense station. I'm very sorry to bother you, sir, but I have two men from—" he hesitated, then continued more slowly, "I don't know where they're from and they have no ID. They say they need to talk to you."

Jake could hear Frank's reply over the soldier's com. "Private, I am in the middle of something here. Pull them to the side and have them wait until I get done. And, son, get some more information the next time before you call me, like at least a name."

It was good to hear a friendly voice. Jake could picture Frank sitting behind his desk, chewing on a cigar. He assumed that Frank had been informed that they were dead.

"Sir," said the soldier, "they did give me their names."

"Well then, who are they?" Frank demanded. "Hurry it up!"

Jake could hear the irritation in Frank's voice. Probably from stress. If he knew Frank, Frank probably blamed himself for all this, for sending them to Craton in the first place.

The soldier hesitated, then spoke. "They are . . ." The soldier trailed off and paused. "Well, sir, they say their names are Rooster Cogburn and Dog."

Jake could hear Frank's open hand slam his desk, and he could picture Frank's face, with a big smile. He heard Frank shout, "Giddy-up horsey! I knew those two coyotes were too ornery to die!"

The soldier's eyes widened and his head jerked back. "What was that, sir? I don't think I quite copied you."

Calm down, Frank, Jake thought. *Don't blow it now.* But he wasn't worried. Frank would take over the situation now. Just part of his plan. He heard Frank again over the com. This time he could hear anger in Frank's voice. A very good acting job to scare the soldier into not asking any more questions and to move Cal and him along. "Soldier, why didn't you tell me their names right away? Didn't you think that was important?"

"Well, sir . . ." the soldier started to murmur before Frank cut him off.

"You send those two men directly to Sector Four head-quarters, the south hangar. No more questions of them and make sure they have a clear flight path." Jake could hear Frank getting louder, and he could hear Frank's fist pounding his desk every now and then, probably for effect. "And soldier, this is a code red priority and a direct order from me. You are to tell nobody that they passed through the defense station. And let me assure you, Private Alexander, if they don't make it to me safely, if anything whatsoever happens to them, you'll be flipping pancakes at an Antarctic Legion outpost for the rest of your Legion career. You got that?"

"Yes, sir, got it, sir, consider it done, sir!" The soldier stood up straight and stepped up to Jake and Cal's spacecraft.

Jake chuckled to himself. Poor guy. He felt a little bad for having to bring the wrath of Cantor down on him. But he would survive. He was a Legion soldier.

The soldier spoke loudly, and as if Jake and Cal hadn't just heard the whole conversation with Frank. "The commander has given you direct clearance to Sector Four headquarters, the south hangar. I'll make sure you have a clear, uninterrupted flight." The soldier paused, then continued, speaking softly. "And Mr. Cogburn and Mr., um, Dog, I deeply apologize for my behavior. I had no idea that the commander was expecting you and that this was such a high priority. You know, with your, well, uniforms, and the condition of your spacecraft . . ." He paused again, then continued, "You know, just the appearance of it all, well . . ."

Jake was enjoying the moment, but he couldn't risk spending any more time at the defense station. Someone could recognize them. They needed to get to Frank as soon as possible. So he decided to interrupt the soldier and save him from any further groveling. "Soldier, it's okay. We understand. Keep up the good work."

Jake closed the hatch, pulled away from the siding dock, and quickly exited the defense station.

Jake and Cal climbed out of their spacecraft in the south hangar of Sector Four headquarters. Jake looked around. Not a soul in sight, except for Frank trotting quickly toward them. Frank must have cleared out all personnel from the hangar.

Frank reached them and started to hold out his hand. "Jake, Cal." He stopped. He looked Jake in the eyes, then reached out and pulled him tight for a hug. "I thought I lost you, son."

Jake felt a lump in his throat. His eyes started to water. He wasn't the one who had just found someone he thought had been killed, but the crackle in Frank's voice and the hug, well, he could feel what Frank felt. "I know, Frank. I know."

Frank hugged Cal, then wiped his eyes with his shirt sleeve. "Just look at this. An old gunslinger like me brought to tears. Doesn't that just beat all."

Jake chuckled, wiping his own eyes. Until now, until seeing Frank at this moment, in tears, he had never realized how much Frank cared about him. He probably was the son that Frank never had.

Frank peered behind them, looking in the spacecraft. "Where's Diane?"

Frank's eyes were wide, his face frozen, prepared to hear the worst. "She's alive," Jake said. "Romalor still has her. I don't think he'll hurt her. Not just yet anyway. He wanted her to help him deal with Vernius. I'm not sure what that's about. But in any event, once he learns that we escaped, he'll probably want to use her as leverage against Earth. Whatever's going on, he'll keep that leverage as a backup. At least for a little while."

"Okay," Frank said. "I have a computer booted up in the hangar office and I've been doing some digging around. You two can tell me what happened up there and we can compare notes. Maybe we can figure this out and figure out a way to get Diane back."

Frank stepped over to look at the makeshift transport spacecraft that they had been flying. Then he looked at Cal and Jake again. "You two look like you've been hog-tied and pistol-whipped. It must have been a pretty big outlaw to do that much damage to ya. Look at those knots on your heads." Frank touched Jake's head.

The touch sent a streak of pain through his head, which then started throbbing again. "Ow," Jake said. He stepped back. "You have no idea."

"All right," Frank replied. "I've cleared everyone out of the hangar. Why don't you two hit the shower room and clean up a bit. There should be extra clothes in there. I'll grab you some grub and a first aid kit. Meet me in the office and I'll patch you up and get your bellies full. That'll help you think better."

"Sounds good to me," Jake and Cal said at the same time.

JAKE AND CAL WALKED INTO THE OFFICE, CLEANED UP, AND with fresh clothes on. Not Legion uniforms, but clothes far better than the sweaty, bloody, torn rags they had been wearing.

Frank was sitting at the computer behind a desk. The office was small, probably used for processing temporary data at the hangar. One wall was all glass, looking out on the hangar floor. The other walls were solid white. No windows, no bookshelves, no pictures, nothing. It was evident the office belonged to nobody in particular. Anyone could use it.

"Grab a sandwich over there," Frank said. "You eat while I tell you what I've found out, then I'll get you two doctored up and you can bring me up to speed."

Jake and Cal each picked up a sandwich and sat near Frank. Jake opened the bread and picked at the meat. His lip turned up, almost involuntarily.

Frank looked up from the computer. "I know, roast beef, but it's all I could find."

Oh well, Jake thought. He was starving. He could eat anything at this point. He took a bite. Roast beef never tasted better.

Frank looked back at the computer. "Here's what I've found so far. First, at some point after the Presidential Mansion gave me the orders that I passed on to you, sending the three of you to Craton, the Legion issued a directive to find and capture you two. It explained that you two were

mixed up in trying to illegally deal a hilaetite crystal to Romalor. It said that Diane was caught in the middle and, therefore,
you were also charged with kidnapping an ambassador."
Frank swiveled his chair to turn toward Jake and Cal. "The
orders were to try to take you alive, but any resistance should
be dealt with by the use of lethal force. Then, not more than
an hour later, the Legion issued a statement that all three of
you had been killed on Craton. That the president's office
would be handling the investigation, but there would likely be
no action taken against Craton, given the earlier directive that
you two were criminals anyway. I received both reports at the
same time." Frank paused and shook his head, then continued, "I, of course, knew the first directive was a lie, but had no
reason to doubt the statement that you were dead. That made
perfect sense. Whoever is behind this probably arranged to
have Romalor kill you." Frank stood up and started to pace,
looking at the floor. "So I started to piece things together and
did some digging around. First, it was Armin Dietrich, the
president's chief of staff, who gave me the order to have you
three diverted from Vernius to Craton. He said it was an order
from the president." He stopped pacing, sat down again, and
looked at the computer. "Then, I called a couple of friends in
the Legion and the Presidential Mansion. It appears that both
the directive and the statement of your death originally came
from the Presidential Mansion. My sources can't tell for sure,
but they say that it looks like the president ordered both the
directive and the statement."

"The president?" Jake questioned. He'd figured this went
pretty high up the chain of command, but he hadn't thought
the president was involved. Everything he knew of Jack
Buchanan showed a man of utmost character, integrity, and
values. Those characteristics were rarely even questioned by
his opponents. He had met Buchanan once, a few years ago,
when Buchanan was the keynote speaker at a Legion cadet
graduation ceremony. Of course Jack would have been on his

best behavior at such an event, but something about him made Jake trust him.

Jake got up and poured two tall glasses of ice water. He handed one to Cal and then drank. Ah, that was good. So cool, so refreshing. He had never been so happy to have a simple glass of water. They had found some warm, stale water stored away on the transport they took. That kept them going. But it was nothing like this. Jake pulled his chair around the desk beside Frank so that he could see the computer and took another bite of his sandwich.

"I can't believe that President Buchanan is behind all of this," Cal said.

"I couldn't either," said Frank. "So I had more sources dig deeper. When they did, they found that it looked like the orders were actually made by Dietrich on behalf of the president. So I did my own checking and found that Dietrich and Romalor were pretty close during the negotiations of Treaty 5274."

"The hilaetite treaty," Jake said.

"That's right," continued Frank, looking at Jake. "As you know, Craton was the last to sign the treaty. Dietrich, a young ambassador at the time, was credited with getting Romalor to sign the treaty. Word has it that Dietrich's ties to Romalor and the relationship they developed was why Romalor signed. So I'm convinced that Dietrich is the mole in Earth's government, probably going back to the attack on Sector Four headquarters that killed your uncle, Jake."

"That all fits," Cal said.

Jake pictured Dietrich in his mind. Not the picture of evil that he always imagined was behind this. Dietrich wasn't a fighting man, at least in the sense that Jake thought of fighting. But he wasn't a man who was very well liked, and like anyone in a position of power, he probably wanted even more power and, of course, money. Money and power. The two motivators that had caused most of the pain and suffering in Earth's

154 | BRYAN PROSEK

history and throughout the galaxy. Yes, he supposed that even Armin Dietrich could cause the death of so many, including Uncle Ben, with money and power as the motivators. "I've always said that it was Romalor who led the attack. And we saw the giant crystal on Craton. Romalor is developing some type of weapon with it. By all accounts, it has to be the same crystal that was taken from Sector Four headquarters. That Uncle Ben died for."

"Yes," agreed Frank. "Now what we need is hard evidence. Something linking Dietrich to Romalor. Not just our speculation. Even if anybody would believe us, Dietrich wouldn't let us get close enough to anybody to talk. We need evidence to show somebody first."

"Yeah, and I doubt that Romalor will be willing to waltz into an Earth courtroom and testify against Dietrich," Cal added with a slight smile.

Cal got up and poured them each another glass of water and got himself another sandwich. He handed the glass to Jake.

Before drinking, Jake held the glass against the side of his head. The cold felt good. It eased the throbbing, but he still had a headache. Although now it was probably more from lack of sleep than anything. "Romalor played us a video com of a man, Sloan, talking to him," Jake said. "Sloan explained how he would arrange to set us up. Sloan said that he had friends in high places that could do that. He must have been referring to Dietrich."

"Good, good," Frank said. "Did Sloan say anything or do anything that you can remember that might lead us to a connection with Dietrich?"

Jake and Cal both shook their heads.

Frank continued, "Was there anything in the video that might give us a clue? Think."

"It's hard to remember," replied Jake. "We've both been

smacked over the head with a club by a seven-foot Cratonite. That tends to make a person forget a lot."

Cal sat back down, shut his eyes and put his face in his hands. Jake reran the video in his mind, from start to finish, at least what he could recall of it. Nothing out of the ordinary struck him.

Cal uncovered his face, his eyes wide. "Wait, I do remember something! Sloan was sitting at a desk during the call. Behind him on the wall was the bottom half of an emblem. The top was cut off by the video com angle. But the part of the emblem that I could see was the earth, or half of it, and underneath the earth was a giant X."

"Okay, good," said Jake. "Do a search on the computer for an earth emblem with an X."

Frank got up from the computer. "Here, you go at it, Cal. You're a lot handier with these things than I am."

Jake got up and moved to the front of the desk so that Frank could stand where he had been sitting. Cal sat down and began typing. Frank stood, looking over Cal's shoulder. A couple of moments later, the search results appeared.

"What all did we get?" asked Jake.

"Well," said Cal, reading the results to himself, "there are a number of book titles, articles, miscellaneous stuff." He paused and read some more to himself before continuing, "Wait, here's something. A Senate Bill 365 trademark registration of a business logo." He hit a few keys, and a picture of the logo came up on the screen—the earth with the letter N above it and the letter X below it. "It says the holder of the registration is EarthNX Corporation."

Frank slapped the desk. "Bullseye!"

"That's it," added Jake. "Sloan was sitting in the offices of EarthNX when he made the call."

"Of course," said Frank. "It all makes even more sense now. This mess has the fingerprints of Edgardo Ramirez all over it. I bet EarthNX sold Romalor the crystal, and Ramirez probably is developing that weapon for him, at a nice price, of course. If that isn't selling out Earth. Whether it's robbing a stagecoach or intergalactic espionage, the motive never changes. Money!"

"And power," added Jake.

"Dietrich, Romalor, and Ramirez," Cal said. "It all fits together."

"And don't forget our mysterious friend, Mr. Sloan," added Jake.

"You two need to get to the EarthNX offices," Frank said, "and find something solid connecting Dietrich to this. The president won't have any trouble believing that Romalor and Ramirez are behind this, but it's going to take hard evidence to convince him of his chief of staff's involvement."

"Even if we find something, will the president listen to us?" Cal asked. "I mean, Dietrich and he go back a long way."

"Good point," Frank replied. "I was thinking that as well. I think we should take it to Marco Veneto first. He's a Legion man. He'll listen. He'll want to protect Legion soldiers if he has solid proof that you didn't do anything. And he'll be able to get the president's ear."

"All right, then," Jake said. "It's settled. Cal and I will check out EarthNX and see what we can find. Once we find some evidence, hopefully Veneto will get the president to lift the directive and send the Legion for Diane, and for whatever weapon Romalor is working on, before it's too late."

Frank added, "And in the meantime, I will talk to Veneto to bring him up to date."

"Is that a good idea?" asked Cal, leaning back in the chair and looking up at Frank. "You know, telling him that we are alive and here on Earth. I mean, the original directive still stands."

"I think it's our only option," Frank replied. "He has to be brought in sometime, and the sooner the better. That way, if something goes wrong for you at EarthNX, at least we might have him in our corner. I know for a fact that he and Dietrich don't see eye to eye, to say the least. If there is any chance that Dietrich is implicated, I think he'll give us the chance to prove it."

"Makes sense to me," said Jake. He walked over and picked up another sandwich. This roast beef wasn't half bad. He was beginning to develop a taste for it.

"You two need to hit EarthNX after dark," Frank said. "Even then, it won't be easy. Ramirez has an army of guards the size of a small Legion division, and probably better equipped. And we can have no communications. The Legion will be monitoring everything. Let me doctor you two up, then you can stay here and get some sleep until dark. I'll keep everyone out and wake you when it's time. I'll have a quantum light fighter ready for you. It won't be the most inconspicuous mode of transportation, but it'll be dark and EarthNX isn't far from here. Besides, if something goes wrong, you may need the firepower." Frank paused and then added, "There won't be any help. Even if I can get Veneto on our side, he can't and won't go to the president without hard evidence. You'll be on your own until you can bring something back."

Jake nodded. He didn't like it, but it was their only option. Frank was right. There was nobody else they could turn to for help. In addition to being Earth's army and air force, the Legion was the sole law enforcement agency on Earth. If Cal and he couldn't clear their names with the Legion, there would be no place they could hide on Earth, and very few places they could hide in the galaxy. And if they were on the run, what about Diane?

9

THE COMPLEX

Even though they couldn't use quantum drive close to a planet's surface, it was a short flight for Jake and Cal from Sector Four headquarters to EarthNX, located in a remote region of former southern Spain. Due to the top-secret nature of its work, EarthNX was located away from any other buildings or industry.

Jake could see the EarthNX complex lit up on their scanners as they approached. It covered nearly forty acres and consisted of at least twenty different buildings. At least that's what was picked up by the scanners, visible above ground. "This complex is huge."

"Yeah," Cal replied. "And the Legion granted the company a no-fly zone covering almost ten square miles, including the complex. What the scanners don't pick up are the company's numerous underground facilities and testing areas that are connected to the above-ground complex."

"The information Frank gave us said that the complex is heavily guarded twenty-four/seven by an elite group of guards," Jake said. "And since EarthNX makes most of the Legion's weapons, it equips its guards with the best and most current technology. I even saw where it is believed that the company has its own fleet of quantum light fighters."

With the night vision on the video screen, Jake could see the large, thick green concrete poles surrounding the complex. Each one was about ten feet high and they were placed about twenty yards apart. An invisible shield, Frank had said, based on the same technology as Earth's defense shield, ran between each pole, forming a wall around the complex. He thought back some more as to what Frank had told them before they left. Attached to every tenth pole were two small black boxes, one on the inside and one on the outside of the shield, that operated the shield between those ten poles within the boxes' grid. The shield was never set at its maximum strength; therefore, if a person were to walk into it, it would not necessarily kill him. It would give him a good jolt and knock him backward. Of course, if he were to insist on continuing to run through the shield, it would eventually kill him. Or if a vehicle were to run into the shield hard enough, it would explode the vehicle.

Jake set their quantum fighter down in a small clearing in the woods just outside the no-fly zone. They would have to go on foot from there. Jake helped Cal slip on the large backpack that Frank had stocked with everything they would need to gain access to the complex and try to locate the main terminal.

JAKE AND CAL HAD MET FRANK BACK IN THE HANGAR AFTER A few hours of sleep—or attempted sleep. True to his word, Frank had a quantum light fighter waiting in the hangar for them, and there was not another soul in sight.

"What's all of that?" Jake had asked as he surveyed a large table beside the quantum fighter. Numerous gadgets and small weapons were laid out on it, in addition to two sepders.

"This is what you're going to need to get in and out of EarthNX alive," Frank replied.

"I thought it was a corporation, not a military complex," Jake said as he looked closer at all the high-tech equipment.

"It's both," Frank said. "I want you two cowboys to get in and out of Dodge in one piece, preferably without needing to use most of this. Now listen up. Here's what you have." He held up a small, square, flat transponder device that fit in the palm of his hand. It had a few keys on a small keypad and a larger screen than a typical transponder. Frank continued, "This contains a map of the EarthNX complex. It identifies all above-ground buildings, and what is known of the below-ground buildings. I have marked two possible locations for the main computer terminal. Hopefully, one of them is it. You need to head to these two buildings first."

"Why can't we just hack into any old computer on site?" Jake asked.

Cal answered, "Because we won't be able to, at least not in the time we'll have. That's what this is for. Right, Frank?" Cal picked up a small black box with several wires hanging out of it and a screen on one side.

"Exactly," Frank replied. "You'll need to find the main terminal. With a little luck, Cal will be able to figure out where to connect these rerouting wires. Once connected, Cal will be able to access the entire computer system through the monitor in the main terminal. You'll be able to download any information you need onto this chip." Frank ejected a microchip from the black box. "This rerouting device will only work at the main terminal."

"Oh, right," Jake said. "We just waltz into the main terminal, hook up a few wires, download to the chip, and walk out. It's as simple as that." When it came to computers and technology, Jake had his doubts. He knew that if anyone could pull this off, Cal could. But he also knew that when computers were involved, something would always go wrong. Guaranteed. Why would this mission be any different?

"One more thing," Frank added. "You'll need this to deactivate the fence shield." Frank held up a blue square object. If the object had been round, it could have passed for a very soft bouncing ball, except that once squished, it took a few minutes for it to return to its original form. Frank went on to describe what the fence shield was and how it worked. "Locate one of the boxes on every tenth pole. Put this over the box." Frank showed them how one side of the square had a slit in it. "Push it down and mold it onto the box. This will activate a metallic chemical compound mixture that will seep into the shield box. It'll take about five minutes. After five minutes, test out the shield. The compound blocks the shield frequency temporarily so you can pass through, but it doesn't trip the detection signal, so the guards won't be alerted to a shield failure."

"You said temporarily?" Jake questioned. More technology gadgets. More things to go wrong, especially when the word "temporarily" was used. He preferred to just blow up the fence, but he knew that they needed stealth this time.

"Yes," Frank answered. "This blue square you see here is the compound. It will eventually dissolve after it slowly seeps into the box. Once it's gone, the box will return to its normal operation. It should keep the shield down for five minutes or so. Plenty of time to walk through."

"And how do we get out?" Jake asked. He knew there was always a catch to these types of gadgets. The more gadgets you used, the more you needed, and the more plumbing you had, the easier it was to clog the drain.

"The same way you get in," Frank said. "I was able to get you two." He held up another blue rubbery square. "But only two. So don't mess one up."

Oh, great, Jake thought. One shot to get out, then they were stuck. But enough pessimism. Frank had done the best he could, and this mission already had enough question marks and risks involved. Jake looked over the table a little longer, then he felt a rush of adrenaline when he saw what was at the end of the table. "Frank, are we playing cowboys and Indians? Cool!" Jake reached down and picked up what looked like a longbow, but was made out of a dark silver metallic substance. The string looked like a thin cable wire. Beside the bow was a belt containing several arrows. But the arrows had no feathers on the end. They just flattened out like a putty knife, with a small groove in the middle. The arrows didn't have normal tips. Rather, on the end of each arrow was a small dart. Now this was his type of gadget. Technologically advanced, no doubt, but no computers or dissolving substances involved. Just a good old bow and arrow.

"You'll probably need to knock out a few guards from a distance," Frank said. "Too far for hand to hand, and any of these guns could be too loud. This, my friend, is silent." Frank touched the bow. "It looks different from the old-fashioned longbow that I taught you to shoot, Jake, but it shoots the same, with three times the distance and accuracy. I've been making it myself for years, using materials imported from the planet Bernasia. I know it looks like nothing more than a stiff metal rod, with arrows that won't fly, but give it a try. It's as light as a feather, and you can hardly feel the string on your fingers."

Jake picked up an arrow, set it in place, and aimed at the hangar door keypad at the far end of the hangar, about seventy yards away. The bow felt comfortable, very comfortable, balanced and light. He pulled the string. The string was stiff, but surprisingly flexible and easy to pull back. He loved the feel. He let the arrow fly. The arrow nailed the center of the pad. Sparks flew. The door opened a couple of feet, then stopped, short-circuited.

"Nice," Jake said, satisfied with both the feel of the bow and its accuracy.

"Nice?" Cal questioned. "Now we can't get out of here."

Frank didn't laugh or even smile. "The darts will just knock the target out for a few hours. That's all these guns will do as well." He ran his hand over three different-sized guns. "They're the Legion's latest in what you could call stun guns. They work off of plasma technology, but they won't kill. They only knock out. But they do it instantly. The darts work just as quickly. The sepders are normal though, so no shooting with them. Remember, no matter what corner you get backed into, you cannot kill anyone, or we're no better than Dietrich and Ramirez. Now, you two need to get going."

Frank loaded all the equipment and weapons into the backpack. Jake kept the bow and strapped the belt full of arrows around his waist. That was the last time they would see Frank until they found something to clear themselves. If not, it would be the last time ever.

JAKE AND CAL MADE THEIR WAY THROUGH THE WOODS. JAKE could see the lights of the EarthNX complex off in the distance. He didn't need the transponder to find the complex. The lights led the way.

Jake and Cal approached the fence shield. They were on the edge of the forest. Jake surveyed the area. There was about ten feet of open ground between them and the shield. Once through the shield, they would have to cross about fifty more yards of open fields before they would be able to reach the nearest building for cover. Seeing what they were doing would not be a problem, as the entire complex was well lit. The problem would be moving undetected by the guards. There were two guards visible from where they lay in the woods, one on each side of the nearest building. Cal looked at Jake and pointed to the closest pole containing a black box.

Jake nodded. Jake likewise pointed out the two guards, and Cal nodded.

They crawled on their stomachs through the grass, slowly covering the ten feet from the cover of the trees to the pole. Jake readied his bow and pulled two arrows from his belt. He placed one in the bow and nodded to Cal. Both men were still lying as close to the ground as possible. Cal placed the blue rubber square over the outer box and pressed it down hard, molding it to the shape of the box. The rubber immediately started to disappear as it dissolved into the box. Jake watched as Cal marked his watch, and the two of them lay motionless for five minutes. *All right. Here we go. This better work*, Jake thought. He had no doubt that he could knock out the guards with Frank's high tech bow and arrows, but would the fence shield deactivate and stay deactivated long enough?

Cal looked at his watch and nodded to Jake. Jake slowly moved the end of his bow toward the shield. If the shield was still active when he hit it with the bow, a detection signal would go off inside the complex and their mission would immediately end. And if they waited too long to move, the shield might reactivate before they downed the two guards and passed through. Jake slowly moved the bow past the pole. Nothing happened. Jake sighed. He rose to his knees and aimed at the guard on his right, slowly pulling the bow wire back. He let the arrow fly. The dart-tipped arrow struck the guard's neck. The guard grabbed at it. Before he could utter a sound, he dropped. The second guard turned toward the first guard. The second dart-tipped arrow struck the second guard in the neck. He dropped just as quickly as the first. Jake nodded to Cal, and they both crouched low and sprinted to the side of the building for cover. Jake held up his hand, signaling Cal to pause. Jake looked around. No noise and nobody in sight. They had made it in, undetected.

"VENETO RESIDENCE," FRANK HEARD AS HE WATCHED THE housekeeper appear on the video com.

"This is Commander Frank Cantor calling for Mr. Veneto. Is he in?" Frank asked.

"Let me see if he's available, Commander," she replied.

Frank watched the video com. The picture on the other end was of a desk and the back wall of Marco Veneto's home study. From this view, it was a study filled with only the highest quality furnishings and very meticulously maintained. Mr. Veneto had expensive taste, which was a bit surprising for a career Legion man. He was also meticulous in his organization and maintenance of his property. That quality in a Legion soldier was not surprising.

It seemed to Frank like it was taking forever. He looked at his timepiece, then at the video com. *Come on, come on*, he thought. He wondered how things were going for Cal and Jake. Did they make it in? If Veneto wasn't home, was he at Legion headquarters because Cal and Jake were caught, or worse? He couldn't be having those thoughts. He had to remain positive. Stay focused on the objective.

Marco Veneto appeared in front of the video com. "Frank Cantor, it's good to see you. I understand that you are doing a bang-up job commanding Sector Four. That doesn't surprise me one bit. That's why I wanted you there."

"Thank you, sir," Frank replied. He kept his tone circumspect and respectful. He needed to break the ice and build trust, quickly.

"So what has you calling at this hour?" Marco asked.

"Well, sir, I was wondering if I could talk to you—face to face that is?" Frank said. "Not over the com."

"It's getting pretty late, Frank," Marco replied, "but I assume you wouldn't be asking if it wasn't urgent."

"Yes, sir, it is urgent," Frank said. "It's regarding Armin Dietrich. I think you will want to hear what I have to say."

There was a long pause. Frank tapped his foot repeatedly. If he couldn't get an audience with Veneto, what chance would their plan have?

Marco's voice came over the com. "How soon can you be here?"

Frank sighed with relief. "Within the hour, sir," Frank said. "I'll come by aircraft."

"That'll work," Marco replied, "but my landing pad is being resurfaced. You'll have to use the pad at the park across the street. You'll see my aircraft parked there. There's a small coffee shop nearby. I'll meet you there in an hour."

"Thank you, sir," Frank responded. Over the first hurdle. Marco Veneto was his first and last option for trying to save Jake, Cal, and Diane. If Marco wouldn't hear him out, and then convince the president, nobody else would. "I'll see you soon."

JAKE LOOKED DOWN AT THE TRANSPONDER IN CAL'S HAND. CAL pointed to the closer of the two buildings that Frank had marked as the best possibilities for housing the main computer terminal. Jake nodded. Jake knew where they were on the map, and where the targeted building was on the map. Now if they could just get there, undetected.

They slowly eased their way along the back side of the building they had run to. Jake noticed that, unlike the dome-shaped buildings found in most towns and cities, the EarthNX buildings were square or rectangular, with the tallest being no more than four or five stories. As they reached the edge of the building, Jake popped his head around the corner, then jerked it back quickly. One guard, not looking in their direction. Jake looked at Cal and put his fingers to his eyes, and then held up one finger. Cal nodded. Jake loaded an arrow in the bow. He would have to be quick, and he would have only one shot. Even with the quiet arrows, a miss would surely alert the guard. By the time he could get off a second shot, the guard would raise an alarm. In one quick, smooth motion, Jake stepped around the corner, aimed, and released the bow wire. Good, another perfect shot in the neck.

Jake and Cal sprinted to the next building. The targeted building was one more over. They edged to the corner of the current building and Jake did another check. This time one guard, but he was on the roof of the targeted building, out of arrow range.

Jake whispered, "I'll shoot two arrows into those barrels over there." He pointed to a stack of barrels off to the side of the targeted building. "When he walks to the far edge to look down, we can make a run for that door on the other side. It should be out of his view."

Cal nodded.

Jake pulled out two arrows. He put the nocks together, but slightly angled the dart tips so that one would hit slightly above the other. He wanted to make noise this time. Enough noise to draw the guard's attention, but not enough noise to attract any other guards.

Jake aimed and let the arrows fly. The plan worked perfectly. They were at the doorway, undetected, in no time.

Cal pulled what looked like a ball of clay out of the backpack and molded it to the door keypad. "These doors are high-tech. The decoder won't work on them, but Frank gave us this." He pulled out a small laser, the size of a pencil, and clicked the back. A red light hit the clay-like substance. The substance smoked a little, then the keypad made a very faint "pop" and the door opened. They quickly ducked inside. Cal pressed the door close button.

Jake turned on his light rod and whispered, "Now where? We don't have interior building maps."

"If the main terminal is in here," Cal said, "it'll be on the lowest level. Let's go down."

Ahead and to their right, Jake saw a vertical transportation unit. It was an open-air unit, using the same technology as the sides of skyscrapers. In fact, it was the same unit as used in skyscrapers to reach the top floors in seconds. EarthNX did have money if it could afford such units in buildings no taller than these. It would be quick, but the stairs were the safer option. Jake tapped Cal on the shoulder and pointed to a service stairwell near the transportation unit. They took the stairs down as far as they could go, two flights.

"This looks like the basement," Cal said. "Good."

They exited the stairwell into a long, dimly lit hall. Jake liked the looks of it. Enough light to see what they were doing, but not enough to easily give them away.

"The lights are a good sign," Cal said. "Power must have to stay on down here twenty-four/seven for some reason. Hopefully, it's for the terminal."

Looking down the hall, there were several doors on either side. Older doors with knobs. At the end of the hall were two large doors. They proceeded down the hall. Jake turned the handle on the first door. It wasn't locked. He opened the door and held up his light rod. It looked like a storage area. It was full of old and new computer equipment. Cal did the same with the next door. It contained backup heating and cooling units.

"More good signs," Cal said. "I bet the terminal is in the room at the end."

They quickly made their way to the double doors. Jake turned the handle. It was locked. Jake watched as Cal proceeded to disable the lock in the same manner he had before.

As Jake reached to open the door, a deep voice shouted from the other end of the hall behind them. "You two, stop where you are. Get your hands where I can see them and slowly turn around."

Jake and Cal raised their hands. Jake was wondering if it would be an army of guards standing there. If so, this would be the end. He and Cal turned slowly. Good, it was one guard, armed with a long plasma rifle. They had a chance. Not a good one, but a chance.

"That's far enough," the guard said. He approached them. The guard pressed the com button on his belt. "This is F4306. I have a situation in building eight, basement level."

A response came over the com immediately. "Copy that, F4306. We are proceeding to your destination. ETA, seven minutes."

The guard looked at Jake and Cal. "Okay, slowly lay down the backpack and the bow, and also those." He paused and looked closer. "Sepders? What are you guys, Legion?"

Neither of them spoke.

"Who are you and what are you doing here?" the guard asked.

Jake and Cal just stared at him. Jake thought, *I need to do something.* They only had seven minutes. Actually, less. But what? *Think, Jake, think.*

"Look," the guard said, his voice louder, "you can tell me now, or when my company gets here, we can beat it out of you. Your choice."

Cal stepped in front of and a little to the right of Jake and spoke. "Okay, we were hired by Edgardo Ramirez to infiltrate the complex and reach the main computer terminal. It was a test. He wanted to test his guards to see if you could stop an infiltration."

What are you up to, Cal? Jake thought. I need to play along, but what's my move?

As Cal raised his hands a little higher, his jacket pulled up and Jake could see one of Frank's plasma stun guns tucked into Cal's belt at the small of his back. *Cal, you sly dog. Good move.*

Cal continued, "You caught us, so you passed. We'll give a full report to Mr. Ramirez, with a glowing review of you, officer . . ." Cal stopped for a moment. "What's your name?"

The guard didn't move. "You're not going anywhere until I say so," the guard said.

Jake could see that the guard was focused on Cal now. This was his opportunity. He pulled the gun from Cal's belt with his right hand. As he raised it up toward Cal's left shoulder, Cal ducked. That gave just enough clearance over Cal. Jake fired. Before the guard could react, the plasma blast hit him directly in the chest, and he dropped instantly. His plasma rifle fell to the ground and he toppled over backward. He fell so quickly that Jake thought for a moment that maybe it was a regular plasma gun and he had killed the guard. But from what he could see, there were no burns.

"Nice shot," Cal said.

Jake immediately ran to the guard and felt for a pulse. He found one. *Good*, he thought. He quickly pressed the com button on the guard's belt, and with the best imitation of the guard's voice that he could muster, he spoke deeply. "This is F4306. The situation has been neutralized. No further need of assistance."

He waited. No way this would work. Surely they were either already so close that they heard the blast or would continue on anyway. Or they would recognize that it was a different voice. A voice came over the com. "Copy that F4306. Returning to our posts."

"That was close," Cal said.

Jake sighed. "Too close."

They hid the guard in a closet and headed through the double doors. The room was dimly lit as well. Jake held up his light rod. He could see all sorts of machines and equipment in the room. They appeared to be computer terminals. All right, they'd found it. The main terminal.

Cal slammed his backpack on the floor. "All that for nothing."

"What do you mean?" Jake asked. "Isn't this the main terminal?"

Cal shook his head. "No, it's the backup center. And the main terminal is never in the same vicinity as the backup terminal. The main terminal must be in the other building."

Jake shook his head. What else could go wrong? But hey, they had come this far, and as far as he knew, they were still undetected by anyone currently conscious. So why couldn't they get to the other building and locate the terminal there? He pulled the transponder out of the backpack and spoke. "Okay, then, here's the other building. Let's get going."

FRANK LANDED HIS AIRCRAFT ON THE PARK'S LANDING PAD. There was only one other aircraft there. *That must be Marco's,* Frank thought. Frank looked around and spotted the coffee shop down the street.

Frank entered the shop. He saw Marco seated in a booth in the far corner. There were a couple of other people at the counter seats, but nobody else in the shop. That was perfect. They would have privacy.

Marco set down his coffee cup, stood, and shook Frank's hand. "You look good, Frank."

"Thank you," Frank replied. "As do you, sir."

The waitress approached and looked at Frank. "Coffee, sir?"

"Yes, please." He felt like he needed the whole pot, but he would start with one cup.

She poured Frank a cup and warmed up Marco's.

Frank said to Marco, "Thank you for meeting me on such short notice, and at this hour of the night."

"Don't even think about it, Frank," Marco replied. "It must be important or you wouldn't be going to all this trouble. What's up?" Marco scooped a little sugar into his coffee.

Frank poured cream into his coffee. "Well, sir, I'm not sure where to begin or how to say this. It's about those two Legion privates accused of various crimes, including dealing in black market hilaetite crystals."

Marco scooted up to the table and set down his cup. "You mean Jake Saunders and Cal Danielson?"

Frank nodded and continued, "And I know you aren't a big fan of Armin Dietrich. I mean, I don't want to put words in your mouth or anything, but the way you two feel about each other isn't any secret."

"No, it isn't," Marco replied. "But I don't think you came all the way over here at this hour of the night to discuss my relationship with the president's chief of staff. And what does my relationship with him have to do with Saunders and Danielson anyway?"

Frank paused for a moment. Maybe he should stop. Accusing someone at Dietrich's level of, among other things, conspiracy and treason, wasn't something to be done lightly. And what if Veneto felt that such an accusation was also an accusation against the president? What if Veneto went to the president immediately? He could be reading Veneto entirely wrong. Veneto might not have that much of a vendetta against Dietrich. If Frank continued, and if he was wrong about Veneto, then everything could be over for Jake and Cal right then and there. But wasn't everything over for Jake and Cal if he didn't make the attempt? There was no other way to get the president to listen to the evidence. He had come this far, and disclosing what he knew to Veneto was the plan he, Jake, and Cal had agreed on. He had to continue.

Frank took a sip of coffee, cleared his throat, then spoke.

"As soon as I received the report on Saunders and Danielson, about their crimes and their death, I started doing some digging. I didn't believe for a moment that Saunders and Danielson were guilty. I've known them too long. I had to clear their names. So I started putting two and two together." Frank paused again and took another sip. "Sir, I have very strong reason to believe that Armin Dietrich, not Saunders and Danielson, is behind the transfer of a hilaetite crystal to Romalor. Not the little crystal that Romalor returned. That was just so Dietrich could set up Saunders and Danielson. But I mean the large crystal taken from Sector Four headquarters eight years ago." Frank scooted closer to the table. "It was sold to Romalor for use in some kind of super weapon. When Vernius recently detected the crystal on Craton, the setup was needed to cover up the transaction of eight years ago. The setup not only explained Vernius' detection, but also drew any attention away from anyone in Earth's government being involved, namely Dietrich."

Marco sat up straight. Frank could tell he had Veneto's attention, one hundred percent.

Marco put his hands on the table, leaned forward, and spoke softly. "Frank, do you know what you're saying? This is the president's chief of staff you are accusing. I would like nothing more than to get him out of the president's inner circle, but accusing him of conspiracy, treason, involvement in an attack on Earth? I don't know. And why would Dietrich help Romalor develop a super weapon that presumably could be used against Earth?"

"That part, sir," Frank replied, "I haven't figured out, but I think I will, once I have the hard evidence in hand."

"What hard evidence?" Marco replied. "What do you have that proves all of this?"

Before Frank could go on, the waitress returned. "Can I get you gentlemen anything else? Would you like more coffee?"

"I'm fine," Marco said, not looking up.

Frank looked at the waitress and scooted his cup toward her. "Yes, please. Thanks."

JAKE AND CAL MADE THEIR WAY UP AND OUT OF THE BUILDING the same way they had come in. Once out the door, they hung tight to the side of the building. Jake wanted to be careful to stay out of view of the guard on the roof. Jake looked at the transponder again. The new target building was three buildings to the left and one building up from where they were. A diagonal path across the open alley was the most direct route and would put them up against the building just to the right of the target building. He could easily scout out the path from their current vantage point to determine if any guards were in sight. However, they would have to cross the main street in the complex, which was the widest. It would put them in the open longer than Jake liked. But it was still their best option, Jake thought.

Jake motioned to Cal, pointing out the path they would take. Cal nodded. Jake then slowly moved along the edge of the building and checked around the near corner to survey for guards. Jake spotted two guards who would be able to see them make their next move. One was on top of the adjacent building. The other was around the corner from their present location. That guard was close. The two guards would have to be knocked out simultaneously or one would see the other and signal. Because of their locations, Jake could not use the bow on both. There would be too much time between shots. He signaled to Cal and Cal gave him an understanding nod. Jake would knock out the guard on the roof with the bow while Cal struck the other with his sepder. They crept to the edge of the building. Jake loaded his bow with another arrow while Cal readied his sepder. The timing would have to be perfect. They worked on simultaneous takedowns in the Legion all the time. Just for this purpose. But never when one soldier was using a bow and arrow. Such primitive weapons were unheard of in the Legion. Well, it's now or never, Jake thought. Jake nodded, and they both moved in unison. Jake's arrow hit its target in the back of the neck. The guard dropped almost immediately. At the same time, Cal struck the other guard on the side of the head with the broad side of his sepder, so as not to kill him. He also dropped.

They both ran low and fast diagonally across the open street to the cover of the building as planned. The target building was now the next building over, with a door facing them. Jake surveyed again. He gave the all-clear sign, and they both darted to the door. Cal quickly disabled the keypad and they were in. They wasted no time finding the stairwell and descending to the basement. Like the last building they were in, they exited the stairwell into a long, dimly lit hall. Also like the other building, a double door was at the far end of the hall. Just in case of a patrol guard like the last building, Jake thought he better stay by the stairwell, where he could see down the hall. "I'll wait here until you get inside."

Cal nodded and quickly went to the other end of the hall and disabled the door keypad. Once Cal was inside, Jake followed.

"Bingo," Cal said. "This is it. The main computer terminal. Now, let me see."

Cal played around with various controls for a few minutes and searched the room. Finally, he smiled and sat behind a glass-topped table. He touched the table in a couple of spots, and it lit up. The entire table was the computer screen, with touch screen controls. Cal pulled the rerouting box from the backpack and inserted the microchip. Jake watched as Cal crawled under the table where the main terminal monitor was located. After a few minutes of connecting the rerouting wires to various terminal wires, Cal crawled back out.

176 | BRYAN PROSEK

"There, that should do it," Cal said.

Jake continued to watch Cal and occasionally looked out one of the double doors down the hall to make sure no guards were coming.

Cal sat down and started working the computer. To Jake, the computer seemed fast and easy. Or maybe Cal just made it seem that way.

"Here's something," Cal said. "It's as top secret as you can get, with more firewalls and blocks than I've ever seen. I guess we'll see how well Frank's box works."

"Is it letting you in?" Jake said after only a few seconds. Then he looked out the door again.

"Patience, my friend," Cal answered. A moment later, Cal spoke again. "Yes, we're in. Wow, would you look at this. This is a whole new design for the defense shield."

"You mean the EarthNX fence?" Jake asked.

"No," Cal replied. "The *Earth* defense shield. It looks like it's being designed as a proposal to the Legion. The Legion doesn't know about it yet." Cal paused for a moment, then jumped out of his seat, still looking at the computer table. "Look at this! It's being designed as a defense against a super weapon, possibly in the possession of Craton."

Before Cal could go on, Jake interrupted, "That explains the missing piece. That's why Dietrich and Ramirez had no problem selling the hilaetite crystal to Romalor. They probably also designed and sold him the plans for the super weapon as well. Then, once the weapon becomes functional, they plan on selling the Legion this new defense shield. Romalor gets what he wants, the galaxy's most powerful weapon, and Earth is safe from Romalor."

Cal finished Jake's thought. "And Dietrich, Ramirez, and this Sloan guy walk off with trillions of quads. Unbelievable."

Jake left the door and walked toward Cal. "And in the meantime, Legion soldiers, an ambassador, and who knows how many other people are killed. All for greed."

"Well, it's going to stop now," Cal said. "Let me download this onto the microchip. Now we just need to find the evidence connecting Dietrich to all of this."

Cal sat back down and started flipping through files on the computer.

Jake peeked out the door. "Let's pick it up. The patrol guard just came out of the stairwell. He's probably just doing routine checks, but he'll look in here once he sees the keypad disabled."

"I think I found it," Cal said. "Money transfers."

"Hurry it up," Jake said. He knew Cal was going as fast as he could, and he trusted nobody to work a computer faster, but he didn't want to risk yet another confrontation. Sooner or later the whole complex would be alerted.

"I just need a couple more minutes," Cal answered. "Here it is. Transfers coming into EarthNX from Romalor. Probably in payment for the crystal. Yes, the first was eight years ago. And also for the weapon plans. And here are the transfers out. They go to three different accounts. The name on the first account is, let me see, Edgardo Ramirez. Of course, he takes a share off the top. Why wait for a dividend from the company? The second account is titled to . . ." Cal paused for a moment, then continued. "It takes a minute. Here it comes. Sloan."

"Okay," Jake said as he peeked out the door again. "The pieces are fitting together. But the guard is still coming. He's checking in the other rooms on his way. There's only one more room before he gets to this one."

"I'm accessing the last account now," Cal said. "It should be Dietrich's. Then we can download them to the microchip and get out of here. Here it comes now. The name on the last account is . . ." Cal paused again.

Jake took a couple of steps toward Cal and the computer table. He looked at the table and could see the computer trying to access the account. As the name appeared on the screen, Jake looked at Cal. Cal's eyes widened and he looked at Jake. Jake looked back at the screen. The name on the screen was Marco Veneto.

"We have to contact Frank. Now."

"Now where was I?" Frank asked after the waitress had left them.

"What evidence do you have for all of this?" Marco replied.

"Yes," Frank said. "That's right." He slowly looked around the room to make sure nobody had sat down within hearing range of them. He was safe. There were now two other tables occupied. And both of those were occupied by young couples, probably topping off a late date. He took a drink of coffee and puckered. He realized he hadn't added cream. "Well, through my investigation, I found a number of leads connecting Dietrich to Romalor. And Jake and Cal were able to connect Romalor to a man named Sloan and to EarthNX. That completes . . ."

Marco interrupted Frank in the middle of the sentence. "Jake and Cal? You mean Jake Saunders and Cal Danielson? You've talked to them?" Marco added some more sugar to his coffee and stirred.

"Yes, sir," said Frank. "They're alive, and are back here on Earth."

"Impossible," Marco said. His eyes widened.

"What's that, sir?" Frank asked.

"Well, I mean, that's great news. Are they okay? How about the ambassador?"

"They're fine," Frank replied. "A few bumps and bruises, but they'll live. Romalor still has the ambassador. And that's part of the reason why I am here. As I was saying, now that we have connected the triangle, Romalor, Dietrich, and EarthNX, plus this Sloan, whom I assume is the middle man that brought them all together, we need to find the hard evidence connecting Dietrich to the group. I believe that evidence is at EarthNX. Jake and Cal are there right now searching the main computer terminal to see what they can find."

Marco straightened up, took a drink of coffee, then scooped in more sugar. "They're at EarthNX right now? Have you heard from them yet? Have they found anything?"

"No," Frank said. "We agreed to go silent, figuring the Legion would be monitoring the airways."

"Good thinking," Marco replied. "Who else knows of this?"

"Nobody," Frank said. "Just Jake, Cal, and me, and now you." Frank couldn't read Veneto. He was asking lots of questions, which made it seem like he was believing Frank. Yet, he seemed apprehensive, worried. But maybe he was just mulling it over. Trying to figure out what to believe. But Veneto's questions weren't the questions Frank expected.

"Good. I think we should keep it that way for now," Marco replied.

"That's what we thought too, sir," Frank said. "We figured that the president wouldn't listen to me with it being his chief of staff who's involved, unless we had hard evidence. And even then, I'm skeptical that he will listen. We figured our best option was to bring you up to date, hoping that you would have no problem speaking out against Dietrich, and that you could get the president's ear. Assuming, of course, we provide you with the evidence first." Frank finally poured some cream in his coffee. "Once the president is involved, I assume you and he will have no problem reversing the report on Jake and Cal, dropping the charges, and sending the Legion after Diane, not to mention stopping Romalor from developing this super weapon." Frank hesitated. He hated to be direct and ask the decisive question, but he was running out of time. He had to find out where Veneto stood. "Can we count on you, sir?"

Marco looked at his coffee, stirred it some more, then took a drink.

Good, Frank thought. *He's really thinking on it.* Just maybe Veneto would see it his way.

Marco cupped his coffee cup with both hands, leaned forward, and spoke softly. "Frank, you are one of the best commanders, if not *the* best, that I've known. Even with my history with Dietrich, I am hesitant to go after him, for fear of what the president will do. But if everything you say is true, and I have no reason to doubt that it is, then our planet is in grave danger, some very good people have been killed, and some very good soldiers have been wronged. Frank, you get me that evidence, and I promise you I will take it to the president and put an end to all of this."

Frank felt like hugging him. They had just cleared one of the biggest hurdles in their plan. Now, if Jake and Cal could just come up with the evidence and make it out of EarthNX safely. "Sir," Frank said, "you don't know how much this means to me. Thank you, sir. Thank you."

"I'd best be getting home now," Marco said. "You contact me the second you hear from your guys. Okay?"

"Yes, sir," Frank said.

"GET THIS DOWNLOADED TO THE CHIP, QUICKLY," JAKE SAID. He peered out the door again. "The guard's almost here."

"It's loading," Cal said. "I can't make it go any faster."

Jake could hear the guard's footsteps. Jake motioned for Cal to hide. Jake left the door cracked open a bit. He could now see the guard through the crack where the door met the wall. Jake flattened himself against the wall next to the door on the guard's right. He pulled out his sepder. He could see the guard examine the disabled keypad, pull out his plasma gun, and slowly open the right side door. The computer was running, but Cal was gone. The guard moved to the right of the door and continued to open it. Jake slowly raised his sepder, with the flat edge of the blade toward the guard. He swung. The guard ducked. The guard immediately came up with an elbow into Jake's face. Jake stumbled backward against the wall. Jake could taste blood in his mouth. The guard was quick, and Jake could tell that he was well trained. Jake started to bring his sepder up, but the guard got his plasma gun up first, aimed at Jake's head. Jake froze.

The guard spoke in a husky voice. "All right. I can't stand punks like you. You have three seconds to start telling me who you are and what you're doing here, or I burn a hole in your head." Without a pause, the guard started counting. "One, two, three!"

Jake heard a plasma gun fire. He cringed, expecting to feel a burning blast in his face. But everything was silent. He felt nothing. He relaxed his face and looked at the guard. The guard's face was frozen for a second, then his eyes rolled back. The guard's plasma gun dropped to the floor, and he fell forward, just missing Jake's feet. Jake looked up, and there was Cal facing him with his plasma stun gun still pointed to where the guard had been standing.

"Thanks, buddy," Jake said.

Cal nodded. "I think it's all downloaded. Let's get out of here and get hold of Frank."

"Can we call him now?" Jake asked. "If he hasn't talked to Veneto yet, then we might as well risk being overheard. It's our best chance. And if he has talked to Veneto, then it won't matter. Veneto will have men all over us in no time."

"Yes," Cal said, "but we can't here. The basement is too heavily shielded because of the main terminal. We can't get a signal out."

Cal dropped the microchip in his coat pocket and they proceeded out the door, down the hall, and up the stairs. As they approached the door where they'd entered the building, they could hear hover vehicles stopping outside. Jake peeked through a small window by the door. It was still dark out, but Jake could clearly see the tanks and guards circling the building.

"Looks like we're too late to warn Frank," Jake said. "Hover tanks. Five of them, plus twenty or thirty guards. It looks like they're trying to surround the building."

"Yeah," Cal replied, "and it sure didn't take Veneto long to tell Ramirez and Ramirez's guards where we are. Any ideas?"

Jake tried Frank on the com, but he still couldn't get a signal. "The com's dead."

"EarthNX must keep the signals jammed in the complex," Cal said. "They probably have a sub-tronic frequency that they use. There's no way we could duplicate it with our coms even if we knew what it was. We're going to have to clear the fence shield before we can get Frank."

A guard shouted from outside, "Saunders and Danielson, we know you're in there. Come out with your weapons down and we won't fire. Mr. Ramirez just wants to talk to you. If you don't come out, we're coming in, full fire."

Jake looked at Cal. "They won't fire, he says. Sure, and John Wayne isn't the Duke."

"Now you sound like Frank," Cal replied. "But you're right. Veneto wants us nothing but dead."

"I have an idea," Jake said. "Let me see the backpack. Frank said he gave us a few extras just in case." Jake pulled out a few gadgets that Frank had stuck in the backpack. "Now let me have your plasma gun."

Jake pulled wires from a transponder and hooked them to a backup com. He then opened the backup com and reconfigured it. He cracked the plasma gun with his sepder and stuck one wire into the cracked gun. As soon as he did so, the gun started to slowly charge.

"The gun's charging," Cal said.

"Yep," Jake replied. "The same thing a plasma gun does when the trigger is pulled, except then it's instantaneous. I read how to do this in a Legion survival manual. Hope it works."

"I didn't know you read," Cal said.

Jake looked at Cal and grinned slightly, then laid the contraption by the front door.

"We have about ten minutes, in my estimation," Jake said. "Once the gun hits full charge, the makeshift reactor will detonate, blowing a sizeable hole in the front door. It shouldn't be enough to blow up anyone or anything nearby, but it should distract them for a moment. Follow me."

Jake headed into a large conference room to their right.

"Help me stack these chairs," Jake said as he grabbed a couple. "Put them under that ceiling vent."

"Okay, but why?" Cal asked.

"I noticed the vent in a room earlier," Jake said. "If I'm not mistaken, this is the same vent design that I crawled in eight years ago in Sector Four headquarters that led me to the ceiling where I saw it all happen. If we go backward through the vent system, it should lead us out and to the ground. We bust open a grate and we're gone. The explosion should give us enough time to run clear before they see us, if we time it right."

"There's a lot of 'ifs' in what you just said," Cal said as they continued to stack chairs. "I hope you're right."

The guard shouted again. "That's it! We're coming in! Men, move forward. Bring those tanks up."

Jake and Cal quickly climbed the stack of chairs, removed the vent cover, and crawled into the air duct. Cal turned on his light rod, and they crawled. Jake could hear the hover tanks move into position to blast the door. As they descended down the final air duct to ground level, Jake heard the makeshift bomb explode. *It worked*, he thought. But would it buy them enough time? When they reached the end of the air duct, Jake could hear the chaos and noise at the front of the building. *The noise should be loud enough to drown out a sepder blast,* he thought. He fired, blasting open the grate at the end of the air duct. They were at the back of the building. Fortunately, the guards hadn't made it all the way to the back yet, or they had, but moved to the front when they heard the explosion. Jake and Cal ran clear of the building.

They were on the opposite side of the complex from where they'd entered, but they ran directly toward the fence shield on that side anyway. "Let's get out of the complex," Jake said, "then we can make our way back to the quantum fighter." Jake kept scanning for guards as they ran from building to building. None were in sight. *They all must have been sent to close in on us at the target building,* he thought. When they had cleared the last building, there was only the grass field between them and the fence shield. They ran for it, side by side. Jake heard a plasma gun fire and saw Cal go down, clutching his side. Jake stopped instantly, turned toward the shot, and raised his plasma stun gun. Another plasma blast whizzed by Jake's head. That gave him his target. He saw the guard near the next building over, fired, and the guard dropped. Jake quickly surveyed the area. No other guards in sight. He grabbed Cal by the arm, swung the arm around his neck, and dragged Cal to the fence. "Hang on, buddy. Let's get into the woods, then I'll take a look at you."

Jake was glad he had watched Cal disable the fence shield the first time. He got what he needed out of the backpack and did it himself this time. They were through the shield and into the woods in no time. The pitch black night would help them. That, along with the dense forest, should get them back to the quantum fighter safely, if Cal didn't die first.

Jake laid Cal down and pulled off his burned jacket. Jake was half afraid to look. He had seen the damage a plasma gun could do.

Cal grimaced. "How bad is it?"

Jake looked down at the spot, then let out a sigh and smiled.

"What are you smiling at?" Cal said. "I've just been shot."

"Cal, you wore one," Jake said, still smiling.

"Wore what?" Cal asked.

"A vest," Jake said. "You wore a protective vest. The plasma didn't get through it." Jake dropped to the ground on his knees, finally able to relax a bit. He felt exhausted all of a sudden.

Cal sat up. "Ouch, my side burns, though."

"That's just from the impact," Jake said. "It'll stop soon. You're fine."

Cal's eyes suddenly widened. He jumped up and grabbed his jacket and started searching frantically through the pockets.

"What's wrong?" Jake asked.

"The chip!" Cal replied. "I put the microchip in my pocket."

Cal froze as quickly as he had started the search. Jake looked. Cal was slowly pulling his hand out of the pocket of the jacket. Cal opened his hand. There was the chip—melted, destroyed, useless. Jake felt the exhaustion really hit him now. All that work, and defeated again.

"That was all we had," Cal said solemnly. "That was our only chance to clear our names, be free, and . . ." He paused for a moment, then continued, "and get the Legion to save Diane. She's as good as dead. We're as good as dead."

They both just sat there, silent, staring at the ground.

Jake thought about Diane, his Uncle Ben, Romalor, and now Frank. What had Veneto done with him? Jake's whole adult life had been spent on a quest to figure out and expose the cover-up around his uncle's death and make those involved pay, especially Romalor. Now, he had no place to turn, no place to run, and every single friend he had was either dead or close to it. He took a deep breath and thought of Uncle Ben again. No, it wasn't going to end like this. Not here, not yet. He and Cal were still mobile, and they still had a quantum light fighter. He wasn't going to quit. He stood up, picked up his sepder, and looked at Cal. "No, we're not giving up. Diane's not going to die. We're not going to die. We have a quantum fighter now and we know where Diane is. We're going to get her ourselves. And get the crystal. Then with that, we're going to expose Veneto. We can and we will still do this. First we need to contact Frank and warn him. As soon as Veneto knows that we've escaped, microchip or not, he'll need to contain all three of us. He'll have Frank locked down immediately."

Cal slowly nodded and stood up, picking up his own sepder. Jake noticed a different look on Cal's face. It wasn't the childlike, computer game geek that he was used to. Cal looked more mature, more determined, more like a battle-tested Legion soldier. Jake felt a warmth come over him. He felt more confident, seeing that look on Cal's face.

Jake and Cal started making their way to the quantum fighter. Jake hailed Frank on the com.

"I thought we agreed to go dark," Frank said. "We shouldn't be talking on the com."

"It doesn't matter now," Jake replied.

"Why? What do you mean?" Frank asked. "Everything is going as planned on my end. Does that mean you found something?"

"Yes," Jake said. "You could say that. But it's not what we thought. We were wrong. Dietrich's not the government mole. Frank, it's Veneto." The com was silent. "Are you still there, Frank?"

"Yes, I am," Frank replied. "I'm so sorry, guys. I've already told Veneto everything. He sure did play it cool. He played right along and finessed everything out of me. Man, I'm such a fool. How could I have misread him? How could I have been so narrow-minded?"

"Frank," Jake said, "don't worry about it. We all were convinced it was Dietrich."

"Are you two all right?" Frank asked. "Where are you? Veneto's going to have Ramirez's men all over you."

"He already has," Jake answered, "but we're fine. We made it out, but we lost the evidence. We have nothing to prove Veneto's involvement, or anything else that these guys have done."

Jake went on to explain Veneto's, Ramirez's, and Sloan's plan dating back to the attack on Sector Four headquarters eight years ago, the development and sale to Romalor of the super weapon, and the plan to sell Earth a defense system to protect Earth against the weapon.

"Frank," Jake continued, "Cal and I have to try to get Diane out. It's her only chance now. And we have to try to get the crystal before Romalor uses it. You need to get someplace safe. It won't be long before Veneto knows we've escaped. He'll assume we talked to you and told you everything. That makes you a threat to him. He'll have you locked down, or worse."

"Don't you cowboys go fretting about me. I can handle the outlaws just fine. You're right. You need to get out of here and go get Diane and the crystal. That has to be your first priority now. I'm going to clear you through the Sector Four defense station right now, before Veneto shuts everything down. You won't have long. Don't stop. Use B16 for clearance."

"Okay, got it," Jake replied.

It was silent for a moment. Jake knew there was little chance to escape the Legion, make it through Romalor's troops, and rescue Diane. It was a hopeless mission for two men and one quantum light fighter. And even if they somehow made it through all that, where would they go? They would still be wanted by the Legion. Veneto would have every planet in the galaxy looking for them. If Frank stayed alive, they would likely never see him again. He knew they all three were thinking the same thing. Nothing more needed to be said. They had to try. He had to stay confident.

The silence was broken by Frank's voice. It cracked. "Jake, Cal . . ." He paused for a moment, then continued. "Boys, I just want to say that—"

Jake interrupted before Frank could finish. "Don't say it, Frank. You and I still have that new John Wayne movie to watch together. Cal and I *will* be back."

10

ALONE

J ake and Cal approached the Sector Four defense station.
"I better use the audio com, no video, so they don't
recognize us," Cal said.

"Good idea," Jake replied.

Cal set the com on the station's frequency. "Station Four, we are requesting clearance. Our clearance code is B16. I repeat, bravo one six."

"Copy that," Jake heard over the com. "Let me check the code."

The com was silent. Did Frank get the clearance code to the station? Or did Veneto stop him first? If the station didn't have the code, they would have to stop and answer questions, possibly be inspected.

They had been wanted by the Legion before, but if Veneto got in touch with the defense stations first and reported them, they would really be wanted now. They would be recognized instantly. Jake could feel the anxiety building inside him. It shouldn't take this long. He was sure they couldn't find the clearance code.

The com crackled. "Bravo one six, you are clear. You may proceed."

Jake breathed out heavily. It felt like he had been holding his breath forever. Their fighter quickly passed through the station and exited into space. "We're clear. Are the coordinates in?" Jake asked.

"Yes, all set," Cal replied.

Jake looked at the coordinates on the control panel to be sure. He recognized the numbers instantly. Craton. He punched the quantum drive control and Earth disappeared in a flash.

Neither Jake nor Cal spoke during the flight. Jake just watched the control panel and stared into space. They were heading toward what he had been wanting for eight years. If they were to succeed in retrieving Diane and the hilaetite crystal, he would have to face Romalor. What lay before them was an impossible task. Two men trying to rescue Diane and save Earth from annihilation. All with the entire Craton military in front of them and the Legion chasing behind them. Was this really what he'd been wanting? Was this what Uncle Ben would have wanted for him? No use debating it now. Even if he wanted to turn back, he couldn't. There was no place to go.

And he didn't want to turn back. He wanted to save Diane, to save Earth, or die trying.

Jake looked at the coordinates and their location on the control panel. Good, close enough, but out of visual range. He released the quantum drive control.

Cal turned quickly toward Jake. "Why did you drop out of quantum drive? We should be in visual range of the planet in about two minutes."

Jake kept his eyes on the viewing screen, which was set to external. "I'm sure Marco has warned Romalor by now that we're probably coming. I want to see what Romalor's sending to meet us."

Cal grinned slightly. "A greeting party."

"Yeah, right," Jake said. "Are you reading anything?"

Cal looked down at the sensor readings. "That's odd. This is showing one massive spacecraft heading our way. Why would he send such a thing?"

Jake leaned over and looked at the sensor. He saw the blob for a moment, then it started to break apart.

"Oh, no," Cal said.

Nothing more needed to be said. It wasn't one large spacecraft. It was a squadron of Craton fighters. Jake estimated around two hundred. "We'll never get through or around them." What could they do? He had to think of something, and quickly. He cut the engines. "I have an idea. Is it possible to go from a dead stop immediately into quantum drive?"

"Theoretically, yes," Cal replied. He shook his head. "But it's never been done before, or that is, it's never been done before successfully. It's a precise calculation that is different each time due to different variables, like the type of spacecraft, the region of the galaxy, the weight of the spacecraft, to name just a few."

"But it can be done, right?" Jake asked.

Cal bit his lip and shook his head harder. "The quantum drive unit has to be put on a slow charge first. The speed of the charge is another variable. Then you have to run the numbers to determine the exact point on the quantum drive's charge that the engines need to be ignited. At that exact point, the engines must be ignited at full power and the quantum drive must be shifted to full power. If any one of the variables is miscalculated or if the engine and quantum drive aren't thrust to full power simultaneously or if they aren't thrust at the precise correct time in the quantum drive charge, then it doesn't work."

"Okay," Jake replied slowly. "So it doesn't work. What's the worst that could happen?"

Cal looked at Jake with his eyes wide. "The worst? The worst that could happen is what has happened on every failed test attempt. The spacecraft's plasma coils explode, which, in turn, vaporizes the spacecraft and all its contents immediately."

"Okay," Jake said. "You still haven't said that it can't be done. Let's give it a shot."

"Give it a shot!" Cal said. "This isn't something you just 'give a shot.' Legion engineers with a lot more experience than me have tried and tried again. As I said, always unsuccessfully."

"Yes, but none of those engineers were Cal Danielson," Jake responded. "Let's go. We don't have much time." They had gotten this far. If this was their only chance of getting by the Craton fighters, he would do it. The only other option would be surrender, and that really wasn't an option. Romalor wouldn't take any more chances with them. They would probably be dead before they ever left their fighter. Besides, he was beyond being concerned about failure or the fear of death. He was going to see this through to the end. Romalor's and Veneto's end, or his end. He turned back to the viewing screen. The Craton fighters were coming into view. All two hundred of them. Heading straight at them in four or five waves.

Cal shook his head and started working the calculations on the spacecraft's control panel.

The hailing signal sounded. Jake opened the audio com but did not answer.

A deep, almost growling, voice came over the com. "This is Raxmar, first officer to Romalor Leximer. Surrender your spacecraft immediately. You get but one warning and this is it."

Jake did not respond. Instead, he turned to Cal. "Are you ready? You heard the man. One warning."

Cal didn't answer, just kept on working. Jake looked at the screen. The Craton spacecrafts started to separate from their formation to flank Jake and Cal's fighter on either side.

"Come on, Raxmar. Open us just a little hole," Jake whispered.

He watched the screen. He knew without asking Cal that they needed just the slightest gap in the Craton line for a heading. If they jumped to quantum drive with a spacecraft in their path, well, that would be a problem.

The Craton fighters now completely encircled them, with fighters above and below them as well, and they all came to a halt. *They're probably just waiting for the word from Raxmar,* Jake thought. He searched the viewing screen again. "There!" he shouted, and pointed at the screen. He'd found the gap they needed, and it was in the right direction, straight toward Craton. He entered the heading.

Once again, Raxmar's voice came over the com. "Consider yourselves warned."

Jake looked at Cal. "It's now or never."

"Okay, I got it," Cal said. "Or at least, I have my best guess at it. I have no idea if it'll work, though."

"Well," Jake replied, "we're dead if it fails and we're dead if we don't try, so go for it."

Cal started to charge the quantum drive. A few seconds passed, then Cal said, "Brace yourself. Three, two, one . . ."

They heard Raxmar's command over the com. "Fire!"

Cal shouted, "Now!" He shoved the engine and quantum drive controls to full power simultaneously.

Jake's head jerked back as the spacecraft gave one hard jolt. In an instant, the Craton fighters disappeared.

"It worked!" Jake shouted. "You're the man! If we live through this, you'll be famous."

Cal just shook his head and sighed.

"There it is," Jake said, as Craton came into view. "Since we left two hundred fighters back there, hopefully they don't have too many more here waiting for us."

"Yeah," Cal replied, "but it won't take Raxmar long to figure out what happened, and those two hundred will be back. Or at least most of them. I'm sure they eliminated a few when we disappeared on the 'fire' command. You know, caught in the crossfire."

"Yeah, that's at least one positive to your too-close-for-comfort-timing," Jake said with a slight grin.

FRANK SAT IN THE HOLDING ROOM AT SECTOR FOUR headquarters. He had never seen a holding room from this vantage point. It was square, with solid metal walls, silver-colored, and a flat ceiling also made of silver-colored metal. There was one door, with a small square window at eye level, the only window in the room. The door was a single access door, with a door keypad only on the outside. He sat behind a bare table. The chair he was sitting on and the table were the only furniture in the room. A young private was posted inside the room, holding a plasma rifle. He stood facing Frank with his back to the door. Frank recognized him. Before the door had closed, he'd noticed two more privates posted just outside the door, each holding a plasma rifle as well. There were no connections to the outside world except the com on the private's belt. He had to connect with the private. Get the private to let him use the com.

"Private," Frank said, "there has been a grave mistake. You have to believe me. I know you're only following orders, and those orders have come directly from Marco Veneto, the president's chief Legion advisor. I commend you for doing what you're told. But Mr. Veneto is the one in the wrong, not me."

The private did not respond. He continued to stand at attention, his gaze focused on the wall directly behind Frank.

"Look," Frank said, "Jimmy, you know Cal Danielson and Jake Saunders. Jake helped train you. You know they aren't capable of doing even one of the things they've been accused of. And you know me. I've known your parents since you were a kid. I used to visit with them on occasion. I even remember playing that galactic war game with you on your computer. You couldn't have been over thirteen. Please, listen to me. Not for me or even for Cal and Jake. Listen to what I'm saying for your own sake, for your parents' sake, for the entire planet. Everyone is at risk."

Jimmy finally looked at Frank uneasily. "Commander," he paused for a moment, "I respect you more than any Legion officer I have ever met. And I don't doubt that some of what you're saying is true. But even if I believed everything, it's out of my hands. I have to follow orders."

Okay, good, Frank thought. This was starting to work. At least Jimmy was talking to him. That was a huge step. Jimmy was breaking protocol, and probably going against his orders, just by doing that. "I'm not asking you to disobey your orders. Did you receive any order that said that I was prohibited from contacting anyone?"

Jimmy closed his eyes and rubbed his forehead. "Well, sir, I suppose not. My orders were to keep you in this room and not let you out of my sight until I heard from Mr. Veneto directly. I believe those were the general orders to all the privates guarding you."

"Okay, then," Frank said, "all you have to do is to let me make one call on your com. If the person takes my call, I will talk briefly and be done. If he doesn't accept it, then I'm done. Either way, it'll be quick. It's just one simple call."

Jimmy looked at Frank, then at the ground, then at Frank again. He shifted his rifle to the other shoulder. His response was choppy. "I guess that won't hurt anything, and it *is* still within my orders." He slowly unlatched his com from his belt, took two steps forward, and laid it on the table in front of Frank. "Who are you calling, anyway?"

Frank looked at Jimmy. He really didn't want to say, for fear that his answer would cause Jimmy to change his mind. But he also didn't want to seem like he was hiding something so that Jimmy would feel like he was doing something wrong. Instead of answering, he decided to try to reach the president first. That way, there would be less likelihood that Jimmy would backtrack.

Frank looked down at the com and punched a few digits. A voice came over the com. "This is Jack Buchanan. Who is this and how did you get this com code?"

Frank looked up at Jimmy. Jimmy's face grew pale and his eyes widened. He was staring at Frank. Frank hoped Jimmy would remain shocked and speechless until he finished.

"Mr. President, this is Frank Cantor, Legion Commander of Sector Four."

"Commander Cantor," the president replied, "I know who you are, but I understand that you have been relieved of your command. How and why are you calling me?"

"The how doesn't really matter right now, Mr. President," Frank replied. "As for the why, I'll be brief, sir. Please, you have to hear me out. The entire planet could be at risk." Frank made a fist and squeezed, waiting for the reply. Everything hinged on what the president said next. If the president wouldn't let him continue, then he was finished. Jake and Cal would be completely on their own in an impossible situation. The president had to let him talk. Even then, it was far from guaranteed that the president would believe him.

"I'm listening," the president replied.

Frank tapped his fist lightly on the table and whispered, "Yes." He looked up and took a deep breath. "Mr. President," he began, "I don't know how to say this, but the recent events regarding Jake Saunders, Cal Danielson, and myself," he paused for a moment, then continued, "well, sir, the reports and statements are all wrong. I don't care about myself. I'm not telling you this to save me. It's Jake and Cal, and Ambassador Diane Danielson who are at risk. Imminent risk, sir."

"Ambassador Danielson?" the president questioned. "Are you saying that she's alive? And Saunders and Danielson. You know where they are? Mr. Veneto filled me in on the events of this evening. Commander Cantor, I would suggest that you be more cooperative with Mr. Veneto if you want to help anybody."

It was now or never. Frank needed to come right out with it, before he lost the president. "Mr. President, Marco Veneto is the problem. He's the one that's behind all of this. Not Saunders or Danielson or me. He, along with Edgardo Ramirez, and a man that we only know as Mr. Sloan, orchestrated Romalor's attack on Sector Four headquarters eight years ago to steal the hilaetite crystal. Then Ramirez built Romalor some sort of super weapon to use it in. And as soon as it's complete, Ramirez is going to try to sell the Legion a new defense system to protect Earth from the weapon. Don't you see, everyone gets what they want: Romalor gets his weapon, Earth is protected, and Ramirez, Veneto, and Sloan get rich." Frank paused and looked up at Jimmy who was still pale and speechless. Then he turned his attention to the com again. "Meanwhile, a lot of very good people and soldiers are being killed. Sir, Danielson and Saunders are on their way to Craton as we speak to try to free Ambassador Danielson and somehow disable the weapon, which, by all accounts, is operational. And they are alone. I'm sure Veneto is following them with some fighters, but not to attack Craton. He's following Saunders and Danielson to stop them. Sir, Veneto is not trying to save Earth. He's trying to save himself."

"Commander Cantor," the president said, interrupting Frank, "these are very serious allegations against one of the highest ranking government officials. One that I hand-picked for the job. Have you any proof of what you say?"

Frank hung his head and spoke softly. "No, sir. We did, but it was destroyed."

"That's what I figured," the president replied. "Frank, even if I wanted to believe you, you know I can't act without more to go on than your word. I trust Marco wholeheartedly. I'm sorry, Frank. Without more, there's nothing I can do."

He was losing the president. Frank knew the president was right. What did he expect Buchanan to do without any evidence? Maybe if Frank gave him a plan, an option. A way the president could find out the truth without accusing Veneto. It could at least buy Jake and Cal some time before Veneto caught up with them, but would it be soon enough to get Jake and Cal some help? It was worth a try at least. It was all he had left. "But Mr. President, I have an idea. If you just—"

The door to Frank's holding room burst open. Marco Veneto rushed in, and with one slam of his fist, smashed the com lying on the table.

Marco turned to Jimmy and shouted, "Private, consider yourself relieved of duty! The guards will take you to the next holding room. You'll stay there until you are dishonorably discharged from the Legion and tried for treason! Now get out of my sight!"

Frank looked at Jimmy. "I'm sorry, son. Just know that you did the right thing."

Frank just sat there as Marco turned toward him. Okay, here it comes. Veneto's face was red and his teeth clenched. Frank thought that the veins in Veneto's neck would pop any second.

Marco shouted even louder. "And as for you, EX-Commander Cantor! Who do you think you are, contacting the president, trying to sabotage my operation? A Legion operation that was authorized by the president, might I remind you. I ought to have you shot dead right now!" Marco turned to the guards in the hallway. "Put this man in solitary confinement. I don't want him to see, hear, or talk to anyone until I return! Do you understand me?" Marco didn't give the guards a chance to answer. "With all the commotion this man's caused," Marco pointed at Frank, stabbing the air with each syllable, "I'm leading the Danielson/Saunders recovery mission to Craton myself! I need to make sure it gets done right! Now get him out of here!"

CAL TURNED TO JAKE. "I THINK OUR BEST SHOT OF LANDING undetected is to put the fighter down here." Cal pointed to a spot on the control panel grid map. "We can then find Diane, disable the weapon, and return to the fighter. If we stay undetected, Raxmar won't know exactly where we landed. That should buy us enough time to get in and out."

Jake started to talk, but he was jolted almost out of his seat. The fighter shook. Jake grabbed the control panel to brace himself.

"A plasma burst," Cal said. "It hit our forward shield."

"So much for undetected," Jake said.

"I see two Craton destroyers," Cal responded. "Slower than their fighters, but they sure do pack a punch."

"Can we outmaneuver them?" Jake asked.

"Yeah," Cal replied. "We're quicker, but I don't know if we can get close enough by ourselves to take them out. And we can't land with them on our tail."

"Let me take care of that," Jake replied. He flipped a switch to take over the main controls. He was very confident in his quantum light fighter flying ability and air combat training. He wanted to instill that confidence in Cal. However, the truth was, he had little hope of being able to take down a destroyer, let alone two, when they were only one fighter strong.

Jake knew that destroyers were combat spacecraft, with quantum drive capability, but they usually didn't enter battle alone. They were generally used as heavyweight support for the smaller and quicker fighters. Alone, they weren't quick enough to take out fighters and they were vulnerable against a fleet of fighters. But with a fleet of fighters as protection, they could inflict heavy damage on another fleet of fighters or another destroyer. And he was sure the Craton fleet of fighters would be there any minute.

Jake maneuvered the fighter behind one destroyer for a shot, while avoiding the destroyer's weapons. There, an opening to shoot. No, there isn't time. There's the other one. The other destroyer was on his tail. Jake maneuvered the fighter behind that destroyer. They played this game of cat and mouse for several minutes.

"We're running out of time, Jake," Cal said. "Raxmar and those fighters will be back any minute."

Jake could hear Cal's nerves in the sound of his voice. "Yeah, I know," Jake replied. He tried to stay focused on landing a shot. "I imagine Romalor sent out these destroyers just to stall us. I'm going to try to outrun them to the other side of the planet."

Jake knew that they were too close to the planet to use quantum drive, but he moved the fighter to full throttle. As he did, the fleet of two hundred or so Craton fighters dropped out of quantum drive near them. Raxmar was back, and he wasn't hailing them this time. Jake knew that all talking was over.

Now all Jake could do was try to avoid being hit. He got off a shot here and there and even landed a few. With so many targets, how could he miss? But he knew that he had no real plan now. It was just survival. Survival for what, he didn't know. No help would be coming. Veneto wanted them dead as much as Romalor did. By now, he figured Frank was probably in hiding or behind bars. It was hopeless.

Jake pulled out of a tailspin, shaking off two fighters and barely missing a destroyer's plasma blast. He glanced up and saw a small fleet of around fifty Legion quantum light fighters drop out of quantum drive. But they didn't offer any assistance. They just stopped, as if to observe the fight.

"I recognize their code on the sensor readings," Cal said. "That's part of Captain Reynolds' Charlie division. He's a Sector One Superior Guard. But that's not even close to an entire division. Veneto must have sent only a skeleton crew."

"I'm not surprised," Jake said. "Veneto has no intention of the Legion engaging Craton in combat. They're just here to retrieve us, or make sure we're dead."

"I'm hailing Reynolds," Cal said, "but he's not responding. It looks like their audio com is open. I'm sure they can hear us. But they're ignoring us."

"Maybe they aren't picking up the signal," Jake said. "Try talking."

"Captain Reynolds, is that you?" Cal said, speaking into the com. "We need assistance immediately. We can't hang on much longer. Please engage."

The com was silent.

Jake was dodging, diving, and spinning. Three Craton fighters were on his tail. He couldn't shake them.

Cal shouted into the com this time. "We're Legion soldiers! Craton has a weapon that will destroy Earth. Engage the enemy. Please engage!"

Jake listened. No response came. The fleet of quantum fighters just sat there.

"Might as well save your breath," Jake said. "They have orders from Veneto. They'll never help."

Cal slammed his fist on the control panel.

"Hold on!" Jake shouted. He turned their fighter straight toward the side of one of the destroyers. He was going to shake those three fighters one way or another. Either he or they would be taking out a destroyer. He continued straight toward the destroyer. Closer, closer. Now! He pulled up into a reverse somersault as the nose of his fighter was about to hit the destroyer. The three Craton fighters had no time to do the same. They hit the destroyer, one after another. All four space-craft exploded into a ball of fire. There would be no time to celebrate. There were still more than one hundred eighty fighters and a destroyer left.

CAPTAIN REYNOLDS TURNED THE AUDIO COM FREQUENCY. "Mr. Veneto. We have the target spotted. It is under heavy fire from the Cratonites. Should we engage in order to retrieve the target and return it to Earth?"

"No," was the command he heard in reply. "I am in progress toward your coordinates with twenty additional fighters. I'm heading up the mission myself from here on. You are to hold your position until I arrive."

"Sir," Reynolds said, "if we don't intervene, the target will be destroyed before you arrive. And from what I see, we'll need more than twenty additional fighters if we are to successfully retrieve the target from the Cratonites."

"You have your orders, Captain," Marco replied.

"He turned us off, sir," Private Gomez said. He was the other pilot in Reynolds' fighter. "It seems like Mr. Veneto has no intention of saving Saunders and Danielson. No intention of taking them back for trial. It seems like he wants the Cratonites to handle them."

Reynolds was frustrated. Gomez was right. That's exactly what Veneto wanted. Guilty or not, Saunders and Danielson deserved a fair trial. A chance to be heard. He hated having to sit there helplessly and watch fellow Legion soldiers be destroyed. But Mr. Veneto was not only his superior, he was the chief Legion advisor. Reynolds looked at Gomez. "We have our orders."

"Saunders and Danielson are hailing us again, sir," Gomez said. He adjusted the com frequency.

Reynolds heard Cal over the com. "Captain Reynolds, our shields are down to twenty percent and we have little plasma left. We're out of time! For the sake of two fellow Legion soldiers, engage. But if not for us, for the sake of Earth, engage the Cratonites."

Gomez looked at Reynolds. "Captain, we have to help them."

Reynolds wanted to more than anything. But he was a Legion captain. Trained to obey orders. If the chief Legion advisor wanted Saunders and Danielson dead, there must be a reason that was bigger than they were. He didn't know the whole story, so he had to trust his superiors. But he didn't have to like it. "No," Reynolds replied. "I don't like this any more than you do. But you heard the orders. Chief Advisor Veneto is personally taking over command of the operation. He'll be here soon, and his orders were very clear. Under no circumstances are we to engage Craton. There's nothing more we can do."

JAKE KNEW THEY WERE ALL BUT FINISHED. HE GLANCED DOWN at the control panel. Almost out of fuel, plasma for their guns, and shield strength. He continued to fly in a basic survival maneuver. Four Craton fighters had encircled them and were slowly closing in. Jake knew that the Craton pattern was designed not to let the target escape the entrapment. His pattern was designed not to escape, but to stay alive long enough for help to arrive. But that assumed help was coming. It wasn't. It was only a matter of minutes, maybe seconds, until the Cratonite fighters would close the circle tight enough that they would fire, unable to miss.

Jake looked at Cal. "I'm sorry I got you into all this. You're the best friend a boy, and a man, could ever ask for." He knew this wasn't entirely his fault. They were somewhat victims of the circumstances. They were in the wrong place at the wrong time, being sent to Craton. But it was he who had persuaded them to land on Craton. He wanted a shot at Romalor. Now, he, Cal, Diane, and Frank would all pay. There was nothing more he could do about it.

Cal didn't speak. He turned toward Jake and gave a single nod of his head.

Jake knew that meant "the same to you." The Craton fighters moved in closer.

———

GOMEZ TURNED QUICKLY TOWARD REYNOLDS. "SIR, WE'RE being hailed by the Presidential Mansion on the video com." He turned on the com without waiting for a response from Reynolds. The president's face appeared in the com.

"Captain Reynolds," the president said, "this is President Jack Buchanan. I have temporarily relieved Chief Advisor Veneto. Until you've been further notified, I am in command of this operation. Your new orders are to do everything in your power to protect the lives and mission of Privates Cal Danielson and Jake Saunders. Do whatever you have to do to get them safely onto the planet of Craton, and bring them home. Understood?"

Reynolds sat up quickly. He felt his heart race. Not only was he about to head into battle, which he loved, but he was about to have the chance to save two fellow Legion soldiers who were in harm's way. This was the order he was waiting for. He looked into the com, holding back a smile, and answered, "YES, SIR!"

Reynolds quickly flipped the com onto audio only and turned the frequency to direct a command to the rest of the fleet. "Men, we have a green light to engage. I repeat. We have a go. Now let's take down these Cratonites!"

Reynolds could hear the fighter pilots, in unison, over the com. They gave a war cry as they flung themselves into the battle.

JAKE CLOSED HIS EYES AS THE FOUR FIGHTERS CLOSED THE circle, waiting for the kill shot. He heard the plasma blast and braced for one final impact. Everything seemed to go silent. He sensed flashes of bright light through his eyelids. Is this what death was? Slow-motion, painless? It's just over? No, it wasn't death. It was nothing. Nothing had happened. He opened his eyes. The viewing screen was directly in front of him. He saw each of the four fighters engulfed in flames. Through the flames flew four Legion fighters with Captain Reynolds in the lead.

"We thought you boys could use a little help," Reynolds said over the audio com.

Jake smiled. "Nothing like waiting till the last second."

"You two don't have a lot of time," Reynolds said. "Romalor just sent out another hundred fighters. We're outnumbered almost six to one. The president has sent a couple more divisions, but it'll be a while until they get here. You two know where things are on the planet. We'll keep these fighters off your tail as long as we can. The Legion fighters will be more useful to you out here buying you time, so you'll have to go it alone down there. And, one more thing, the president thinks the weapon is operational. The Legion started to pick up some sort of tracking signal. The president fears that as soon as Romalor realizes the Legion is onto him, which he may already have, Romalor will test the weapon out on Earth. You two need to get going. Good luck."

"Thank you, Captain," Jake replied, "for everything." Reynolds was in visual view of Jake now. Jake saluted. Reynolds returned the salute. Jake knew that while his and Cal's chances of success had increased, the increase wasn't by much. But he also knew that he and Cal probably had a better chance of survival on the planet than Captain Reynolds would have out there, being so outnumbered. Captain

Reynolds was willing to give up his life to ensure Cal's and his success. But he didn't have time to think. He had to focus and move out.

Cal punched in some coordinates, and Jake turned the fighter and shot toward the planet.

"Are we clear?" Jake asked.

"We're clear of all but one," Cal replied. "It's Raxmar. He's on our tail."

"Hang on," Jake said. "We need to lose him before we can land."

Jake punched the throttle. They were now down at the planet, flying barely over fifty feet off the ground. They were near the military complex mountain, on the east side, just outside Craton City in a desert region. There were a few hover car roads, but mostly sand, rocks, and hills. Jake stayed low, dodging rock formations and hills, hoping one would catch Raxmar, and trying to avoid Raxmar's plasma blasts. Jake tried a reverse somersault, but Raxmar did the same and stayed right with him. Jake tried to roll away and come in behind Raxmar, but Raxmar rolled right with him. Jake couldn't shake him. *He's good*, Jake thought. *How can I lose him?*

Up ahead, Jake could see a long hover car tunnel going through a small mountain. Jake had an idea. If he could lure Raxmar into the tunnel, maybe Raxmar would make a mistake and crash, provided Jake didn't do so first. He had to take the chance. Jake accelerated the fighter down and entered the tunnel. It was completely dark, but for the faint light at the opposite end where they would exit. Raxmar followed, right on their tail. *Great*, Jake thought, but he hoped Raxmar wouldn't fire. He feared that a missed plasma blast could bring the entire mountain down on both of them. Now I just need a break, a mistake by Raxmar.

As Jake approached the other end of the tunnel, he could see a large hover vehicle speeding toward the tunnel in the opposite direction, coming right at him. The vehicle was a scrap hauler, with a small cab in front and a cargo bed that grew larger and larger along its sides and top. The back end of it was larger than their quantum fighter and would fill the tunnel. Just before it entered the tunnel, Jake knew the driver had to see their fighter coming at him. Rather than try to stop, the driver simply bailed out, letting the vehicle continue on. As the front of the vehicle entered the tunnel, Jake punched the fighter to full throttle and pulled it up. The top of the fighter sparked as it scraped the rock top of the tunnel and the bottom sparked as it scraped the front of the hover vehicle. Their fighter had just enough room between the top of the vehicle and the roof of the tunnel to make it out. Jake glanced back. He could tell Raxmar had punched his fighter to full throttle as well. But by the time Raxmar reached the vehicle, the larger back end of it was inside the tunnel, filling the entire circumference. Raxmar struck the cargo bed, which pushed his fighter up into the roof of the tunnel at full throttle. The vehicle and fighter both exploded, bringing down the whole side of the mountain. Raxmar was no more.

11

REVENGE

J ake sat the fighter down behind a rock outcropping between Craton City and the military complex, making sure it was hidden from the complex. He and Cal made their way up the same path they had before, climbing toward the building that housed the weapon. Once there, they quickly found an outer door.

Cal took a decoder from his belt and used it to pop the lock like the last time they were there.

Jake kept a lookout while Cal worked. He knew it was only two or three minutes, but it felt like fifteen, before he heard the lock pop. Cal stood back. Jake slowly opened the door just enough to peek inside. He saw twenty to thirty guards working at the computer console surrounding the weapon.

Cal peeked in as well. "They're programming it to fire," he whispered.

Jake pulled an amplifier from his belt and stuck it in his ear. He could hear one of the guards working on the programming. "Our tracking system has been following Earth's orbital pattern and should have all variances calculated by now. Give me the coordinates for Earth. Once they are input, we should be ready to power up the weapon system."

Another guard turned to the first. "Are you sure we should be doing this? We haven't completed all the tests on the weapon. We could blow up our own planet."

The first guard replied, "You go tell that to the general and see if you return."

"Any ideas?" Cal whispered. "There are too many of them for us to take on alone."

"Yeah, I know," Jake replied. "But with all the guards out in fighters, and that many with the weapon, the rest of the complex can't be very heavily guarded. Let's find Diane. She's probably in the same holding block where they kept us."

Jake was right. The complex was close to deserted. He peered around each corner before he and Cal turned down a new hall. If there were guards patrolling, he and Cal waited for them to move on.

At the end of one final long, dimly lit hall was a single solid door with its own keypad locking it.

"That's the entrance to the holding block," Cal said. He pulled the decoder from his belt again and quickly had the door open.

They passed through the door into another long hall with a row of doors on each side and one large door at the end facing them. Jake remembered this hall very well. It was where their holding cell had been. Red lights on a door's keypad meant it was occupied. Green meant it was empty. Most lights were green.

They looked in the small square windows of the doors with red lights. Jake took one side and Cal the other. Jake saw nothing but Cratonites and a couple of species he didn't recognize.

"Nothing but Cratonites," Cal said. "Come on, let's try this door." He again used the decoder on the door at the very end.

Jake barely opened the door, peering through a crack. It was a smaller, but more brightly lit hall with a few doors on each side. Only one with a red light, and with two guards standing on either side of it. He closed the door gently. "That must be it," Jake whispered to Cal.

Jake didn't want to risk being heard, so he didn't want to fire sepders. Jake pulled a knife from his belt. He was glad Frank had taught him knife throwing along with bow and arrow skills. His "old west" training would come in handy. "I'll make some noise. You take whichever guard comes to investigate. I have the other." They pressed their backs against the wall on either side of the closed door. Jake tapped on the door. He immediately heard footsteps—just one guard. Jake held up one finger to Cal and then pointed to Cal. The guard slowly pulled open the door. Jake nodded, and Cal kicked the door open hard. Cal instantly struck the guard in the temple with the pommel of his sepder.

The other guard turned and started to pull his plasma gun. Jake stepped into the open doorway and let his knife fly. It stuck in the guard's neck. The guard grabbed for the knife with both hands, grimacing, but he quickly fell to the floor without making a sound.

They both ran to the door. Jake looked in and saw Diane lying on the bed. Cal decoded the door and opened it.

Diane looked up, her eyes wide, her face expressionless. "Cal, Jake." She paused for a moment. "Is that really you two?" She smiled, jumped up, and ran to them. "Oh, I thought you both were dead. I can't believe it!"

She met Cal first, and they embraced. Jake watched. He had never seen two people hug so hard. He felt warm, comforted. Less than an hour ago he had given up all hope and braced himself for death, as well as the deaths of Cal, Diane, and Frank. Deaths that he blamed himself for, at least in part. Now there was hope. Still a long way to go, but hope nonetheless.

Cal pulled back, still holding onto Diane's arms and looking at her face. "I didn't think I would ever see you again. Are you all right?"

"Yes, yes, I'm fine," Diane said, smiling into Cal's face.

Jake could see Diane's eyes move from Cal to him. Her smile softened, and her eyes filled with tears. Jake smiled and nodded his head. Diane closed her eyes and nodded back. Jake wanted to hug her, embrace like she and Cal had. But did she feel the same way? He thought the smile and nod was her way of saying that she did. But now wasn't the time, anyway. They were far from out of danger, and time was running out. How long could the Legion hold off the Cratonite fighters? How long until the weapon was ready to fire? How long until Cratonite guards found them? They had to get going. They had a job to do.

Diane stepped back from Cal. "How did you two ever get here? Where's the rest of the Legion?"

Cal shook his head. "It's a long story, but suffice it to say that we're it. You're looking at your rescue party."

Jake was refocused, and he wanted Cal and Diane to refocus as well. "We need to find a way to draw the guards away from the weapon and give us time to disable it."

"There must be a central grid with schematics of the complex," Cal said. "That would tell us how the lockdown mechanisms work and where to trigger them from."

"What do you mean?" Jake asked. "What lockdown mechanisms?"

"The guards have to have the ability to lock down this holding block in the event of an attack or attempted escape," Cal replied. "They don't want prisoners running around the complex in such an event. If we could lure the guards to the holding block, then lock it down, we could trap them in their own system. We already know there aren't many guards here besides those in the weapon room. If they think there's a rescue attempt, most of those guards will have to come. But we'll already be out. We lock them down, and go to the weapon room."

"Okay," Jake said. "Sounds good. This schematic, where would it be?"

"In some type of control room," Cal replied. "Probably near Romalor's central command center."

"I saw a room like that one time when they were bringing me down here," Diane said. "Come on. I can show you where it is."

Jake and Cal dragged the two dead guards into Diane's room and locked the door. Then they made their way to the room Diane had seen, using the same caution as before. It was just below Romalor's central command center. Cal decoded the door, and the three of them quickly stepped inside. The room was filled with electronic equipment, computer terminals, tabletop computers, and computer screens. Cal slowly walked around the room, inspecting each item.

"Don't touch anything," Cal said. "It's all probably alarmed." Cal looked some more. "Here it is." He opened a rectangular panel. Jake looked over Cal's shoulder. Inside was a diagram and three rows of various colored touch screen controls, each separately numbered. "That's it. This is exactly what I was looking for. The only problem is that it looks like locking down the holding block from here will set off an alarm which could cause a lock down of the entire complex so we can't get out." Cal paused and looked at the panel closer. "However, it looks like the holding block can also be locked down from the central command center. That won't set off any additional alarms."

"That's likely where Romalor is right now," Jake said. "He seems to be directing the battle at the moment."

"Yeah, I know," Cal replied, "and the problem is, the lockdown must be activated from inside the room. Looking at this diagram, it's probably a switch at the bottom of the inside door keypad. So this isn't an option. One of us would have to activate the lockdown while the other two disabled the weapon. It's suicide for whoever goes into the central command center. Romalor and who knows how many guards will be there."

Jake stared at the floor for a moment with one hand pressed against the wall. He quickly raised his head and pointed at Cal. "No. It'll just be Romalor. You've seen how thin his ranks are here. He won't be wasting any guards in the central command center with him. I'm going."

"But Jake—" Diane started to say before Jake cut her off.

"You two set this explosive on the keypad of the room they had Diane in," Jake said. He handed Cal a small device from his belt. "How long do you estimate it'll take the guards to get from the weapon building to the holding block?"

Cal paused for a moment, then replied, "With an alarm going off, and the guards fearing a break-in and escape attempt, but yet being cautious, I would estimate about four minutes. But that's an offhand guess."

Jake chuckled and shook his head. He knew that Cal's "offhand guesses" were more accurate than most technicians' computerized calculations. "Perfect," Jake said. "When I hear the alarm, I'll wait five minutes. That'll give them time to get well inside the holding block and down the hall toward Diane's room. Then I'll blast into the command center and activate the lockdown. You two will have to take out any remaining guards in the weapon building, disable the weapon, grab the hilaetite crystal, and get to the fighter. By the time you do all of that, if I'm not at the fighter, you have to go without me. Our priority has to be to get that crystal off the planet."

Diane looked at Jake. "But Jake, what about Romalor? I've been here a while now. I've seen what he's capable of. There has to be another way."

"Yes," Cal said. "Give me some time. Let me think of another way."

"There is no more time," Jake yelled. "Now go. Get moving!"

Jake wasn't sure why he was yelling at them. They were his friends. They were trying to protect him. Maybe he was yelling to make it easier for them to deal with losing him. Whatever the reason, he knew what they were thinking. That there was no way he could defeat Romalor alone. The moment he had been anticipating for more than eight years was finally here. But now that it was here, he didn't know if he could succeed. He too had seen what Romalor was capable of. Could he really beat Romalor? He had no time to ponder it. He had to remain confident. And besides, there was more at stake now than simple revenge. He had to buy time for Cal and Diane to get the crystal and escape. That had to be his main goal now. And if he was lucky, he would be leaving with them.

"All right," Cal said, "let's get going."

Diane looked at Jake. "Jake, please be careful."

"I just got you back," Jake replied. "You be careful." He walked up to Diane and handed her a small plasma gun from his belt. "Here, I know you know how to use this." He paused and looked into her eyes, those eyes that he so dearly loved. "Don't worry about me. I told Frank we would be back. I plan on keeping my word."

―――――――

JAKE WAITED OUTSIDE THE MAIN DOOR TO ROMALOR'S central command center, atop the military complex. He didn't need to enter quietly. He planned on blasting the keypad with his sepder. He readied the timepiece on his belt to mark when Cal would detonate the explosive in the holding block. Cal would do it remotely, probably from a spot near the weapon building. He would mark off five minutes, and then enter. He remembered what Romalor said about guns not working inside the central command center. That meant he wouldn't be able to take Romalor by surprise as he entered. But it also meant that Romalor wouldn't be able to take him out before he had a chance to activate the lockdown. According to Cal, the lockdown switch was right inside the door underneath the keypad. Romalor would probably be over near the operations area by his desk, and there shouldn't be any guards. At least all of that was what he hoped. After the lockdown was activated, it would all be up to Cal and Diane. All he would need to do then would be to stay alive long enough to allow Cal and Diane to get to the fighter with the crystal before Romalor could release the lockdown. It would be hand-to-hand combat, the sepder versus the goliath. In all the commotion, the need to get the crystal off the planet, trying to free Diane, trying to save Cal's and his life, he'd almost forgotten the scene eight years ago, his Uncle Ben's death, and the person directly responsible for it all, Romalor. But standing there waiting, it all came back. He could see his uncle's dying face and Romalor's grin as if it were yesterday. This was what he had been waiting eight years for. The time had come. He wanted Romalor.

Jake heard the alarm. He marked his timepiece, then pulled out his sepder, gripping it with both hands. He readied it, cocking it behind his head, in case Romalor came out the door. He figured Romalor would let his guards deal with the alarm, but Jake remained at the ready just in case. He watched his timepiece and waited. It seemed like forever. What if the guards were in the holding block already? Maybe he had better enter and activate the lockdown now so they wouldn't get out, he thought. No, it just seemed like a long time to him, standing there. He had to trust Cal's estimation. If he activated the lockdown too quickly, the guards wouldn't be in the holding block yet. He waited. He looked at his time-piece. Four minutes. He felt his muscles tightening, his armpits getting damp. What was this? He was nervous. Why? He'd never felt like this prior to a fight before. But he'd never had to wait and think like this before either. Or was it that he had never fought anyone like Romalor before? He looked at his timepiece again. Four minutes, fifty seconds. Ten, nine, eight, seven. He counted in his head as he watched the timepiece. Four, three, two, one. It was time. He blasted the keypad with a sepder shot, kicked open the door, and stepped through the doorway. The lockdown switch was right where Cal had said. No guards were in the room. Just one Cratonite sitting behind the desk, his back to the door. Jake flipped the lockdown switch quickly and then looked up. At the same time, Romalor turned in his chair. Jake was face to face with Romalor Leximer. This time, they were all alone.

CAL AND DIANE STAYED OUT OF SIGHT, HIDING IN THE corridor that led from the main complex of buildings to the one-room building that housed the weapon. Diane watched as the guards left the weapon building. *Hopefully, they're heading toward the holding block,* Diane thought. If so, the plan was working. She looked at Cal. She knew that from his vantage point, he could see into the weapon building as the guards fled. He held up two fingers. *Great,* she thought. Only two guards remained. Cal stepped out into the corridor by the interior door to the weapon building and disabled the door keypad. Ever so slowly, he cracked open the door just enough to see inside. He signaled to Diane again that there were two guards, both with their backs to the door. Cal had his sepder ready. Diane pulled out the plasma gun Jake had given her. Her hand shook slightly. She focused on it, gripping the gun harder, but she couldn't stop the shaking. She certainly knew how to use a gun, and she knew she was an excellent shot. She had practiced quite a lot with her dad. But she was not battle trained. She had never killed anyone before. But she had to do this. Cal needed her. Earth needed her. She saw Cal look at her hand and then her face. She gave him a nod. She was ready. At least as ready as she would ever be. Diane watched as Cal counted on his fingers. One, two, three. On three, he kicked the door open. Both guards turned toward them and reached for their plasma guns holstered in their belts. Cal swung into the open doorway on his knees from the left and fired his sepder. One blast took out the guard on the left. At the same time, Diane jumped into the doorway from the right, feet spread, both hands on the plasma gun, arms outstretched, and elbows locked. She fired. She hit the second guard square in the chest. He dropped without making a sound.

Cal closed the door, and they ran up to the main control terminal.

"How long do we have?" Diane asked.

"I'm not sure, exactly," Cal said. "Jake must have gotten the guards locked down, or they would be back here by now. And once activated from the central command center, the lockdown can be deactivated only from that room. So as long as Jake can keep Romalor occupied—or better yet, dead—we have time."

They stared at each other. Diane knew what Cal was thinking. She was thinking the same thing. How long could Jake really keep Romalor occupied? Did Jake stand a chance? She wanted so much to run to the central command center and help him. She thought she had lost him once and that was horrible enough. Now that he was back, she couldn't stand the thought of losing him again. But Jake didn't know that. Maybe she should have told him. Would he fight better knowing he had someone waiting for him? No, she had to stop thinking about it. She was needed here, with Cal. If they couldn't get the crystal off the planet, nothing else would matter anyway. There would be no more Earth.

Diane turned toward the massive weapon system. She looked at it closely. It had been dark the last time she was in that room. Now, in the light, she could make out the details.

She looked up. There, located on top of all the components, still enclosed in its housing, was the hilaetite crystal.

Cal pointed to a part of the computer system right in front of them, where the two guards had been working. "This looks like the main control terminal."

Diane looked at the terminal. She could see changing numbers, in Craton's language. "That clock is counting down," Diane said.

Then a voice sounded from the computer. "Weapon activation in ten minutes." The numbers continued to count down and the roof of the building opened.

Cal's eyes grew large. "They've already set the weapon to fire!"

"At what?" Diane asked.

"From what Jake and I overheard," Cal answered, "Earth!"

Were they too late? Was all of this for nothing? Diane didn't know what to think. "What do we do now?"

"I'm not sure. We need to figure out how to shut it down before that clock hits zero," Cal said.

"Can't we just climb up there and unhook the crystal?" Diane asked.

"No," Cal replied. "I'm sure it has a failsafe. Since it's already armed to fire, if we try to disconnect the crystal without first shutting the system down, it'll most likely fire immediately. We have to shut it down, but the language on here is all Craton." Cal looked over the computer screen. "This looks like the main terminal at EarthNX, built right into the computer table with touch screen commands. I think it's the same design. EarthNX probably made it. This is good. You can read Craton, right? There should be a control labeled 'source module' or 'main power' or something like that. Can you find it?"

Diane looked at the computer closely. "Yes, I can read Craton. But this isn't Craton." She wasn't sure what it was.

She had never seen any language like it before. She looked closer. "It looks familiar, though." Then it dawned on her. "It's Craton letters, but they're coded somehow. The letters aren't in any order that makes words."

The computer sounded again. "Weapon activation in seven minutes."

ROMALOR STOOD UP. TO JAKE, HE DIDN'T LOOK A BIT surprised. There was no way Romalor could have known they were in his complex, but Romalor seemed as if he was expecting Jake.

Romalor smiled. "Jake Saunders, you are a stubborn one. You have returned. Why, might I ask?"

"To stop you from using the crystal, and to expose the truth," Jake said, slowly raising his sepder.

Romalor drew his goliath and held it in both hands. He stepped toward Jake. "The truth about what? About how Earth is so full of corruption that it sold me the crystal? Or how Earth used you to cover it up and left you for dead? Why would you defend such people? The planet is prideful, ignorant, and greedy. All your people want is money. And when they get it, they just want more."

Romalor started walking slowly to the side, still facing Jake, his goliath at the ready.

Jake held his sepder in both hands, his arms fully extended, pointing it at Romalor. He also moved slowly in a sideways motion, the two of them circling each other. "Earth is not corrupt. Only certain people are. And those few will answer for what they've done." Jake could feel the anger start to boil. That old familiar anger. The same anger that he used over and over in his mind to kill Romalor. And the same anger he often heard his superiors tell him he needed to let go of.

"Answer to whom?" Romalor replied. "You're just one

person. It's too big for you. You can't fight everyone. How can you stop me, my guards, your Legion, and your so-called government? You've been abandoned. Go. Leave now while you can. You and your friend. You can find some remote planet to spend your remaining days on in peace. Why risk your life for Earth? Why should you care what happens between Craton and Earth anymore? Neither planet wants you. I'm giving you a chance to live."

"Just like you gave me a chance in the Pit? I care because there are a lot of good people on Earth that I care about. A lot of innocent people. Innocent people that you'll continue to murder, like . . ." Jake stopped.

"Like your Uncle Ben," Romalor finished the sentence. "That was eight years ago. Let it go."

Jake didn't respond. The comment made him angrier. An anger he didn't try to hold back. This was what he had wanted for eight years. What he had lived for for eight years, a chance to do to Romalor what Romalor had done to his Uncle Ben. Anger had fueled him all this time. He didn't want it to stop now.

He blocked out all the words from his Uncle Ben, from Captain Gorski, and from others who had tried to teach him to fight without anger, telling him that his thirst for revenge would be his undoing. Jake didn't want to hear those words now.

"Do you really want to fight me? You're just a boy. I will destroy you." Romalor chuckled.

Jake's eyes narrowed. The muscles in his face tightened. "Go for it."

CAL SLAPPED THE COMPUTER TABLE. "WAIT, I HAVE AN IDEA!" He reached to the back of his belt and pulled off a small transponder.

"What's that for?" Diane asked.

"It's a portable transponder," Cal replied. He punched a couple of buttons. "It can be used as a multitude of things, like a triangular locator, a coordinate locator, sensor detector, portable video com, and to play games, which is what I'm setting it for right now."

"Do you really think we have time for you to practice Quantum Flight Attack or whatever games you have on there?" Diane asked. She knew Cal was planning something more than playing a video game, but she had to say it anyway.

"Here it is," Cal said. "Remember that game I was telling you about, Intergalactic Combat? The one that uses real military codes?"

Diane nodded. "Yes, yes. Do you think it'll work?" She knew where Cal was going with this now.

"Well," Cal said, "part of the game requires you to decode the military signals of Craton. If the maker did use the real codes, I may be able to connect the transponder to the computer system and use it to decode the language on the computer controls. If it works, it'll unscramble the letters so you can read them."

The computer sounded. "Weapon activation in five minutes."

ROMALOR MADE THE FIRST MOVE, LUNGING TOWARD JAKE WITH four basic swipes of his goliath. Jake recognized them. Two straight down and two on each side of Jake. Jake blocked each swing easily. Romalor, with a smirk on his face, came at Jake again. This time with more advanced moves. An overhand roundhouse followed by an underhand roundhouse, and then two more swings, one to Jake's left and one to his right. Again, Jake successfully blocked each swing.

Romalor snickered. "I see you have had some training. So

let's do away with these childish moves and get on to the real stuff." Romalor charged again at Jake, this time switching hands with his goliath in mid-swing, making a lower swing that Jake blocked with a backhand move. Romalor then made a 360-degree spin, followed by three more thrusts of the goliath.

Jake blocked each, and then went on the offensive himself, swinging his sepder from side to side, roundhouse swings, back swings, all of which Romalor countered and blocked.

Romalor then came at Jake with an above-the-head swing. Blocked by Jake. Underhand swing. Blocked by Jake. Then Romalor spun around and caught Jake on his left forearm. Jake felt an instant sting followed by a slight numbness in his arm. A trickle of blood oozed from the wound. The sting made him even angrier. He lunged at Romalor twice, swinging hard each time. Romalor didn't even try to block the swings. He just lowered his goliath to his side and jumped backwards each time.

Romalor stood there, his goliath still at his side. "Come on, Jake. Is that all you have? Your uncle fought better than that with a bad leg. I don't think he would be too proud of his little nephew, now would he?"

Jake couldn't think of anything except running his sepder through Romalor. He just felt rage. He raised his sepder again and yelled, "Romalor!" He charged Romalor and swung back and forth repeatedly. Romalor, with his goliath at his side, ducked and jumped back and to the side, then to the side again, all the while with a smirk on his face.

Romalor raised his goliath and charged again. He let go with three lightning fast swings, the third one striking Jake on his right shoulder. Another sting, more blood, a deeper gash.

Jake immediately went after Romalor again, swinging furiously. Romalor used his goliath this time, blocking each one, seemingly effortlessly, all the time still grinning. Jake stepped back and hunched over. He breathed heavily. He tried not to show his fatigue, but he needed to gasp for air. His lungs burned.

Before he could catch his breath, Romalor was on him again, with swing after swing of his own. Jake blocked the first, second, third, and fourth, but by the fifth his arm moved more slowly, his sepder felt like a lead weight. He couldn't get it down to his side in time. Romalor's goliath slashed into his side, opening a small wound below his rib cage. Jake winced. This time there was no numbness, just a sting and a deep pain. He doubled over and stumbled backward. He breathed hard and deep. He was angrier than ever at Romalor, and now angry that his sepder, his skill, his body, were failing him. He had waited eight years for this moment. He could taste revenge. It was so close, yet it was out of reach. Romalor was defeating him. Romalor was slowly killing him.

Romalor laughed. "Had enough yet? Too bad your Uncle Ben didn't stick around long enough to teach you to fight better."

That was it. He felt pain all over. But was it from the wounds or from his hatred of Romalor? Or perhaps both. He wanted to take Romalor down so badly. But his breathing came heavy and his wounds ached. He could feel the adrenaline leaving him. No! He needed the anger, the adrenaline, the motivation, but he was losing, badly.

CAL PULLED UP THE GAME ON THE TRANSPONDER, FOUND THE docking port on the computer, and connected the transponder. He hit "play" on the game.

Diane looked at the computer. All the computer symbols started changing simultaneously, faster and faster until they were a blur. They kept changing and changing, even the numbers on the timer.

"It isn't working," Cal said, shaking his head. "The game

is sending a signal, but it's not decoding the computer system. The system must be too complex."

"Weapon activation in three minutes," Diane heard.

Cal shook his head again and looked at Diane. "It's no use."

Suddenly, every symbol, every word on the computer table stopped changing.

"It worked!" Diane shouted. "I can read them!" She pointed to one of the touch screen pads. "This is Craton for 'power source.'"

"Weapon activation in one minute," the computer voice sounded again. "Fifty-nine, fifty-eight . . ." The voice continued to count down the numbers.

Cal quickly worked the pad that Diane had pointed to and those nearby. "Tell me when this says 'power source accessed.'" He pointed to another area on the table screen, then he continued to work the touch pads. "This system was designed by EarthNX, and now that we've located the power source pad, I know where the other relevant pads are in relation to it. EarthNX designs all its weapons with the same power source configuration. Thank you, Mr. Ramirez."

"Twenty-four, twenty-three, twenty-two, twenty-one . . ." Diane heard.

"There!" she said. "It says, 'power source accessed.'" She could feel herself tensing up. Her stomach started to churn. She knew Cal was working as fast as he possibly could, but she wanted him to go even faster.

Cal continued to work. "Now tell me when it says something like, 'weapon activation in progress.'"

"Ten, nine . . ." she heard.

"There! Now!" Diane shouted.

"Okay, here it goes," Cal said. He typed frantically. His fingers were flying on the touch pads.

The voice continued, "Five, four, three, two, one . . ." The voice stopped. The timer froze at the Craton number one. Cal and Diane leaned heavily on the table and hung their heads. Neither spoke. Diane closed her eyes and breathed deeply, trying to calm her nerves.

She opened her eyes, looked at Cal, and smiled. "You did it, little brother. You did it."

Cal smiled back. "No, we did it." Cal put his arm around her and squeezed her shoulder. "Now we can disconnect the crystal and get out of here."

Diane didn't move. "I know Jake said to leave if he wasn't here in time, but do you think we can go get him?"

Cal smiled. "I never intended to leave him behind. Take my sepder. It's armed. Leave me the little plasma gun. You go now. I'll disconnect the crystal. Maybe you can get there in time before Romalor . . ." Cal stopped there. Diane knew what he was thinking. She was thinking the same thing.

JAKE STARTED TO RAISE HIS SEPDER FOR YET ANOTHER CHARGE. He just wanted Romalor dead. No matter how he did it. He was going to go at him swinging harder than ever this time. Then something stopped him. He lowered his sepder. He could see himself practicing with his toy sepder with Uncle Ben. He was just a boy. He heard Ben's voice. "Jake, you have to think when you fight. Use your head." Then he could see himself training in Sector Four headquarters. He could hear Captain Gorski. "You always let the taunting get to you. Then you fight with anger, not with intelligence. If you keep letting your enemies get to you, you're going to get yourself killed one day."

"What's the matter? You give up?" Romalor asked, tapping the back of his goliath on the palm of his hand. "You're as weak as your uncle. He at least fought to his death, even if it was a useless effort."

Jake ignored the words. Uncle Ben and Captain Gorski

were right. He was playing right into Romalor's hands. Romalor was taunting him. Making him angry. That way he wouldn't fight with intelligence. No more anger, he told himself. He needed to focus on what he was doing. He needed to focus on his opponent. Learn his opponent's weaknesses, then use those weaknesses to gain an advantage.

Jake held up his sepder in attack position. "No, I don't give up."

"Excellent," Romalor said.

Romalor came at him. Romalor swung, Jake blocked. Romalor swung again. Jake blocked. Again and again Romalor swung. Jake could feel each swing increase in strength. But Jake blocked each one. Romalor spun and swung. Jake blocked down as Romalor came up with his foot and planted it in Jake's chest. As Jake went over backwards, he tucked his chin and formed a ball, rolling into a reverse somersault and coming up on his feet, his sepder at the ready. He looked at Romalor. That was it. Romalor always attacked with his goliath held high. If he could come up under the goliath, there would be an opening to Romalor's chest.

Jake gripped his sepder in both hands. His eyes narrowed and his face tightened. He wasn't angry. He was determined. He extended both arms straight out in front of him so that his sepder was pointing straight at Romalor. His eyes followed his sepder from the handle to the tip, then straight across the floor to Romalor's chest.

Romalor's grin disappeared. He raised his goliath to attack. Jake watched Romalor's eyes. They met Jake's.

"It's time to end this," Romalor said. "Now I will kill you."

Jake spoke slowly and deeply. "You will try."

Jake charged, still focused on Romalor's chest. As he met Romalor, Romalor swung. Jake went under the swing by falling to his knees. Without stopping he went right into a somersault. As Jake's head popped up out of the somersault, his sepder was directly in front of his face, outstretched, still gripped in both hands. It was pointing directly at Romalor's chest, unobstructed. In one continuous motion Jake continued to come up out of his somersault. He thrust his sepder forward, plunging it deep into Romalor's chest. As quickly as he stuck it in, he yanked it out.

Romalor stood motionless, his eyes wide. He looked down at his chest, now oozing blood, then up at Jake's face. His arms fell limp at his sides and his goliath fell to the floor with a clang. He dropped to his knees, then fell over on his back. His eyes still open, Romalor breathed his last.

Jake had thought about this moment almost every day for the last eight years, but he didn't feel anything like he'd thought he would. He expected to feel the triumph of revenge finally complete or the thrill of a great victory in battle. Instead, he felt sorrow. He wasn't sad that Romalor was dead or that he had killed him. It was different. It was a sorrow that the events he had seen when he was only fourteen had consumed his life and led him to this moment. A sorrow that he had lost eight years of his life obsessing over Romalor, living to get his revenge, putting everyone he loved in danger. What a waste. How many people had he ignored? How many people had he abandoned and hurt?

Jake stepped closer to Romalor's body. Reaching down, he grasped Ben's medallion. With a quick jerk, he snapped the chain from Romalor's neck. Holding the medallion, he read it out loud: "To Uncle Ben. The best dad ever. Love, your little buddy, Jake." Tears filled his eyes. All these years, he had never mourned the loss of his uncle. He was too preoccupied with hatred. Whether he had done that subconsciously, or whether he did it to avoid the pain of Ben's loss, or whether he had been using that pent-up sorrow to fuel his anger, his motivation, it didn't matter. It was over now. Now, he felt only his love for his Uncle Ben and a void from losing him. All the pain he had been avoiding, holding back for eight years was coming out. Jake dropped his sepder and clutched the medallion even harder. He felt a tear trickle down his cheek. He whispered, "I miss you, Uncle Ben."

"Are you okay, Jake?" came a soft, familiar voice from behind him.

Jake turned and saw Diane. He slowly nodded. "I am now."

Diane walked to him. Putting her arms around him, she pulled his head to her shoulder and squeezed. Jake put his arms around her and held her tight. How he had longed for this moment. Holding Diane in his arms. He wanted to speak, but he couldn't. He just clenched his eyes tight and pulled her closer. So, too, the realization of all the lost years with Diane hit him. Lost time. Time he could never get back. Another loss that he could chalk up to his selfish quest to find and destroy Romalor.

Jake pulled his head back and put his hands on her shoulders. "I'm sorry, Diane. I'm so sorry for everything I've put you through. Everything you've been through these past few days. Everything I have put you through the past eight years. You, Cal, Frank, everyone. I've only thought of myself."

"Oh, Jake," Diane replied, "no, don't be sorry. You have nothing to be sorry for. You did what you had to do. What you always do. Make right that which is wrong. You couldn't live with yourself if you didn't. That's what makes you, you." She paused for a moment, then continued. "That's what makes me love you."

The words hit Jake hard. A good hard, very unexpected. And he'd had no idea how beautiful they would sound until now. He'd thought he would never hear Diane say those words to him. He was silent, trying to think of what to say. He said the first thing that popped into his mind. "You love me?"

"Jake," Diane paused for a moment, "I have always loved you."

Jake cupped her face in his hands and looked directly into her eyes. "I love you too, Diane Danielson. I love you too."

Hearing himself say those words, he knew that he should have said them long ago.

They both smiled and stood there, staring at each other.

"I guess the old man was right," Jake said with a smile.

"What old man?" Diane asked.

"The old man in the pub when we first arrived on Craton looking for the weapon," Jake answered. "He told me to be careful seeking what my mind desires. For the heart is much wiser than the mind. I should have listened to my heart a long time ago."

Cal stepped into the room. "This is a beautiful moment. Really it is. And I've been waiting for it for years. But there's a couple of hundred warships out there trying to kill our Legion soldiers and a death ray pointed straight at Earth. Correct me if I'm wrong, but don't you think we ought to lend our guys a hand?"

Jake looked at Cal and then back at Diane and nodded. He felt good. He felt energized. He wanted to go into battle, not in anger and not for revenge, but to protect his friends, his comrades, his planet. And above all, he had a new motivation. Diane. "Let's finish this once and for all."

12

THE CHASE

J ake, Diane, and Cal lifted off the planet in their quantum light fighter and headed back toward the battle. The best they could tell, over half of the Legion fighters had been destroyed, and the rest were barely holding on. Jake noticed one Legion fighter not in the battle, but sitting just outside range of any plasma blasts.

Cal pointed to where Jake was looking. "Our sensors show that that's Veneto. He's just watching."

"That's not surprising," Jake replied. "He's probably hoping that Craton defeats the Legion fleet, and that we fail down on the planet. His only hope is that whatever turned the president against him will be reversed, if there's still no proof."

"I'm picking up a large group of spacecraft on the sensors," Cal said. "They just dropped out of quantum drive. They're Legion! Now we've got 'em outnumbered."

Jake looked back at Veneto's spacecraft. As he did, it disappeared into quantum drive.

"There goes Veneto!" Jake shouted. "Follow him."

"Shouldn't we get backup?" Cal asked.

"There's no time," Jake said. "Go, go!"

Cal punched their fighter into quantum drive, headed in the same general direction Veneto had gone.

"There he is," Cal said, pointing to the control panel. "I have him on the sensors."

"Can we close the gap?" Jake asked.

"If we go to maximum drive," Cal responded. "He's not at full throttle. He must not know he's being followed. You take the control and I'll navigate." Cal punched the pilot exchange control.

Jake took over the main controls from his seat. He turned his head around to Diane, who was bunched up in a little storage area behind their seats. "You okay back there?"

"I would ride out on the wings if it meant getting off that planet," Diane said.

They closed the gap on Veneto's fighter to where Jake could see it on the viewing screen.

"Now he knows," Cal said. "He just punched it to full throttle."

"Try hailing him," Jake said.

"He's not responding," Cal replied. "I'm using all frequencies. I know he had to hear it. He's ignoring us. What should we do? Shoot him down? He has to have a lot more fuel than us. We are dangerously close to empty. We can't follow him forever."

"Let's try to get close enough to take out his engine without blowing him up," Jake replied. Jake wasn't so sure that was a good idea. Cal was right, they didn't have much fuel left, and their fighter was heavily damaged. But it was the only idea he had.

"Uh-oh," Cal said. "This isn't good."

Jake looked up at the screen and saw Veneto's fighter entering an asteroid field.

"Hang on!" Jake shouted. "We're going in."

"Do you really think this is a good idea?" Cal asked. "We hardly have any power left in our shields."

No, Jake thought. It probably wasn't a good idea. But could they ever find Veneto again if they let him get away? He would have a whole galaxy to hide in. Jake didn't answer. He just flew. One asteroid came at them from the front. Jake maneuvered to the side, avoiding it. Then another came toward that side. Jake maneuvered back, then jerked up quickly, barely missing an asteroid underneath them. He went up, then down again, side to side, all the time keeping one eye on Veneto's spacecraft and one eye on the asteroids.

"Look out!" Cal shouted.

Jake looked at the screen. A large asteroid was coming straight at them. Jake pulled the fighter straight up vertically and then continued pulling into a reverse somersault. When they were upside down, halfway through the somersault, he saw in the viewing screen an asteroid that had been directly behind them. They were now heading straight for it. Jake immediately rolled the fighter to the right into four spiraling rolls as he continued through the reverse somersault. When the fighter righted itself and came out of the final roll, he saw nothing but space in front of them—space and Veneto's fighter.

"I'm detecting something large in front of us," Cal said. "Something very large. Too large to be any spacecraft we know or an asteroid or anything of the sort. But not quite large enough to be a planet."

"There haven't been any planets charted in this region of the galaxy anyway," Jake said. "Have there?"

"No," Cal replied.

Jake could see a light appearing on the viewing screen. The closer they came to it, the brighter it became.

Jake pointed at the light. "Is that what you're detecting?"

"Yes," Cal replied. "It looks like a star, but that would be even more bizarre, to find a new star out here. And so small for a star."

Veneto continued to fly toward the object. Jake followed.

"I still think it's too large to be a spacecraft," Cal said. "But the light it emits is too white to be natural. It's too clean."

Jake watched as Veneto's spacecraft suddenly stopped. It didn't just drop out of quantum drive, Jake thought. That was an immediate dead stop.

"Why did he stop?" Cal asked.

But no sooner did Cal ask the question than their fighter instantly stopped as well. Jake flew forward out of his seat. He felt a sharp pain in his jaw as his face hit the control panel. He looked over and Cal was in the same position. "You guys all right?" he asked. He turned around to see if Diane was okay. She looked like she was.

"I think so," Cal said.

"Yeah," Diane said. "I'm jammed in here so tight, I didn't move."

"Why did we stop?" Jake asked.

"I don't know," Cal replied. "The engine just stopped. I can't do anything. No controls work. I can't even hail anyone or anything." He continued working the control panel.

"What do you suppose it is?" Diane asked.

"This can't be right," Cal said. "The final sensor reading before we lost power. We were close enough to get a reading of the object." Cal paused for a moment and worked the controls some more.

"What? What is it?" Jake asked.

"According to the sensor," Cal said, "ninety percent of the object consists of hilaetite."

"What?" Jake said. Something that large, made entirely of hilaetite? Where did it come from? Where did they get the hilaetite? How did they keep it from being volatile? And the weapons it must have. They must be enormous.

Jake heard a voice. "You are not welcome here." But the voice wasn't coming over the com. It was coming from space. From all around him. Amplified. How could that be?

"Did you hear that?" Diane asked.

Cal and Jake both nodded.

The voice continued, "We will release control of your vessels. You will have ten seconds to turn your vessels around and go back to where you came from, or be disintegrated."

Cal looked at Jake. "What? Disintegrated?" He turned back toward the control panel in front of him. "Wait, we have control back. The sensor shows the voice came from the object. What should we do?"

Jake looked at the screen. He could see Veneto's fighter, then the object. Veneto was proceeding toward the object. *He's ignoring the warning*, Jake thought. Jake saw a burst of bright light emit from the object. He couldn't believe a light could be brighter than the object itself, but it was. A second later, Veneto's fighter disintegrated right in front of him. There was no explosion, no fire, no residue. The fighter, with Veneto in it, just vaporized before his eyes.

"Let's go!" Jake shouted. "We're getting out of here!"

Jake turned the fighter, and Cal punched it into quantum drive.

13

THE MYSTERY

F rank held open the door to the largest conference room in the Sector Four headquarters building. The room was empty except for the magnificent marble conference table extending the entire length of the room, chairs around it, and an open video com screen on the wall at the far end of the room.

"Get on in here and pull up a seat," Frank said.

Jake, Cal, and Diane walked in and sat down beside each other about halfway down the table. Frank sat down opposite them, laying an electronic data pod on the table in front of him.

It was much easier for Jake to be in this building, now that everything had been set straight. He didn't care to go in the room where it all happened anymore. The events of the past few days had helped him put all that behind him. Now he just remembered the good times with Uncle Ben. The fun they had together. That's what Uncle Ben would have wanted. Jake put his elbows on the table, folded his hands, and leaned forward toward Frank. "So how did you convince the president that Veneto was behind everything? I heard you were in a holding cell at the time."

"I didn't," Frank replied. He put an elbow on the table and leaned forward as well. "I was fortunate enough to be able to tell him what we knew. But Veneto cut me off before I had convinced the president of anything. Apparently, Mr. Dietrich had been doing his own investigating for quite some time and had reached the same conclusion, that Veneto was involved, although he didn't know to what extent. And since he had nothing solid, he couldn't go to the president with it. Fortunately, the president listened to me enough to make an inquiry to Dietrich. Dietrich corroborated my story, and, well, you know the rest."

"So Veneto was even behind the attack on Sector Four headquarters eight years ago?" Diane asked.

"Yep," Frank answered. "He opened the defense shield for Craton and put up all the roadblocks at the Sector Four defense station. He did it all from the combat room underneath the Presidential Mansion. Unbelievable, isn't it?"

Jake heard the video com come on. He turned toward the screen, as did the others. A middle-aged lady, well dressed, appeared on the screen, sitting behind a desk. "The president is ready for you, Commander Cantor."

Jake turned back toward Frank. "The president?" Jake said. He never would have guessed that. Frank had asked the three of them to meet him in this room, but he'd figured it was just an informal debriefing, since they had all already filed their reports. What was the president doing talking to them?

"We're ready," Frank replied, looking at the screen.

The screen went black for a second, and then the president appeared. "Thank you all for being here. I apologize that I couldn't be there with you in person, but I wanted to reach out to you as soon as possible. By reaching out, I mean I wanted to thank you. Jake and Cal, on behalf of me, the government, and the entire Legion, I want to apologize to you for what we put you through. You two fought through everything that was thrown at you in order to protect the very government that was trying to put you away. For that, and more, we are sorry." He paused for a moment, then continued, "Frank, I owe you a sincere apology as well, for not believing you as soon as you told me."

Frank spoke up. "No, Mr. President, you owe me nothing. You did believe me enough to make further inquiries. I thank you for that."

The president continued, "To all four of you, this planet, its government, and its people owe you more gratitude than a simple 'thank you' can ever say. If not for you, and what each of you did, Earth United would no longer exist. This planet would no longer exist. I know that a thank you from me doesn't cover the debt, but I'll say it anyway. Thank you."

Jake, Cal, and Diane all nodded to the president, and Jake spoke. "Mr. President, I think I am speaking for all of us when I say, thank you for coming through for us. And nobody owes us anything. We all just did our jobs."

The president nodded back and raised two fingers to his forehead to salute them. "That you did, son, and more." He lowered his hand and the video com screen went black.

"THAT'LL BE ALL. THANK YOU," JACK SAID. HE WATCHED AS two Presidential Mansion workers closed the video com screen. He wasn't sure if he would have had the courage to do what those four did. He really admired them.

The door buzzed.

Jack pushed the remote door keypad on his desk and the door opened. "Aretha, Clarisse, please come in." He stood up, slowly walked to the front of his desk, and leaned against it, half sitting, with one foot on the floor and the other angled sideways. "Please sit." He motioned to the chair and sofa in front of them and they sat. "I should have listened to you two eight years ago. You warned me to turn over that crystal immediately. You both knew that nothing good would come of delaying a decision, which I did. And look what happened. Look at all the lives I've cost. All the pain, suffering, and hardship I created."

"Jack," Clarisse interrupted, "you can't blame yourself for any of what happened. You had no idea what was going on or who was behind it. Marco, Edgardo, and Romalor would have found a way to do what they did even if you decided to turn over the crystal immediately. It's not your fault."

Jack knew part of what she said was true, but not all of it. It was partly his fault. He should have acted immediately. He should have done what he knew deep down inside was the right thing to do. "But it would have been more difficult for them," Jack replied. "And besides, it's my job to know what they're up to. And I failed. That's why tomorrow, I'm signing a bill to be sent to the Senate for approval, giving the Senate authority over any matter that, in the Senate's opinion, could adversely impact the safety of this planet and its citizens, in which matter the Legion may, in the Senate's opinion, be in conflict."

"Mr. President," Aretha said, "you can't do that. I mean, sure, that sounds great for the Senate, but that authority is too broad. A bill like that will give the Senate an open door to challenge almost anything the Legion does. Not to mention how it will weaken the office of the president."

"Exactly," Jack said. "That's what I want. The Presidency has become too powerful in its control over everything. Too powerful for one person. The planet can't risk one person having that much authority. There needs to be a stronger check on this office in the future."

"Jack," Clarisse said, "are you sure you've thought this through? A lot has happened in the past couple of days.

Maybe you should let things settle for a while before you sign the bill."

He had thought it through. He had thought about it for eight years. This was what he wanted to do. This would be his legacy. Not the attack on Sector Four headquarters eight years ago. "No," Jack said. He straightened up and walked back behind his desk. "I have thought about this. I've thought about it for a long time. It's time to act."

Aretha smiled, stood up, and walked to the front of Jack's desk. "Well then, I guess that's that." She stuck out her hand. Jack grasped it in both of his. "I'll personally make sure the bill makes it through the Senate, unchanged. I think you'll be making a bit of history with this move. Congratulations."

Clarisse stood up and smiled as well. "Yes, I agree. Congratulations are in order."

"Thank you," Jack said. He nodded and smiled at both of them. "Thank you both for your guidance and support. It always has and always will mean a lot to me."

AFTER THE VIDEO COM WAS OFF, JAKE, CAL, AND DIANE looked at each other and smiled. Jake hadn't expected to receive a thank you directly from the president, and he didn't need it. But it made him feel good. He felt wanted again, and appreciated. That meant a lot after almost losing everything. All was well again. He turned to Frank. "So where's the hilaetite crystal now?"

Frank leaned back. "It's on Pergan. And as we speak, it's probably being processed. We won't be seeing that crystal again, and it'll save a lot of lives."

"What about Ramirez and Sloan?" Diane asked.

Frank smiled slightly. "The Legion caught up with Edgardo Ramirez. He didn't put up much of a fight with the entire Legion after him. He'll be spending the remainder of his days behind bars." Frank's smile disappeared. "As for Mr. Sloan, he dropped off the grid again. Nobody knows who he is, where he came from, or where he went. He's a mystery. Now let me ask you cowboys and cowgirl something. I just finished reading everyone's report. Everything is clear and thorough, as usual. Everything except the end. After the new Legion fighter divisions arrived at Craton, I know from the other reports that the Craton fighters retreated back to the planet. Not only were they then outnumbered, but they had also learned of the death of Romalor. At that point, the president ordered the Legion to withdraw because you folks had the crystal. But prior to the Craton retreat and Legion withdrawal, you saw Veneto depart in quantum drive and you gave chase. Everything up to that point is clear. Your report says that you chased Veneto for some time, through an asteroid field and so on. Then you say his spacecraft was destroyed and he was killed, and you returned to Earth. But you folks left out the details. You didn't say how Veneto's spacecraft was destroyed. Did you shoot him down? Did he blow himself up? Did he crash? Or what? What happened?"

They all three looked at each other. Jake was glad he had told Cal and Diane to leave the details out of their reports too. He wanted this to be a private conversation. Just the three of them and Frank. He was afraid of the panic it could cause if what they had seen leaked out to the public. But more so, he still didn't trust anyone in the Legion or government higher up than Frank. He was confident that they had everyone involved with the crystal and the attack eight years ago, except for Sloan, but what if there was someone else, and the thing they saw was part of it? What if that someone found out he, Cal, and Diane knew about it? He was probably just being paranoid, but he wanted to play it safe. He got up and walked to the door, opened it, and checked the hall. Good, it was clear. Jake closed and locked the door.

He walked over to Frank, pulled out a chair right beside him, and sat down. He leaned forward. "Frank." He paused and looked at Cal and Diane and then turned back to Frank and continued, "We saw something out there, the likes of which nobody has ever seen. We need to talk."

ABOUT THE AUTHOR

Bryan Prosek is a science fiction writer and business attorney. Along with his debut novel, *The Brighter the Stars*, he has published books and articles in legal trade journals and magazines. When he isn't writing or practicing law, you can probably find him watching science fiction movies or television shows. He loves the big screen and the small screen. There's a good chance that he'll be watching one of the numerous Star Trek movies or series, but he could be watching anything from Guardians of the Galaxy to The Conjuring.

You can find more about Bryan at his website:
www.bryankprosek.com

Taking you to new worlds.

BOOK CLUB QUESTIONS

1. What messages does this book offer about science and technology and its effects on today's society or the future? How are your own ideas alike or different?
2. Is the purpose of this book to be optimistic about the future or to serve as a warning?
3. What did you think about the main characters? Were they believable? Who did you relate to the most/least? Who did you like best/least?
4. How well do you think the author built the world in this book? Did it seem realistic?
5. How did this book influence today's pop culture? Or was the book influenced by pop culture?
6. Which parts of this book stood out to you? Are there any quotes, passages, or scenes you found particularly compelling? Were there parts of this book you thought were incredibly unique, out of place, thought-provoking, or disturbing?
7. Did this book's pace seem too fast/too slow/just right?
8. If you were making a movie of this book, who would you cast?
9. If you got the chance to ask the author of this book one question, what would it be?
10. If you could write a sequel to this book, what would the main plot consist of?

CamCat Books

VISIT US ONLINE FOR
MORE BOOKS TO LIVE IN:
CAMCATBOOKS.COM

FOLLOW US

CamCatBooks   @CamCatBooks   @CamCat_Books

9 780744 301380